Dark Money

The Stopper Files, Volume 5

Eugene Lloyd MacRae

Published by Eugene Lloyd MacRae, 2019.

DARK MONEY

First edition. June 12, 2019.

Copyright © 2019 Eugene Lloyd MacRae.

ISBN: 978-1393300281

Written by Eugene Lloyd MacRae.

Chapter 1

MY NAME IS Dimitri Starkov, and I will see to it that your family is sent to Siberia."

Despite the naked threat, the man in the thousand-dollar-suit simply straightened a lapel as he calmly sat enjoying the warm sun on the Washington, DC rooftop terrace. The succulent scent of buttery croissants from a nearby bakery drifted on the air. "I know who you are Dimitri. You've spent time at my cottage in Maine. Remember? You have to understand–"

"No, I do not." Starkov turned abruptly from his stance looking out over the city. "It is *you* that needs to understand. I own you. I own you—what is your American expression? I own you lock, stock and can"

"Barrel. The expression is...lock, stock, and barrel, Dimitri. And you have to understand that the information your man asked me for is highly sensitive intelligence that will put a target on my back if someone–"

"I - don't - care. I want what was asked for." Starkov advanced across the terrace, scowling, "And my threat of Siberia is not an idle one. Your daughters—who are very beautiful teenagers—and your lovely wife will need heavy clothing to survive the cold winters–"

Mr. thousand-dollar-suit scowled back, "Damn it, Dimitri, we're Americans! And we're not living in your country. This is the United

States of America. You can't just threaten people with the hollow specter of your Siberia–"

Starkov stopped ten feet from his guest and stood with his feet astride. "You have heard of rendition? Your country engages in the practice. In case you are not familiar with the term, that is where you take people from one country to another, and you put them in a deep, black hole. You Americans know this practice well…it is where you kidnap someone you call a terrorist and take them–"

"You listen to me. I'm a United States Senator. And I will not be threatened like this."

"Then how would you like to be threatened?" Starkov asked. "I can issue threats in any way that you desire. It makes no difference to me. And your position does not matter to me. What does matter is that I can…what is that other expression you love in your movies? I can drop a coin…? No, I can drop a dime on you. That is the one. I can drop a dime on you. Do I make myself clear, Mr. United States Senator?"

His jaw grinding, Mr. thousand-dollar-suit sat there, staring bullets at the Russian.

"Or do I make a visit to your lovely family?"

Raising a hand in surrender, Mr. thousand-dollar-suit closed his eyes, "Fine. Just leave my family out of it."

"I will. As long as you give me reason to. *And* as long as you give me the intelligence information I have asked for. Keep in mind that I have helped you to get what you wanted. Now you will help me to get what I want. That is the arrangement."

Chapter 2

OTTAWA, CANADA

MERLIN ARTHUR DRAGON sat in a large comfy chair, his feet up on an ottoman, drinking a coffee and watching his blue, wooly Chartreux cat trying to catch the birds sitting on the other side of the window. Jigs would pounce, and then slowly look under his paws, assuming he had caught his prey. The birds would occasionally flap their wings when he jumped at the glass, but on most occasions they simply looked at the cat on the other side of the window pane, considering him entertainment rather than any kind of danger. Merlin couldn't help but smile, "Jigs, you do realize those are just birds and not chickens?"

The cat looked at him, his ears perking up. He loved the bits of chicken Merlin—and neighbor Jamie Hartman—would occasionally feed him as a treat.

"Sorry, I didn't mean to mention your weakness–"

His special cell phone rang on the small glass table next to him. It was connected to Interpol's I-24/7, secure global police network, and there were only a few people who had the number.

Merlin looked at the phone. He was Interpol's one and only Stopper, tasked with stopping the bad guys by whatever means necessary. The thing was—his assignments usually came through that phone using Interpol's proprietary encrypted messaging app. Not a personal call.

The cell phone rang and jangled on the table.

Voice communications were encrypted as well but this was still unusual. Picking the cell up, Merlin pressed the answer button and held the phone to his ear. He simply listened.

"Mr. Dragon?"

The voice sounded familiar.

"Merlin?"

Recognizing the voice as belonging to Constable Samantha Powless, Merlin wondered what was going on. Sammy was part of the Bear Island Police Service—which meant she was a member of the Temagami First Nation, an Algonquinn Indian band—and was attached to Interpol, working for Evelyn O'Toole. But other than being drawn in accidentally and working with him on his last case, she had nothing to do with his assignments. His blood ran cold and he wondered if something it happened to O'Toole or Director Aubrey Laurent again. They were still in a specialized hospital, recovering from an assassin trying to kill them using a nerve agent developed by the Soviet Union decades ago. The plot was put in motion by an arms dealer seeking revenge on everyone involved in thwarting ones of his plans to steal the wealth from an African nation. That everyone included getting Merlin to come out the shadows so they could kill him.

"Hello?"

"Sammy? What's wrong?"

"You had me worried there for a minute. I thought I had the wrong number."

"I don't usually get calls through this phone. And when I do, it usually turns out to be a problem."

"Sorry about that," Sammy said. "But Director Laurent asked me to call you."

Removing his feet from the ottoman, Merlin sat forward, "Is everything okay?"

"Oh...yes. Sorry about that. I obviously had you worried. No, the director called me and asked me to call you to tell you that you have an assignment. He said your limousine would be waiting for you? Must be nice."

Silent for a moment, Merlin said, "That's it? Why wouldn't he just send me a text message or...just call me himself? This doesn't make any sense."

"What can I tell you? I'm not a part of...well... I guess you could say I'm not part of the loop. All I know is what I know. And that's absolutely nothing."

Jigs pounced against the glass again, held his paws together and then lifted one slowly to peek to see if he had the bird. Disappointment ensued and the wooly Chartreux eyed the birds striding confidently on the other side of the window pane.

Merlin cursed softly under his breath.

"I'm sorry," Sammy said, "I wish I could give you more information. But that's all I have."

Shaking his head, Merlin said, "No, that's not it. I just can't...." He grimaced and slid the ottoman away with his foot, "Thanks for calling."

"I can tell something is wrong. Is there something I can do to help?"

"No." He stood up, "Thanks for calling again, Sammy. I appreciate it."

"There's nothing to appreciate. I'm just doing my job and relaying a message." She was quiet for a moment and then said, "Talk to me,

Merlin. I owe you big time for saving me from a fate worse than death."

"I did? Seems to me I put you in more danger than you deserved."

"Talk to me," Sammy insisted. "What can I do to help?"

Merlin watched Jigs stretch and then jump down, heading for his water bowl. "It's just... I have a cat. When I go on an assignment, I usually have a neighbor babysit for Jigs. But the thing is...she's away right now." He ran a hand over his hair. "I guess I can take him to the vet and board him there but...it sounds dumb, but he's my best friend and...."

"No, it makes sense now."

"What does?"

"What the director said to me. Or at least asked me. He wanted to know if I liked cats. He knew you needed someone to take care of the cat. Actually, I think he knew you wouldn't go on an assignment... maybe even quit?"

Merlin felt sheepish, "Dumb isn't it?"

"Actually, loyalty can be a rare thing in many ways," Sammy said. "Your loyalty for Jigs is part of who you are. Give me the address to your apartment and I'll stay with him."

"Really?"

"Yeah. In fact, I'm going to send a message to Evelyn O'Toole to let her know that I'm going to be on assignment as well. Jigs will have a 24-hour guard from a member of the Bear Island Police Service."

Chapter 3

AN HOUR LATER, the armored limousine dropped Merlin off in a private and secure area at the Ottawa Macdonald–Cartier International Airport. It was raining lightly. Go-bag in hand, Merlin took the airstairs two at a time and ducked into the Bombardier Global 8000. The ultra long-range business jet was on constant standby for his use. The permanent crew consisted of two serving members of the Canadian military; the pilot, Captain Charity Sherrell and the co-pilot, Captain Faith Saab.

Dropping the go-bag on one of the plush seats, Merlin flapped his arms, sending drops of water from his suit jacket flying in every direction. The fresh smell of coffee carried on the air. The main cabin area on this luxurious jet contained just four plush seats, two of them with a table. The area in front of them contained a long sofa, a television, and a mini-bar. Beyond that was a doorway that led to a galley that was fully stocked if he needed a meal or just a coffee. And beyond that was a suite with two single beds, a private washroom, and a true stand-up shower. Merlin removed the damp jacket, setting it on the back of the seat above the go-bag.

The pilot, Captain Charity Sherrell, appeared from the back and headed to the airstairs, "Welcome aboard, sir. Saab is running through the checklist and take-off is in five."

"Thanks, Captain. Any idea where we're heading?"

"Not yet. I imagine the orders are coming through as we speak." The airstairs closed in place with a thick whump. Sherrell efficiently headed up the aisle toward the front, "Please buckle in, Sir."

Sitting in the plush window-seat next to the go-bag, Merlin pulled his cell phone out and quickly composed a text message to the Director; Onboard and in the air. He set the phone next to the go-bag and buckled in for takeoff.

The TechX high bypass turbofan engines came to life in a deep, buzz-saw moan, sending the sense of immense power surging through the cabin.

A moment later, the plane was running smoothly along the taxiway to the runway, rain dancing off the window. As soon as the executive jet was aligned for takeoff on the runway, the power was applied. The turbofan engines growled deeply against gravity.

Merlin was pressed back in his seat by the 16,500 lb thrust from the engines and the water began to streak hard across the heated, water-repellent glass windows. Seconds later, the business jet rose from the tarmac, soaring into the dark clouds. Before they even leveled out above the rainstorm, Merlin sent the text that he was in the air. That done, he put the cell back on the seat.

The cabin bell dinged.

Removing his seat belt, Merlin was up and heading for the galley. He made a coffee and headed back to his seat. After only a few sips of the hot beverage, his cell phone buzzed. Setting the coffee in the cup-holder, he checked for the expected message on the phone. True to form, it gave him the day's code for the electronic locker that was in the suite situated further back in the plane. Setting the phone down. Merlin headed to the suite to get his orders. Retrieving a thick envelope, he returned to his seat.

The envelope was labeled Dark Money; Case #647321. Unsealing the envelope, he slid out a large number of files and reports onto the table and he began flipping through the pages.

Dark Money referred to cash from unknown sources that is spent to influence, and change political outcomes. Dark Money groups spend millions of dollars to shape elections without revealing where the money comes from. They also used dark money to influence things like policy, public health initiatives or get their preferred judges in place. It often came from rich people who wanted to influence things to their advantage, like getting lower taxes or keeping some business enterprise free from government regulations.

Merlin scanned the rest of the page. He didn't really care about politics, even if the underlying corruption from dark money was a threat to democracy. And rich people spending money secretly to get what they wanted wasn't really news to him. But as he scanned the document, he found one section interesting. It referred to the development of techniques now being used to throw elections and referendums. It was developed by the tobacco industry who deliberately hid the fact they knew for forty years that cigarette smoke contains cancer-causing particles. It was an art later refined by biotechnology, fossil fuel, and junk food companies. Interesting but not earth-shattering for someone who listened to the news over the years.

Flipping the pages, Merlin found his target was Dimitri Starkov. He was a Russian oligarch who had rapidly accumulated immense wealth during the era of Russian privatization. In Starkov's case, he was ex-KGB, the main security agency for the Soviet Union, and had gotten his hands on a Russian diamond mine, the largest in the world. Like the other oligarchs, he was close to the Russian government and worked hand-in-glove to push Russian-centered political agendas. He was also suspected of being heavily involved in laundering illicit money into dark money. And then Merlin realized his assignment. Dimitri Starkov was using that dark money to not just influence politics. He was using it in two other ways. One was what the Russian's called Kompromat—short for *compromising material.* They collected damaging information about a politician, a businessman, or some public figure, using it to create negative publicity or for blackmail and extortion if a target was elected or appointed to government positions. The threat of publicly revealing that dark money was the driving force behind a person's success in business or politics could be used as Kompromat.

Starkov was also using dark money to blackmail people in political circles to become Russian agents. Astonishingly, some political figures were so ambitious they willingly—and knowingly—traded access to the money for the power they could achieve. Starkov was operating his scheme in Canada, the United States, and the United Kingdom. There was a fear he had already gotten at least one person on the inside of each government. There was no telling the secrets they could steal or the damage they could do to the security of the free world.

Without a doubt, these governments were feeling their normal counter-intelligence methods were not working as well—or as fast—as they needed. Merlin's mandate was to do *whatever* was necessary to stop Dimitri Starkov and his schemes, a no-holds-barred service. And since he worked for Laurent secretly, that gave these governments plausible deniability.

A light beep sounded and then Sherrell's voice came over the intercom, "Sir...our orders don't have a destination. Apparently, we are to get airborne and wait for instructions from you."

"From me?"

"Yes, sir."

Confusion set in for Merlin. That didn't make any sense. And then it struck him. The Director was still in the hospital. The assignments he gave to Merlin were known only to a few people. In fact, it was usually the head of a country, a President or Prime Minister, who called Laurent directly to get an unsolvable problem solved one way or the other. And as fast as possible. Laurent wasn't in any position in the hospital to do much research to help him out. There could be prying eyes and everything had to be kept in a tight circle. No, Merlin was on his own right now. "Hold on for a few minutes."

"Yes, sir."

Merlin quickly ran through the case reports, looking for clues on where they should go. There wasn't a lot. The Russian wasn't married and had no kids. There was no record of a girlfriend. He had an opulent home in Moscow, an apartment in London, England, and a condo in Washington, DC. There wasn't much personal information beyond that.

Pulling his cell phone, Merlin looked at the screen. Its advanced facial recognition software knew it was him and automatically unlocked the special features. Now connected to Interpol's I-24/7, the secure global police network, he had top-level access to the databases that held information from the nearly two hundred member countries of Interpol. A search on Dimitri Starkov returned an interesting hit on his passport. The United States Department of Homeland Security showed Dimitri Starkov entering the country at John F. Kennedy International Airport ten days ago. It wasn't Washington, DC but it did put him inside the United States. It was highly possible the man would end up in Washington sooner or later.

Merlin hit the intercom button, "Set a course for Washington DC. Set down wherever you can and I'll make my way from there."

Sherrell's voice came back a moment later, "We can fly into Ronald Reagan Washington National Airport in Arlington, That's the primary airport serving Washington, D.C."

"Sounds good."

"Do you want us to radio ahead and rent you a car?"

"That sounds good."

"Any preference?"

Merlin shook his head as he looked at the rain streaking the window, "No. And knowing you two...I'm sure you'll surprise me."

Light laughter and a 'chick magnet' comment came across the intercom.

Chapter 4

ARLINGTON, VIRGINIA

THE SUN BROKE THROUGH the dark clouds as the Global 8000 made the turn to set down on the tarmac of Ronald Reagan Washington National Airport. The rain had stopped but the water glistened off the buildings, traffic, and lights in a variety of colors as Arlington and Washington spread across the landscape. The center of so much political power, it made sense that Dimitri Starkov had a condo here. A question stood out though. What reason, what *scheme* was the Russian working on or hatching in New York?

Forty minutes later, Merlin used his special Interpol passport to move through customs without a single question. Or a search. What it did draw was a questioning *look* from the two customs officers, obviously not used to his level of clearance and authority. His passport was tied into the government offices of every member country of Interpol, allowing him to move freely across every border in the world. Merlin wasn't worried about hiding his identity at this point and he was learning to assert the power and push back on any aggressive stance on the part of the customs officials. Plus, in his job, the phrase 'time is of the essence' was true.

The concourse was busy and noisy as he headed for the rental counter to pick up his car. As usual, he was traveling light. He wore a dark suit, striped tie, and white shirt, planning to blend in with the other executives, lobbyists, and politicians who frequented life around the political power structure. The shirt pocket held three items. A credit card and a debit card for any expenses during the assignment. The other was a Shomer-Tec Carbon Fiber Ventilator. It was made of ultra-stiff hollow carbon fiber tubing and looked like a standard cheap black pen with a standard pen cap and a pocket clip. But concealed under the cap was a sharp point cut on a bias. The other end was covered with a slightly tacky material to enhance the grip. His first, and only, attempt to use it as a last-ditch weapon had failed. But it added to his tools and enhanced his chances of survival in a tight situation.

The suit jacket covered his conceal holster in the waistband of the pants over his back right pocket. The holster held his special, 9mm Beretta PX4 Storm Subcompact handgun. Made from carbon fiber, it could pass through metal detectors without a problem. It also had Smart Gun technology—the grip had an internal scan of Merlin's palm print and the weapon couldn't be fired by anyone else.

The dress boots he wore had shoelaces with blacked-brass tips. One tip on each lace was actually a boot-lace handcuff key.

His 'escape belt' was made of 1.5" nylon webbing, completely non-metallic, and was part of the field kit used by some of Canada's elite forces. The inside of the belt buckle itself held a non-metallic handcuff key and a ceramic razor blade held in place by a Kevlar lanyard. The inside of the belt webbing had dozens of elasticized compartments containing another non-metallic handcuff key, 4.5 feet of Kevlar survival cord, the Escape Stick by Shomer-Tec, a 4-piece, titanium lock-picking kit, and an American Liberty nickel. You turned the nickel to heads-up, slid a fingernail clockwise along the edge and a small blade of hardened stainless steel rotated out. All you had to do was slip it into your pocket and it was doubtful anyone patting you down would be concerned with a small coin, if they even detected it. Around his wrist, he wore a Pyro-Band bracelet. It had an integral ferrocerium rod that served as a connector as well as a fire source. Rapidly scraping the rod with a sharp edge, such as a knife blade, would send out a shower of sparks to ignite tinder to start a fire.

The go-bag he carried contained his Interpol badge, his credentials, another shirt, and a change of socks and underwear.

Merlin spotted the rental counter and made a beeline to get the final item he needed to start. A vehicle.

At the sound of his approaching footsteps, a young woman appeared from behind a divider and glided toward the front counter. The light scent of orange blossoms preceding her as she beamed a smile at him, "Yes, sir, how may I help you?"

The name is Merlin Dragon. I'm here to pick up a rental." He slipped the credit card from his shirt pocket and held it out, "You can use this for the charges."

Taking the credit card, the young woman moved to a computer and began typing. She smiled and gave a nod, "Yes. We have a Porsche 911 GT2 RS reserved."

"Seriously?"

"Yes, sir. Is there a problem?"

"Uh...no...my assistant told me it wasn't available." Merlin shook his head to himself. Sherrell had surprised him with an exotic car. An expensive exotic car that had to cost nearly four hundred thousand dollars.

The young woman smiled, "So she surprised you?"

"Yes."

Working away, the young woman glanced up through her dark eyelashes, "Your assistant is very lucky...working for you I mean."

"She is?" Merlin realized she was flirting with him and his insides tied up. Social situations like this made him uncomfortable. He could never figure out what he should say.

"Yes. And I hope you don't mind me being forward but...you have a very sexy name."

"I do?"

"Yes." She set a folder and a set of keys on the counter, "Is this your first visit to the area?"

"Uh...yes."

"I see." The young woman printed off the paperwork, set it on the counter, and held a pen out, "Sigh there, please. And there."

Merlin complied, handing the pen back to her.

The young woman placed her fingers around his and paused, "Do you need a local guide?"

"A guide?" Merlin could feel the light, suggestive feel of her skin against his.

"Yes," She took the pen and wrote on one of the papers Merlin had just signed. She gave it to him with a smile, "This is my personal cell phone number. Call me if you need *anything*."

"Uh...okay, thanks." Merlin scooped up the paper, the folder, and the keys. He turned.

"Sir?"

Merlin glanced back.

"I just thought you would like to know...you car is in B-16. Hope to see you...*soon*."

As she wiggled a goodbye with her fingers, Merlin hustled away from the rental counter. Dealing with a Russian oligarch, spies, and even an assassin was preferable to the social dance between men and women. *That* he was really lousy at.

Chapter 5

ALL 700 HORSE POWER of the sleek black Porsche growled under the hood as Merlin accelerated on the highway. He began to understand the rationale of Sherrell's thinking. The information package in the glove compartment told him this vehicle would accelerate from 0 to 60 mph in 2.8 seconds. And it would top out at 212 miles per hour. Just a couple of things that might help catch or escape the bad guys. The only problem was the *chick magnet* thing they had joked about. He dreaded being a chick magnet. His tongue would be tied in knots that would take a year to undo. And the car would make him look more like a Playboy instead of helping him fit into the political life of Washington DC. Then again, there was no doubt there was a lot of money in the pockets of local politicians. And yet again, it didn't matter which country you looked at, you found very few politicians at the high levels who came from working-class backgrounds. The higher you went in politics, the more money you needed. Which brought him back to the subject of dark money and Dimitri Starkov. It was impossible for Merlin to solve the world's social issues with anything he did. But maybe he could stop one man from screwing with the security of the free world. The rest he would leave up to others.

It took Merlin an hour through traffic to reach Starkov's Washington abode. It was in an impressive, 19th century, gray brick building with limestone accents and ironwork, sitting on the corner of Pennsylvania and 25th Street in the West End. A heavy canvas canopy ran from the entranceway and across the sidewalk to the edge of the street. It was held up by a number intricately-carved gold-colored posts. An Internet search told him the building was labeled an historic landmark and turned into sixteen luxury condominiums ten years ago. Starkov had the top penthouse unit that included a rooftop terrace. All units had direct elevator access. There was a twenty-four-hour concierge and a secure front desk. He had come here because it was his only point of contact. The question was—now what?

First things first. Merlin parked and got out, waited for a break in the traffic and jogged across the street to the front entrance.

An alert security guard inside got up from the front desk, stuck his thumbs in his belt and watched Merlin approach the glass front door.

Merlin tried the door. As expected, it was locked. He waved at the security guard and pointed at the door, indicating he wanted in.

The guard strolled forward and spoke through the glass, "Yes, sir, what can I do for you?"

"Mr. Dimitri Starkov? I'm here to see him."

Shaking his head, the guard said, "I'm sorry but Mr. Starkov is not home at the moment. You'll have to come back."

"Seriously? Dimitri's not here? Do you know how long he'll be? Can I wait in his place for him–?"

"No, Sir. No can do. This is a secure building and only people on my list are allowed to come inside. You'll have to contact Mr. Starkov personally and make arrangements. My hands are tied."

Merlin grimaced and cursed under his breath, showing pretend frustration. But he knew he couldn't push it any further. He raised a hand and gave the guard a salute, "I understand. You're only doing your job. I'll give him a call." With that said, Merlin turned and walked back to his car across the street. He half-hoped the guard would open the door and change his mind but it never happened.

Merlin got back in the Porsche and sat for a moment. Now he knew for sure Dimitri Starkov had a condo unit here. And he wasn't home right now. He leaned his head and looked up at the eight-story building. Each side butted against a neighboring structure that was one story lower. Using his cell phone, Merlin brought up Google Earth and zoomed in on the target building and the surrounding neighborhood. Not only were the three buildings butting against each other, they formed a triangle that had a tail of another five buildings extending northward. The building attached to the one that held the Russian's condo unit was the same height. All the rest of the buildings were three or four stories lower than his target building. Almost all of them had some type of roof terrace. These folks were using every foot of square space they had available to them. Scrolling around and using the street view, he looked for a way to the top of any building, hoping to finally get on the roof of his target building. Since the buildings were old, he hoped for something like a fire escape still in place. But there was nothing. He spotted a lot of ledges and handholds in the brick work that would allow someone to climb. But he wasn't anywhere close to a climbing ninja and would probably plummet to his death after two stories.

Starting the car, the engine purred as Merlin pulled away from the curb and turn left at the corner. He drove slowly, looking over the buildings. A narrow lane separated the cluster of buildings from the next and he turned in, wondering where it led. The lane met what had originally been a wider back alley that was now paved over and provided parking spots for the tenants of the surrounding buildings. Vehicles were using every bit of space, including a white motorcycle that sat between two concrete pillars. Eventually circling back to the same spot, Merlin parked again. Still nothing stood out.

The building on the right of his target building had a bank branch on the first floor. Getting out again, Merlin walked to the corner and crossed with the crowd, looking up at the floors above the bank, wondering what they held. He followed two women into the bank's front entrance.

The atmosphere inside was hushed, with a few low voices sounding here and there along with the clicks of keyboards. Off to the left, people waited in line for one of the eight bank tellers. The was a line of offices at the far end. On the right was a sitting area and Merlin casually strolled in that direction. Six chairs around a small table formed the small waiting area in front of several offices where bank employees sat behind desks, talking to clients. Taking a chair across from two businessmen, Merlin did his best to fit in as he looked around. Nothing stood out. The only wall he couldn't see was the one behind him. He got up and took a step forward, taking one of the magazines laying on the small table. Turning as he moved back to his seat, Merlin saw two washroom doors and a third door with glass on the upper half that was labeled 'Employee's Only'. Sitting back down, he flipped through the magazine, waiting. As soon as the two men were invited into an office, Merlin tossed the magazine to the table, turned and headed for the 'Employee's Only' door. It was locked. He took a peek through the small glass window. Beyond was a landing with stairs leading to the next floor. The sign next to the front entrance had said the bank closed at four. That meant—if he could get through—he had an hour to explore. Checking over his shoulder to see if anyone was watching, Merlin took the lock-picking kit from his belt. It only took him ten seconds and he slipped through, closing the door quietly and checking through the window to see if he'd been spotted. He was fine. Slipping the tools back into his belt, he began climbing the stairs

He climbed floor after floor, only hearing the occasional set of footsteps on the stairs below. Beyond each landing door was a hallway and he could hear faint conversations or the clicking of keyboards. He reached the top landing and a door labeled 'Roof'. He didn't see any signs warning not to open the door so he put his hands on the panic bar and pushed. There was a clanking sound and the door opened. And he could see why there was no alarm. He emerged to find himself on a rooftop area that had tables with umbrellas, wooden chairs, and benches. The area opened up to the street on the left and behind him, and the other two sides were the wall of his target building and the adjoining building at the back. It was obviously an area the employees could use on days with good weather. Right now everything was wet.

Merlin could see the far wall was his target building and had three large windows. But as soon as he got up close, he realized they were heavy tempered frosted glass. He couldn't see inside. And there was no way they could be opened and no way he could break through without a sledgehammer.

The wall on the right belonged to the next building. But there were no doorways and no windows. The only thing of interest was a six-foot-high, brick barbecue. It stood a foot away from the wall but offered an opportunity to the next rooftop. A bank employee could come walking out of the roof door at any moment but Merlin had to take the chance. He pulled one of the chairs over and managed to climb on top of the barbecue. A small jump allowed him to get his fingers on the top of the wall. It was a tenuous grip and he hung there for a moment, wondering if he would need to call for the fire department if he fell and got wedged between the barbecue and wall. But he managed to maintain his grip and slowly pulled himself up. Once on top, he found himself on another wet rooftop area, filled with lounge chairs, tables, and some greenery.

Brushing damp dust off his suit, he worked his way around to his target building. A five-foot privacy wall separated Starkov's roof area from this one and Merlin scaled it, dropping to an opulent terraced rooftop, much larger and fancier than the other two buildings. It took a few minutes to find the rooftop door to the Russian's unit. To Merlin's surprise, it wasn't locked. He held his breath and took a chance, opening the door. No alarms went off. It made sense and it didn't, unless it was a silent alarm. The building security was meant to keep people from getting in through the front door. And it was up to each individual tenant to secure the roof. Dimitri Starkov was either careless or he didn't care if someone broke in. To Merlin, it meant he was unlikely he'd find anything inside. But it was all he had right now.

Chapter 6

MERLIN DESCENDED a wrought iron, spiral staircase into the Russian's Washington world of ten-foot ceilings, wide-plank teak flooring, fancy furniture, and triple pane windows overlooking the street below. The pleasant scent of sandalwood came from jars of dried flowers place around the unit. The problem was the place held little beyond the furniture. It was more like a staged showroom than a place where someone lived. In the marble bathroom, he checked the medicine cabinet for something hidden spy-like in a bottle or tube. Or maybe prescription medicine that would give him a contact point. But all he found was over the counter medication for a cold, some pain killers, toothpaste, and mouthwash. Nothing incriminating or helpful. He checked three closets and found some towels and linens. The kitchen cupboards had some nice dishware and cutlery but the fridge held little. Starkov definitely wasn't the homebody type. More than likely he had take-out, maybe even held parties or entertained dinner guests where everything was catered and taken care of by outside help. He briefly considered getting hired on to work one of these dinner parties and see who he was trying to influence. But that meant he had to try to find out who was doing the catering and that would take time. The more time that went by, the more damage the Russian could cause. He pushed that to the back of his mind as a last resort and continued to look through the rest of the unit.

He came across a room that had a number of nearly empty bookcases and a large desk with a leather chair facing a computer. The only items on the shelves were books and magazines on Washington nightlife or articles on local prominent figures. There were also a number of Washington Post newspapers. More specifically, they were the Politics sections of the newspaper. A quick glance through them showed most of them folded over to articles of people who were rumored, or who stated, they were looking at running for political office.

Turning his attention to the desk, Merlin pulled open and looked through each drawer. There were some political pamphlets, invitations for dinner parties, charity events, and fundraisers but nothing else. He turned the computer on and looked for documents. There weren't any. He checked out the browser and found he had saved links to the website for The Hill, an American political newspaper, as well as the Washington Post, a major American daily newspaper that featured a particular emphasis on national politics and the federal government. The other links were to websites like TMZ, a tabloid news website specializing in celebrities. There were some government links and a link to the Kennedy Center where he could find out what was playing. His search history showed a variety of names that Merlin assumed were connected to the newspapers on the bookshelf. He checked for emails and found a dozen that were reminders of some of those charity events or fundraisers for various politicians but all but two were long passed. There were a few return emails in the sent box for some of the reminders but that was it.

He tapped his fingers on the desk, thinking. Anything important was probably on the Russian's personal cell phone or a laptop he carried with him. He hadn't expected to find a list of dark money clients, turned assets or spies the Russian had recruited but he had hoped for some scrap of information to start with. But there was nothing. Dimitri Starkov was moving from place to place, light and unencumbered. And playing the game smart.

And then something struck Merlin. He pulled open a drawer and looked through the political pamphlets and invitations. No, not in that drawer. He found what he was looking for in the next. Two invitations that were coming up. Looking back at the emails, he found where Starkov had replied to these two invites. One was in New York tonight. The other was a black-tie fundraiser here in Washington in two days. It looked like he had his answer for the Russian flying into New York. Merlin rummaged back through the drawer and found what he needed; an envelope containing the official invitation for the Washington fundraiser with the Russian's name in curly lettering. Merlin slipped it into his pocket and shut off the computer. His time was running out and he made sure all the drawers were closed and left the room.

He crossed the living area, heading for the stairs to the roof–

A figure in black flew over the back of a long sofa and collided with Merlin.

Reaching out to brace himself, Merlin crashed into a glass table, moving it a foot, and then he crashed face down to the teak floor.

Light running footsteps sounded across the room and began moving upward.

Scrambling around to his feet, Merlin saw the black figure climbing the wrought iron, spiral staircase. He darted across the room in pursuit and took the spiral staircase two steps at a time.

The door at the top slammed shut.

Merlin hit the panic bar with his full bodyweight, banging the door open, and he tumbled onto the roof outside.

The black figure was already climbing the privacy wall.

Rolling and coming up on his feet, Merlin took off at a run. As the figure reached the top of the wall, he saw a face look back.

The figure in the sleek, black tracksuit, and black and silver track shoes—was a beautiful, dark-haired woman.

She disappeared just as he reached the wall and began to climb.

By the time he got to the top, she was bounding across the next rooftop. Tumbling from the top of the wall to the roof top himself, Merlin was up on his feet and running—she had disappeared. By the time he got to where he last saw her, there was no sight or sound of the woman. He cursed under his breath. Whoever she was, she was fast and athletic. And she had to be the reason why the roof door was unlocked. She had already picked it and gone inside before he arrived. Great. Just great. He considered continuing the pursuit, trying to find out where she had gone, but he knew time was running out. He couldn't afford to get locked in the bank and trigger an alarm. It was time to go.

He turned and headed for the brick barbecue. Jumping to the top of the barbecue, he climbed down and moved as fast as possible back through the roof door and down through the bank stairs. He reached the bottom floor and hustled through the door, straightened his tie as passed the sitting area and headed for the entrance. His chest was heaving and he worked hard to keep his breathing under control, trying to look normal. The offices were empty and he could only see a couple of customers standing at the teller wickets.

A young woman stood by the front entrance and she looked at him with surprise, "I'm sorry, sir, but we closed fifteen minutes ago." She narrowed her eyes and looked at his suit, "Where did you come from?"

Merlin looked down and realized his suit was soiled and rumpled from his mad dash across the roof and his climb back down. His voice was raspy as he brushed himself lightly, " Getting a loan here is harder than I thought, I guess."

Her eyebrows rose in surprise, her mouth opened but no words came out. She turned and unlocked the door, pushing it open, "Well... maybe you can try again tomorrow. Sir."

Merlin thanked her and passed through, heading for the lights at the corner as he heard the door locked behind him. He absentmindedly brushed his suit off as he stood there with the crowd waiting to cross. He barely heard the noise or honking of the traffic, or the conversations of the people around him. The frantic, rushing thrum of a motorcycle sound off to the right and then settled into an idle, waiting. All that was just vague background to his jumble of thoughts. Who was the woman in Starkov's condominium? It didn't make sense. If she worked for the Russian, wouldn't she just kill him? She definitely had the drop on him. Maybe she didn't have a gun on her? Then again, maybe she was a girlfriend. He shook his head. That didn't make any sense either. The intelligence agencies were keeping tabs on him and he was sure there would have been a record of a girlfriend. And the way she moved across that rooftop told him she was used to doing that. The bigger question was simple...was his assignment compromised?

Chapter 7

AS HE DROVE, thinking, Merlin passed a Ritz-Carlton Hotel. He made a spur of the moment decision to use it as a temporary base. It was close to the Russian's condominium and it was better than going all the way back to the airport and staying on the plane. He paid for a week in advance with his debit card. At five hundred bucks a night, it was on the high end for him but it also gave him cover for the tentative plan he was forming. After a nice meal at The RIS, an upscale neighborhood restaurant around the corner from the hotel, Merlin sat with a coffee, thinking again. The succulent scent of the meals, and the low, unhurried conversations of the people around him collided with his own thoughts. While they were enjoying themselves without a care in the world, Merlin was trying to find some way of maintaining that sense of peace and security for them. They were having fun while he was fighting monsters.

Paying his bill, Merlin picked up a few after-dinner mints on his way out and stood on the street corner as he sucked on one, doing some more thinking. The night air was cool but comfortable, the traffic was light, and the people coming and going into the restaurant all had a light, happy mood. Life was good for this small section of the Washington DC population. The woman in the black tracksuit penetrated Merlin's thoughts. He half-wondered if she had been following him from the airport—he dismissed that as impossible. But what if the Russian had penetrated Interpol as well? Maybe the impossible was possible after all. Merlin pushed the thought from his mind and pulled his cell phone. He needed something to make him feel better and he could kill two birds with one stone. Tapping a speed dial number, Merlin listened.

Constable Samantha Powless answered after one ring, "Hello?"

"You were expecting an important call?"

"Who are you, Dragon, the cell phone police?"

"No, I was just wondering. You answered on the first ring—"

"If you must know, I was waiting for my stripper boyfriend to let me know he was just outside the door, ready to start his act."

"You sound like a teenage babysitter."

Sammy's voice went low, "The things I had planned for him would make most teenagers blush."

Merlin smiled, "Okay, okay. I know when I'm beat. How is my buddy?"

"I'm fine."

His mouth opened and closed.

Sammy laughed, "Jigs is doing fine. He talked me into getting takeout. A nice chicken dinner for two. He fell asleep purring. And I swear that cat isn't snoring, he's still purring."

"I would say he is. And that's good because that means he trusts you."

"Oh. Good to know."

Merlin could tell that comment made Sammy feel good. He was glad someone felt that way. He cleared his throat, "I was wondering if you could help me with something? With Laurent still in the hospital—"

"So is O'Toole. How can I help?"

"Truthfully, I'm not even sure."

"Just tell me what you need."

Merlin watched a few cars pass by, wondering how he should approach it. Then he said, "I need a cover story for something I'm working on."

"A cover story?"

"Yeah. I need to be... I don't know... maybe someone like a Playboy who–"

"Wouldn't that mean I would need to have a talent like one of those preacher types on television who perform miracles?"

Merlin had to laugh, "Very funny, smartass."

"Tell me more."

"I need to look like someone who is getting into politics. Maybe wanting to run for office for the first time."

"In Ottawa? Or provincial politics down in Toronto?"

"Oh, sorry. No. I'm in Washington DC."

"Really?"

"Yeah. I need to be someone who is getting into American politics. At the highest levels."

"Oh. Okay." She was silent for a moment, "What kind of documentation do you need? Birth certificates? Driver's licenses? A whole school background? I'm not sure what I could do with all that."

Merlin shook his head. Sammy was right. She wasn't in the same position as Laurent was to help him create a persona for undercover work. Or would be if he wasn't in the hospital.

"Sorry. Maybe I can try and–"

"Actually... I don't think there would've been time for the Director to do anything either. I only have a couple of days to try and get this in place. Actually, more like one day."

"That's pushing things. Sorry, I don't mean to–"

"You don't have to keep saying you're sorry, Sammy. I'm the one who should say sorry to you for getting you involved in the first place. And asking you to do something that's probably impossible."

Both of them were silent for a few seconds and then Merlin asked her, "What do you know about how people get stories for websites these days? Especially the ones that offer a digital output for newspapers. Do they still have reporters for various news beats like a crime column or a social column?"

"Yes and no. A lot of newspapers have downsized and eliminated reporters with the loss of much of their advertising revenue to online media. Many just have a skeleton staff compared to their heyday. A lot of stories they run come from freelancers, people trying to make a name for themselves or make some money. Although, from what I read, some of them don't even get paid by some of these large media outlets. It's all about trying to build a following for themselves. Why are you asking?"

Merlin rubbed his chin, thinking, "I was just wondering if I could get myself into some newspaper article. You know, someone up-and-coming trying to get into politics? Or looking to run for some political office?"

Footsteps sounded across the call as Sammy asked, "Any particular newspaper you're thinking of?"

"Maybe the Washington Post? Why?"

"You mind if I use your computer?"

"No, it's fine. What are you thinking?"

"Maybe I could find some freelancer who is willing to do an article on you. I could go through the online articles and see who I can find."

"That sounds like a plan. But it's going to have to be done fast. It can't be under my real name but–"

"How about Rhett Butler?" There was the sound of a keyboard softly clicking away.

"The character from Gone with the Wind? You're crazy." He laughed, "Maybe Rhett Smith or something."

"Rhett Smith is boring."

"Maybe I'm boring."

"True. But we have to overcome that."

"Hey? Hurt feelings here."

Sammy laughed, "You'll live. How about Rhett...Summers. Yeah, that's good."

"Rhett Summers? Okay. At least you didn't turn me into a porn star."

"Fat chance. I cast actors to type."

"Hey?"

She laughed again, "Where are you staying?"

"The Ritz-Carlton Hotel in the West End–"

"I'll give you a call back. Leave your phone on." The call ended.

Merlin kept the phone in his hand and began the walk back to the hotel. If this didn't work, he wasn't sure how he could make contact with the Russian other than a casual, accidental meeting. That would create a whole new set of problems, trying to get close enough to Starkov and gather information without blowing his cover.

Chapter 8

IT DIDN'T TAKE more than an hour before Merlin's cell phone rang. He was in the bathroom, using a damp washcloth to wipe down the suit jacket from his rooftop climb. He had already worked on the pants and they were feeling a bit damp. Dropping the washcloth in the basin, Merlin moved across to the bed where he had laid the phone and grabbed it as it rang for the third time, "Hello?"

"Hi, it's Sammy."

"Hi, what have you got?"

"I was able to make contact with one of the freelancers who writes for the Washington Post," Sammy told him. "His name is Clevon Stuart. The three articles I saw that made me narrow in on him were political articles. They were more general in tone but I figured he would be a good bet. There was a contact email and cell phone number in his byline and I called him."

"Is he willing to help?"

"Uh,,," Sammy didn't say anything for a moment beyond that.

"Are you saying he wasn't?"

"No, he is but..."

"But what?

There was a bit more silence and then the explanation poured from Sammy, "It took some persuasion. Actually, he blew me off at first. Then I remembered you had a debit card and that you had been driving a Lamborghini before and I knew you had some money to work with. He's willing to push a story into tomorrow's addition because I offered him $10,000."

Merlin sat on the bed, "$10,000?"

"Yeah. I could tell it was going to take something big enough to catch his interest. And it's all I had.... "

"It's a good thing you're not my girlfriend. I'd be broke in days. No, make that hours."

"Hey? Hurt feelings here."

Merlin couldn't help but smile and marvel how it had become so easy to talk to Sammy. Then again, he knew if flirting started, that would come to an end fast.

"From your silence I take it I made a mistake? You don't have the money?"

"Uh, sorry. I was just thinking about something else."

"So...I did okay? You're not mad at me?" Sammy asked.

"No, You did fine. In fact, you did a great job because I didn't have much time to get this set up."

"Well, you still don't have much time," Sammy told him. "I take it he's rushing across the city right now. He's going to meet you in the lobby at your hotel at ten o'clock. It's just after nine here so...."

Merlin glanced at the clock on the night table beside the bed, "It's the same time here. How will I know him?"

"Uh...good question. He was so eager, he hung up. Hold on, there's a small picture of him that goes along with the byline under his articles. I can send you a link to the article."

"Okay, send it to me. Now it's up to me to figure out a story he can use." Merlin hung up, dropped the phone to the bed and headed into the washroom to finish cleaning his suit coat. Twenty minutes later, and after receiving a picture of the freelancer, he went down to the lobby and took a look. There were only a few people in the quiet, fancy lobby, and none of them looked like the person he was going to meet. That gave him some time to get ready for the next part of his plan—assuming this part worked—and he headed to the concierge desk, putting in a request for a tuxedo. They had just finished checking on his jacket and shirt sizes when he spotted Clevon Stuart. He was a young, slim black man with short cropped hair, a pair of blue jeans topped by a tweed jacket, no tie, and an air of eagerness about him. Or was that nervousness? Merlin headed for the man and had the impression Stuart was wondering if he was being taken for a fool and no one was going to show up. Merlin stuck his hand out, "Mr. Stuart? I'm...Rhett." He had forgotten the last name Sammy had made up and he felt like slapping himself in the head.

Stuart's eyes lit up as he shook Merlin's hand, "Mr. Summers. Very nice to meet you. I was beginning to wonder—it doesn't matter. There's a coffee shop a few doors down and across the street. How about if we go talk in private?"

"All right. Merlin allowed the man to lead the way. They left the hotel, dodged the traffic, cutting at an angle across the street, and were sitting down within a few minutes, steaming cups of coffees in front of them. Merlin felt the anxiety rise. This could go in any number of directions. The way he wanted it to go, with an article that helped out his plan. Or it could go sideways or even upside down if this young man decided to find out exactly who the man was who was willing to pay all of this money—to use his journalistic talents to dig a little too deep and ruin everything.

Chapter 9

IN THE MIDST OF the rich smells of fresh donuts, steaming coffee, and light happy chatter around them, the freelance reporter got right to the heart of the matter. At least as he saw it. Clevon Stuart shifted in his seat, "I don't mean to be crass—but first things first—are you really willing to pay....? I mean... your assistance said..." He was almost reluctant to mention the figure.

Merlin glanced around, leaned his head slightly and said in a low voice, Yes, I'm willing to pay the ten grand, Mr. Stuart."

Stuart had a hard time not flashing a face-breaking grin, "Can I ask why it's so... important? I mean, why so fast? And call me Clevon. Please."

Taking a sip of coffee, Merlin realized the man was suspecting a sensational story behind his willingness to pay so much money. "The truth is...Clevon...is that I've been thinking of running for Senate for a while now."

"You want to be a Senator?" Stuart reached into an inner pocket of his tweed jacket and pulled out a phone. He began tapping away on it and then looked at Merlin, "I hope it's okay if I take notes?"

"Of course." Merlin watched the freelance reporter tapping away on the phone and mulled over the story that he had been trying to create since Sammy's phone call. But first, he needed to relieve some of the pressure on the reasons for paying so much money for a quick story. He leaned his head in again and spoke in a confidential manner, "The thing is... I just received an invitation to a fundraising event that I suddenly realized offered me an amazing opportunity to do some networking. But I need a higher profile. Something that makes it easier to approach people. Or maybe get them to approach me first. You know, the *I saw you in the news* thing? It seems to me that fame is a valuable commodity in politics these days."

Stuart nodded eagerly, "Okay, okay. I can see that. Can you tell me which event you're going to?"

Merlin became afraid of the freelancer poking around a little too much and he had to prevent that to protect what he was really trying to do, "I'm sorry, I wish I could. But it's a private event and a little hush-hush."

His eyebrows pushing together, Stuart wasn't too happy with that answer.

"But who knows what kind of political gossip I might be able to pass along to you after."

That seemed to brighten him considerably, "All right, I can understand." He turned serious again, "Can you tell me something about your background? I mean... I can't really place the accent...it sounds...Canadian?"

Merlin's mind whirled for a moment, "I guess you're right. I never really thought about it. My family was from New York but my father served in the Canadian embassy in Ottawa for a dozen years. I basically grew up there."

"Okay, okay, so your father was a diplomat. That's good background."

Wondering if he was sinking into quicksand here, Merlin said, "He was a consular officer. But frankly, I'm trying to make on my own. I hope you can understand that?"

Stuart seemed puzzled for a moment and then he nodded thoughtfully, "I can see that." He swept his hand across the table, "Okay. I can see how it can be portrayed in the article; son from a prominent family refusing to use his family name to get ahead in the world of politics. Yeah, that would work. That's a great angle," He eagerly began typing his notes in again.

Knowing he had to throw in some lies that would take time to check on, he said, "I'm not sure if this is the type of thing you need...but...I was fortunate enough to get a scholarship to Harvard University."

"Harvard? Really?"

"Yeah, I played on the hockey team."

"The hockey team? I didn't even know Harvard had a hockey team."

"Well, they do. They play against Dartmouth, Yale, Princeton. We called it the brainiac league."

Stuart laughed.

"I guess that was the side benefit of my father working in Canada. I took an interest in hockey and got pretty good at it. I don't think I would've gotten a single scholarship opportunity without that. After I graduated, I was working in investment banking with Goldman Sachs until a year ago. I did very, very well for myself financially. But that's when I decided to change my career path and pursue politics."

Nodding, Stuart continued to enter his notes, "A midlife crisis type of thing."

Merlin was going to say no but decided to leave it. There were other things more important right now. Such as making sure the article was going to happen when he needed it to happen. But he was also afraid if he pushed too hard it would look suspicious. He said casually, "I don't have any girlfriend. No attachments like that to write about. Can I ask you–?"

"That's okay. In fact, that's even better. I can make something up and not hurt anybody in your life."

"Make something up?"

"Yeah. It's done all the time." He looked up, explaining further. "Let's say...one publicist has a hot female star client who has a movie coming out and she needs publicity to push it. He gets together with another publicist of...say a new hot male star who needs some publicity—they always need publicity—and you work with some gossip outlet to get a story out. Maybe you claim they're dating and the gossip outlet shows up to take pictures of them leaving a restaurant together. Or you can even make up rumors of them getting married. He did that with Suzanne Lunney and Orley Coakley–"

"Really? I saw that on Celebrity America just before a movie I wanted to watch that had him in it. I thought it was real."

Stuart shrugged. "Nope. It's how the game is played. In this case...I can pass you off as a rich, eligible bachelor getting into politics, dating hot women...." Stuart paused and looked at Merlin, "Uh...it is women, right? I mean, nothing wrong with the other...I just don't want to get it wrong...."

"Women it is."

"Okay, playboy and hot chics but you're getting serious"

Merlin almost laughed. He wasn't quite sure he could pass off something like the playboy thing. But in the end, it didn't matter. He tried to return to his concerns, "About the article–?"

"What kind of car do you drive?"

"Car? I'm driving a Porsche right now. I'm not sure of the model."

"Must be nice. But that's good. I'll play with the whole thing and come up with something good to attract eyeballs to the article."

"Are you sure we can get it into tomorrow's edition? And on the website?"

Stuart nodded as he kept working on his notes, "Yeah." He shrugged slightly, "I'm going to have to part with some of the money, but I think it's worth it."

"You're going to have to bribe someone else?"

Another slight shrug, "Yeah. But I've done it before. It's usually small things that I pass on like baseball tickets. Or something at the Kennedy Center. Which reminds me." He reached into a jacket pocket and pulled out a small white item about two inches square and the same thickness as his cell phone. He plugged it into the bottom of his phone, tapped the screen a few times and then held the whole thing out to Merlin, "Just slip your credit card or debit card into the little white reader, follow the directions on the screen, and we can transfer the money."

Merlin was surprised but he pulled out his debit card with one hand as he took Stuart's cell phone in the other. "It's a card reader? You've obviously done this before."

Stuart shrugged again, "Yeah. It's called a Square. Money changes hand in this business all the time. Not this big of course." He seemed almost to regret that last comment.

Merlin looked at the screen and gave it some thought. If the money angle wasn't the problem he thought it might be, maybe he could push it harder.

Stuart noticed the inaction and seemed to squirm in his seat, "Is everything okay? I mean...?"

Finally tapping away on the screen, Merlin nodded. Then he passed the cell phone back to Stuart, "There you go. I just wanted to make sure you understood my commitment."

"Your commitment?" Stuart looked at the screen and nearly fell off his seat. "Forty thousand dollars?"

"You bribe whoever you need to bribe. I've done well for myself and I'm all-in on wanting the next part of my life to succeed. I have a lot of ideas I think will help our country."

Stuart was very eager again as he tapped away at the screen. "Of course, of course. I can understand that." A moment later, he pointed to his left, "Would you look that way for a moment?"

Wondering why, Merlin looked at where the freelancer had pointed and then looked back, "Why–?"

The cell phone flashed. Stuart had taken his picture and now he tapped and swiped. And then nodded. "Perfect, perfect."

Merlin nearly panicked. He hadn't thought of his picture appearing in the newspaper as well. Well, he did but... maybe he hadn't thought of the implications for someone doing undercover work.

Stuart noticed the concern written across Merlin's face. "Don't worry. I know a lot of people want that glamorous headshot but that isn't what we need here. This is a nice candid shot, the sort that the paparazzi get when they're chasing down the rich and famous." He pushed the chair back and it scraped across the floor as he got up. "Now I've got to go to work."

Merlin looked up at him, still wondering if this had been a good idea.

"Don't worry," Stuart said again as he waved away the continuing look of concern, "I'll be back in touch with your assistant. This is going to be good."

Merlin sat there alone as the freelancer disappeared. Everything had better be more than good—it had to be perfect—or he would fail to succeed in his assignment. And now he had exposed himself needlessly to public scrutiny.

Chapter 10

NIGHT HAD FALLEN and Merlin stopped the Porsche in the large, well-lit circular driveway behind several other vehicles and got out. The people Merlin could see heading for the front entrance were talking and laughing quietly but there was definite excitement in the air. A young man in a red vest came running, handed him a numbered token, and took the car keys. As the car jockey jumped in and drove his car away, Merlin slipped the token into a pocket and looked up at the impressive building. It was a two-story, wood and stone, neo-French Renaissance mansion. He had done a little research, discovering the event was being held at the home of Audrick J Pittman, progressive philanthropist and founder of the Audrick J Pittman Foundation. The event was being held for one of the American political parties. But Pittman played it smart, holding fundraisers for both major parties, as well as a few independent ones because he was willing to grease any wheel necessary to do business. And Pittman was very good at greasing wheels for people who needed the wheels greased.

As Merlin headed for the entrance, he was surprised to see a Hollywood movie star he had watched on a television rerun only two weeks ago. And there was another one. And another. They were handing their invitation cards to one of four security guards standing at the elegantly carved front door. These people were serious if they wouldn't let someone that famous in without an invitation.

Although he imagined someone that famous would find a way in one way or another.

He began reaching into his breast pocket for the invitation card—an arm slipped through his arm and a shapely body pressed against his side.

"This is exciting. Who are we supposed to be?"

Merlin was surprised to see the woman in the black tracksuit. Only now she was in a long, black gown that flowed over her tall, shapely form. She was holding onto his arm like they were on a date. An expensive looking necklace sparkled just above her cleavage, and an exquisite looking diamond bracelet adorned one wrist. A ring on one finger seemed out of place, a gold ring with a black onyx stone. In the center of the stone was a green jade cat. It looked more like a man's ring–

"You had better tell me who we are so I don't give anything away accidentally at the door."

His mind whirled as Merlin tried to figure out what was going on. And who she was. The accent had a slight Brooklyn tone to it. She was in her mid-twenties–

The dark-haired woman continued smiling, looking casual—and beautiful—as she said, "Cat got your tongue? You better hurry. We only have three couples ahead of us."

Realizing she was right, Merlin looked at the guards, reached into his breast pocket and pulled out the invitation. "Uh..."

The woman went on the toes of her high heel shoes as she glanced at the card, "Oh. Dimitri Starkov. Is that why you were in his place?" Her face turned serious as she looked over the building again, "Why a boring old fundraiser?" Her eyes sparkled as she looked at Merlin, "Are we casing the joint? Is there some big diamond called the eye of something or other that we're–?"

"Keep your voice down," Merlin cautioned her. "And how do you expect to get inside with me–?"

She tapped the card with a black finger nail that had a gold gradient glitter tip, "It says right there - *and guest. We* are good to go." Satisfied she had made her case, the woman looked at the other arriving couples, taking in their attire.

Merlin saw her raise one eyebrow, considering one of the women on the arm of a famous movie star. Merlin wondered why she was scrutinizing that one since there was actually a woman on each arm. She was so casual and calm—no, make that self-assured about the whole thing—while his insides were now doing cartwheels, "I'm not even sure why there is a *we* in this."

The woman shrugged, "What can I tell you? In for a penny, in for a pound."

"Who are you?"

The woman wagged a finger in jest, "Sorry, a woman never tells. Wait...that's age isn't it?" She put a finger on her refined nose, wrinkled it and laughed. "You can call me...Sonja. That's Russian, right?"

"I guess so."

They were only behind two couples now and the noise of a handheld metal scanner sounded as one of the guards passed it up and down the body of everybody entering. They weren't touching anyone in a pat-down so Merlin wasn't concerned about his Beretta in the conceal holster—the woman left his arm and he wondered if he was rid of her for some reason.

But all the woman in black did was casually walk to a planter and discreetly deposit something from her small purse—she thought about it for a moment and dropped the purse in there as well—before she sauntered back and took his arm again.

"I take it you had a gun?" Merlin asked her as he watched the guards. "Were you expecting to rob everybody once you got inside?"

"No, a woman just can't be too sure who she meets these days."

"Like someone you knock over in an apartment where you don't belong?"

"Look who's talking," she said with a smile. "Two peas in a pod. Or is that two peas in someone else's apartment?"

Merlin had a partial answer. She wasn't tied to Starkov. Unless she was an accomplished actor. "Why were you there?"

"Too many questions. We're next."

Merlin stepped forward with the woman on his arm and held the invitation out to one of the guards.

As the other guard ran the metal detector up and down their bodies, he eyed the invitation, then Merlin, then the woman.

Sonya raised her eyebrows as the man moved the scanner up and down, close to her form, "That thing won't cause infertility will it?" She overtly squeezed against Merlin, "He wants twins."

The two guards looked confused at the question. A moment later, the one holding the invitation waved at the man with the wand to step back. Then he handed the invitation to Merlin, gesturing to the door being opened by another guard. "Please enjoy yourself tonight."

With her holding firmly to his arm, Merlin stepped inside the foyer, slipping the card into his pocket. He glanced back, pretending to look over the hand-carved millwork, and decorative gold gilding, to make sure the guards had turned their attention to someone else. They did and the door closed behind them. He looked at the woman, "What was that all about?"

"That's so they didn't look too closely at the name. For all you know he's been here before. Right?" She squeezed her body against him again, "We make a good team."

"We aren't a team," Merlin said. He began walking with her to the main area, taking in their surroundings. The foyer opened to a large, high-ceiling room filled with people in tuxedos and expensive dresses. The conversation was lively, mixed with the tinkling of glasses, and the scents of crab rangoon and caviar hors-d'oeuvres.

Sonya did a pretend pout, making sure he saw it.

"Okay, okay, you're right. You did a good job back there." He gave her a grudging, "Thanks."

Flashing a smile, Sonya said, "So we *are* a team. Great."

"No...never mind."

As they reached the edge of the crowd, she squeezed against him, speaking low, "And what name do I use for you?"

"Rhett." He tried to put a sliver of space between them, "And please stop doing that."

"Butler? And why would I do that? I can tell you like my body. you looked at it enough already."

"No, not Butler. What is it with you women? Rhett Summers. And I'm not looking at your body."

She pressed suggestively against him, "No. Right now you're feeling me up with your arm and your side." She laughed lightly at the awkwardness that showed on his face.

Merlin knew he was in over his head with her teasing and it would only get worse for him if it continued. He saw a way out of the conversation when a server carrying a tray of pink champagne drinks passed by. "Excuse me, can we have a couple of those?"

"Of course, Sir." The server extended the tray.

Extricating himself from her arm, Merlin grabbed two drinks, passing one to her before taking a sip of his own.

Sonya raised an eyebrow as she took the drink, knowing full well what he was doing. As the server moved away, she leaned her head toward Merlin, her face serious, "Don't think you're going to get rid of me that easily."

Merlin stayed silent, wondering if he could.

Moving closer, Sonya placed one hand on his back—and froze. Slowly pulling her arm back, her voice was low and intense, "How did you get that in here? I saw them–. Who the hell are you?" She looked around.

She had felt his carbon fiber gun and Merlin now wondered if she was about to let everyone know.

Chapter 11

MERLIN TOOK HER ELBOW firmly and moved her toward a massive stone fireplace and away from the other people. He was trying to put some distance so no one could overhear them. "Look, I didn't ask you to join me here. I didn't ask you to–"

Sonya yanked her arm from his grip and took a step back, her voice low and defiant, "And yet here I am. And here you are, carrying a weapon that is obviously very high tech."

Pressing his lips together, closing his eyes, and feeling frustration, Merlin knew he couldn't push this. He obviously couldn't scare her and if he wasn't careful, everything would be out of control in no time. If it wasn't already. He glanced around to see if anyone was watching. "Like you said outside, you never know who you're going to meet." He shrugged, "I like gadgets and...you never know what you'll find inside someone else's place."

Her eyebrows pushed together and Sonya shook her head, "Why would you think you're going to meet someone that dangerous here–?" Her expression changed to one of intrigue, "Are you saying you found that gun inside someone's house?"

Merlin took a quick glance around. She had bought his loose excuse but he had to keep her occupied with her own thoughts. "No more talk of guns. We need to keep our eyes open. Just play along, okay?"

Sonya gave him a devil of a smile and moved close again, "This is more exciting than I expected–"

"Mr. Butler?"

Trying to put a sliver of distance between himself and the woman again, Merlin looked at who was talking. An elegant looking woman in her forties, dressed in a black gown that sparkled with every movement, stood looking at him, a delighted look on her face. A man stood next to her, smiling. But his smile and his eyes were on Sonya's body.

The woman extended a hand, "I'm sorry to intrude on your conversation. My name is Rebecca Henderson. My husband Roland and I saw the article about you in the Washington Post and I just had to meet you."

That startled Merlin and he had to make a quick recovery as he shook her hand, "It's very nice to meet you, Mrs. Henderson. And please call me Rhett." He shook the husband's hand, "Sir." The husband was in his 80s, with a trim build, slicked-back white hair, and steel-gray eyes that seemed to penetrate Sonya's clothing in open appraisal.

Mrs. Henderson put a hand on her husband's elbow and beamed, "Call us Rebecca and Roland." She looked to the woman, "And who is this lovely lady?"

Roland extended his hand to the woman as his eyes roamed her body, "Yes, who is this young lady?"

A tight smile on her face, Sonya took his hand with just her fingers, "I'm Sonya...Tapper. Very nice to meet you." She reached out and shook hands with Mrs. Henderson.

His eyes caressing the side of Sonya's bottom as she bent forward, Roland Henderson reluctantly looked to Merlin, "I take it you haven't been in Washington very long, Rhett?"

"Uh... no. Just a few weeks actually."

"Where are you staying? Have you found your own place yet?" Henderson asked. He glanced at Sonya again and puffed his chest out, "My *fortune* initially came from my time in investment banking and that has allowed me to purchase several luxury condominium buildings in the area. Perhaps I can help you find something if you're still looking. Both of you, of course."

Rebecca tapped her husband on the shoulder, "I'll let you two men talk business." Then she looked at Sonya and held a hand out to her, "Why don't you come with me? I have someone I'd like you to meet."

Unsure, Sonya took her hand, "All right." As Rebecca pulled her away, Sonya stopped in front of Merlin and planted a soft kiss on his lips, "I won't be far...sweetie." She placed her cheek against his and whispered, "How in the world did you manage an article in the Washington Post?" She gave him a wink as Rebecca dragged her away.

Everything was happening so fast that Merlin felt he was losing control of the situation.

Roland Henderson watched Sonya's bottom wiggle away, "I bet that one wears you out."

"You have no idea."

Switching topics, Henderson took a sip of his pink champagne and asked, "Did you ever get to work much with Rolf Templeton when you were at Goldman Sachs?"

Crap was all Merlin could think of. Yes? No? What the hell was he supposed to say?

"Old Rolf is one of those guys who likes to work twenty-four-seven. Reminds me a lot of myself when I was in my younger days just starting at Morgan Stanley."

Merlin felt relief as the man blathered on, and he followed along, smiling and nodding.

"Not that it changed very much when I went over to—" Henderson paused as he looked past Merlin's shoulder. His eyebrows rose as he lifted an arm and snapped his fingers several times.

Glancing over his own shoulder, expecting to see another server heading this way, Merlin instead saw three men. The one in the lead had salt-and-pepper hair and goatee, dark penetrating eyes, and a tuxedo with a double-breasted jacket. The other two men wore tuxedos with shawl lapels. They looked more like bodyguards than guests and the more open jacket style made that impression even stronger.

Henderson frowned and pointedly looked at the lead man as the three drew close, "You're usually here early. Are you losing your touch?"

The man in the pinstripe suit walked up to Henderson and scowled, "It is not my fault." His penetrating eyes bore into Merlin's as the words came hard and slow, "Someone took my invitation. I had to call Audrick and come in the servant's entrance."

From the Russian accent, Merlin assumed he was looking at his target, Dmitri Starkov. His free hand moved casually towards his back as he readied to pull his Beretta. He cursed inside. How did he know? Where there cameras in the condominium? What did I miss?

The attention of the two bodyguards went to Merlin's hand. They were obviously well-trained, probably recognizing his body language. This wasn't just going sideways—this was headed for disaster.

Chapter 12

OTTAWA, CANADA

RETURNING FROM A BUSINESS TRIP to New York, Jaimie Hartman hurried to Merlin's apartment door. She eagerly knocked, anticipating the scene she would set up and invite him to later, one that involved a sexy Can-Can outfit he had brought back from some secret assignment last month—her thoughts were short circuited when the door opened.

An *unknown*, dark-haired woman was standing in the doorway instead of Merlin Dragon.

Sammy Powless raised her eyebrows as she appraised the startled blue eyes woman of the woman standing in the hallway. "Yes?"

Jaime took a moment to get a word out—three actually. "Who are you?"

Blinking once, Sammy said, "Who are you?"

"I asked first."

"I asked second."

Jaimie shook her head, "That doesn't make any sense."

"Why not?"

Hands on her hips, Jaime said, "Because that's not how it works. I asked first and you have to answer."

Sammy crossed her arms, "No. I ask, you answer."

"Why would that be? I asked first and–"

"And I'm the one in the apartment."

"Exactly! Why?"

"Why what?"

Jaimie gave her an irritated look, "Why are you inside the apartment?"

Sammy raised an eyebrow, "I guess someone has to be in here to answer your knock."

"You're impossible."

"Is that some kind of club like the Shriners?"

"What?"

Sammy cocked her head, "Or is this mission impossible, trying to get a decent answer out of you as to *why* you're at my door?"

Jaime straightened her shoulders, "This is not your door."

"Okay, so technically it belongs to the owners of the building. Now why are you knocking on it?"

It took another moment before Jaime's shoulders sagged a bit and she chewed on her lower lip.

Sammy raised an eyebrow, "I'm waiting–"

"Tell him I won't be." Jaime turned on her heels to the right, and strode down the hallway.

Sammy leaned out, watching the woman unlock a door and disappearing into another apartment. She flinched when the door slammed shut, sending a booming sound along the hallway. "Interesting."

Chapter 13

WASHINGTON, DC

MERLIN DRAGON'S HAND was near his back pocket now. All he had to do was flip the jacket up and pull the weapon. He envisioned a quick-draw shootout like in the old west days. The light laughter of two elegantly clad women passing not more than a few feet away gave him pause. It was possible a lot of innocent people were going to get hurt.

Dmitri Starkov's scowl moved from Merlin's face to Roland Henderson's, "And why are *you* talking to *him*?"

Henderson didn't flinch, "And why wouldn't I?"

His dark eyes boring into Merlin's again, Starkov said, "Are you not a Harvard man? Did I not read that about you?"

That startled Merlin. It took a moment before he said, "Yes–"

Starkov's scowl turned back to Henderson, "And you are a Princeton man. Have your values sunk that low?"

It took a tense, stressful heartbeat before Starkov and Henderson burst into laughter. A moment later, the Russian moved in and embraced Henderson, "It is good to see you, my old friend."

Henderson slapped him on the back, the pink champagne sloshing in the glass he held in the other hand, "Now I really have to question my values."

Merlin felt the adrenaline still rushing through his veins from the perceived threat. It was hard to believe it at all been a joke at his expense.

Breaking off the embrace, Starkov held a theatrical finger up as he turned his attention back to Merlin, "And I am graduate from Leningrad State University. Much better than both American schools I would consider no more than high schools."

"And they changed the name of your university to St. Petersburg in the 90s," Henderson reminded him.

Starkov gave him a frown, "You are always sticking the fork in me."

"Knife. Sticking the knife in you. Learn to speak proper English."

Shrugging as he looked back at Merlin, Starkov said, "I speak well enough to bed the ladies." He laughed and stuck his hand out, "I am sorry, Mr. Summers, for having fun at your expense. I read about you in the Washington Post this morning. My name is Dmitri Starkov. Roland and I are old friends and we often kid each other in this fashion. I can see we have made you uncomfortable."

Merlin managed a slight grin as he shook hands. "I have to admit you did have me there for a moment. It's very nice to meet you. Please call me Rhett."

Henderson spoke up, "We are not just good friends, Mr. Summers...Rhett. Dmitri and I have worked together to help a number of people in politics." He gestured to Merlin with the pink champagne glass, "I have to confess I directed my wife to you as soon as I saw you come in and recognized you from the newspaper article. Politics is a business that can always use good, young talent. And I always strike when the iron is hot as they say."

Dimitri nodded as he looked at Merlin, "He is right. But tell me Rhett...did you come with a beautiful young woman tonight?"

Not sure why he was being asked the question, Merlin said, "I did come with someone—"

"Then be very careful. Roland is probably more interested in her talents than yours." He laughed heartily and slapped Henderson on the chest with the back of his hand.

Henderson laughed in turn, "She is a beauty, Dimitri."

Merlin had the impression these men weren't just having fun with each other, they were dangerous predators in every sense of the word.

Starkov turned to the two men who were with him, "Anatoly? Sergei? Go and enjoy yourselves. Find yourself some young ladies." He laughed.

Both guards continued eying Merlin for a moment, still obviously not convinced he wasn't a danger. Eventually, one of them nodded, tapped the other from his subtle defensive stance and they went in search of enjoyment. There was one more suspicious glance back from the second man and then they disappeared into the crowd.

Another voice emerged from the crowd, "Dimitri? I thought I heard your laugh." It was Rebecca Henderson, with Sonya not far behind. Rebecca Starkov gave a hug, "How have you been? We haven't seen you in ages."

"It's only been two months," Starkov said as he wrapped his arms around her.

Merlin noticed both the Russian and Roland Henderson had their eyes on Sonya as she stood behind Rebecca.

Sensing their interest in her, Sonya took several quick steps in her high heels and slipped between the hugging couple and Roland Henderson to Merlin. She planted a soft kiss on Merlin's lips again, then placed her cheek affectionately against his and whispered, "I saw two of his men. Are we in trouble?"

Before Merlin could give her any kind if reply or indication of their present situation, Starkov turned his head, taking in Sonya's legs, "And who is this young lady who is so passionate?"

Rebecca let go of the Russian and made the introductions, "That is Rhett's lady friend, Sonya Tapper. Sonya, this is Dimitri Starkov, a very good friend of ours."

Sonya kept a hand on Merlin's shoulder as she turned to face the Russian, "I'm very—"

Starkov moved in on Sonya, taking her hand and kissing it, "I am very pleased to meet you, Sonya Tapper." His eyes looked to Merlin, "You are a very lucky man. I will have to be a rival for her affections."

A look of delight on her face at the action, Sonya said, "I'm very pleased to meet you, Mr. Starkov."

The Russian moved in, wrapping his arms around her, "Please, call me Dimitri. I am sure we are going to be very, very close."

Now trying to put some room between their bodies, Sonya said, "Yes...well...Dimitri...." Her eyes went to Merlin, looking for help.

Merlin gave her a subtle smile and shake of his head.

Starkov gave Merlin a mischievous grin, took Sonya's arm and wrapped it around his as he said, "I am going to steal your woman for just a few moments. She needs to fully experience the marvelous culture of my country." He began leading her away, openly flirting with her, "I will get you some of the caviar. I made sure they had some of the finest Russian caviar and without my help, you won't know which is the one to choose."

Not expecting that, Merlin felt some frustration. Making contact with his target so soon had been fortuitous. But now he had no way to work to get closer to Starkov—

Rebecca tapped him on the chest, "You don't need to worry. Dmitri flirts with everyone. It's in his passionate Russian nature."

She looked to her husband, "I'm going back to talk with Marcia Williams. If you need me, come and get me."

As she moved away into the crowd, Roland Henderson bobbed up and down on his toes. He seemed to be enjoying Merlin's apparent concern about his woman, "I wouldn't be so sure about not worrying."

Merlin gave a shrug as he slipped his hands into his pockets, "If you knew her like I do, I'm more worried about him. At his age, she could easily ride him to death."

Henderson snickered at the ribald comment.

Internally, Merlin found it—should that be funny or disturbing—that the woman he had only 'met' after she knocked him over in the Russian's apartment as he worked his assignment, was now a central focus of his Russian target. And this other well-to-do man that he'd only met—who found it humorous—was no doubt contemplating how *he* could get in a position to do his own riding with Sonya Tapper. His impression that these were two predators in every sense of the word was heightened. Anyone getting involved with these two would be like flies in a Venus flytrap, flying innocently into the political world and swallowed whole. And here he was, tempting the thing to snap shut.

Chapter 14

MERLIN PUSHED THE WOMAN from his mind. The expression 'she had made her bed and now had to lie in it' seemed to be extremely appropriate and she had to deal with what she had set in motion herself. Refocusing on why he was here, he took the opportunity to find out more about his target and addressed Roland Henderson. "You said you and Dimitri work together to help people getting into politics. You two have a partnership or a company to do that?"

Henderson shook his head. "No, nothing so formal. Dmitri is a Russian and he has to be careful how he delves into American politics." He held a hand up. "I don't mean to suggest that there would be anything inappropriate in getting involved. He just feels it works better if he remains in the background. Dmitri owns Telekom AG in Stuttgart, Germany, a company that manufactures telecommunications equipment—"

"Telecommunications equipment?" Merlin couldn't remember anything like that in the information pack he had read while flying down on the Global 8000 jet.

"It makes a wide range of things like public switching and transmission equipment to everything you need to set up an office like local area networks, land lines, cell phones. The whole gamut."

"Interesting." And it was, considering what the Russian was involved in.

"Dimitri has outlets in Europe, England, and here in the United States." Henderson leaned his head toward Merlin in a confidential manner. "Government contracts are far more lucrative than the regular ones he wins in the business world, if you get my drift. By helping me helping people like you, we have someone on the inside. He gets to sell his equipment to government agencies and I get to help people like yourself. It's my way of giving back to this great country for giving me so much."

Merlin had the feeling Roland Henderson was doing it for reasons beyond patriotism. What exactly he got out of it wasn't apparent at this point. But there was no doubt the man was also testing out Merlin. The phrase 'we have someone on the inside' was very explicit and very much to the point. There was no beating around the bush or trying to hide it in softer terms. Merlin sipped his drink and nodded after a moment, "I can see that. It makes sense. As you well know, in the investing business we always push the envelope. As long as no ethical or legal boundaries are crossed. It's all part of doing business."

Henderson saluted Merlin subtly with his drink, "Spoken like a true professional. You'll go far in politics young man."

"Well...going far and getting started are two different things."

"That's very true." Henderson gestured to a server and when he came over, he placed his nearly-empty glass on the extended tray. "Hold on just one moment, young man, I'm going to want another one of those drinks."

The server blinked his eyes at being used as a temporary table but he stood there, waiting patiently.

Digging into a pocket, Henderson pulled out a business card, handing it across to Merlin," There you go."

Taking it in hand, Merlin read the card; Roland K Henderson. Blackstone Strategies LLC.

Henderson took another drink from the tray, "And thank you for waiting, young man." He turned his attention back to Merlin, "The article mentioned you wanted to run for the Senate. Your next round of elections is two years away."

Merlin felt the 'kissoff' was coming and he wondered how he could counter it.

"You have a lot of work to do in those two years. You give me a call tomorrow and we can arrange to meet and talk things through. There are a lot of opportunities in this city but you have to have a laser-like focus on where you're going."

"Okay." Relieved, Merlin slipped the card into his pocket.

"Now, if you'll excuse me, I see someone else I need to talk to."

"Of course. Go ahead." As Henderson left, Merlin sipped at his drink, considering the crowd. There were definitely a lot of people who looked to be well-to-do here and they covered all age ranges. It was a perfect fishing hole for someone like the Russian. Voices rose and fell in a general buzz of conversation and laughter. Glasses rang lightly as they were placed back on trays carried by an army of servers who moved in and out of the crowd almost unnoticed. Merlin decided to try and engage Starkov again—since that's why he was here—and he began moving along the edge of the crowd looking for him. Anytime someone looked in Merlin's direction, he looked over the decor, not wanting to mingle and get sidetracked. But ten or fifteen minutes went by and there was still no sign of the Russian. The room was larger than he had anticipated and more crowded. At one point, he caught sight of Roland Henderson emerging from a room. Merlin stopped and watched.

Henderson closed the door behind him carefully, like he was trying to go unnoticed, despite the crowd. Smiling at someone, he disappeared into the crowd.

Merlin tried to see where he went–

"Oksana Pavlovich."

The husky voice with the Russian lilt was close to his right ear. A pillow pressed against his arm.

Merlin looked to see who it was.

A pair of bold, blue eyes sat under a fringe of platinum blond hair.

Glancing downward without moving his head, Merlin realized the 'pillow' was actually one breast of a set barely contained by the black dress the gorgeous woman wore.

"Aren't you going to tell me your name? I told you mine."

The husky voice had a suggestive quality to it and Merlin felt his brain tie into Gordian knots. He pulled back slowly, not wanting to offend, and turned to face the gorgeous woman. His mouth opened slightly but nothing came out.

Heart-shaped lips parted, "Are you afraid your wife will see us talking?"

Merlin managed a faint, "I'm not married...."

A golden eyebrow raised slightly, "Even better." She reached out and touched his arm with her fingers, walking them slowly upward, "Now why don't we start again? My name is Oksana Pavlovich. And your name is...?"

"Uh...M–" He closed his eyes for a moment, opened them and said, "Rhett. Rhett Summers."

"Well, Mr. Rhett Summers, I don't seem to have a drink in my hand. Would you be a dear and get me one?" The heart-shaped lips settled together in a waiting smile.

It took a moment for Merlin to react, although it was more wooden than fluid. He turned his head, looking for a server, saw one and raised a hand.

The server smile, working his way through the crowd and held his tray out.

Merlin placed his nearly-empty glass on the tray, picking up two full ones, "Thanks."

Nodding, the server turned and moved back through the crowd.

Two drinks in hand, Merlin turned back to the gorgeous blonde. And stood there. His eyes accidentally dropped to her pillows. And he brought them back up immediately.

"Are you going to give it to me? The drink, I mean." The lips parted and a pink tongue gently caressed the upper lip.

Merlin took in a breath and let it out, handing one of the drinks to her. "Of course, I'm sorry."

Her fingers caressed his for a moment before she took the drink, "Don't be sorry, just be good... Mr. Rhett. That's all a girl can ask." She took a sip, her eyes remaining on Merlin's. When she lowered the class, her tongue moved lightly across her upper lip again, removing the glistening liquid. "Do you want to tell me about yourself?"

"Uh...not much to tell...I guess..."

"Would you prefer to go somewhere...more private...to talk...?"

"More private–?"

"That will be enough of that, thank you very much." It was Sonya Tapper. She removed the drink from Merlin's hand and passed it to the blonde, "Hold onto that, will you?"

Oksana Pavlovich was startled but her fingers curled around the stem of the glass.

Sonya pulled her head back as she looked at the woman's large breasts, "Whoa." She gestured with a finger back and forth, "What are they? 700ccs? I'll bet those puppies set you back a pretty penny."

The golden eyebrows pushed together.

"Or whoever paid for them."

The heart-shaped lips parted in protest–

Sonya dismissed her with a raised palm. "Whatever." She grasped Merlin's elbow and she turned him, moving them away through the crowd. "Let's go."

Merlin went from being tongue-tied to confused, "What was that all about? And where are we going?" There was no answer as he was steered through and around people toward the front entrance, "Are you jealous or something?"

Sonya scoffed, "Oh, puleeese, Miss Boobsalichious back there doesn't have anything to do with it. You can go back there and squeeze them—I bet she names them hush and puppy— all night long. But right now, I'm leaving and I just need you to give me a ride."

"A ride?"

"Yes, a ride." She pulled open the door and hustled Merlin outside, "Give the car jockey your token so he can get your car. I'm so *done* with this place." She crossed her arms firmly and stood there waiting.

Merlin did as he was told, handing the token to a car jockey. He was going to talk to her, find out what had happened but her coldness told him not to try. And besides her anger, she looked fine. And now he could go back to working on his assignment without her being glued to his side.

A few tense moments later, the black Porsche pulled up and Merlin traded places with the driver.

Sonya Tapper walked around the back and got in the passenger side, still silent and brooding.

The powerful engine roared as Merlin pulled away. "Where do I take you?"

Sonya's voice was tight and harsh. "Not in the backseat like your friends assume." She gestured to the left. "Take me two blocks that way. I took a cab here and I'm not walking in these heels back there."

"Okay." Merlin took a left turn and pressed down on the accelerator. The sleek Porsche took off like a rocket, pressing them back in their seats. A moment later, he glanced at her. He had to ask. "What do you mean not in the back seat like your friends...?"

Her mouth worked to hold back anger before Sonya spit out the words. "I had a tough time getting away from the big Russian guy. And then your friend Roland Henderson cornered me. He basically suggested that spreading my legs for him would help your political career. I'm not spreading my legs to help you in any way, shape, or form."

That stunned Merlin, "I didn't ask you to. And I don't expect you to." He slowed for a red light, "And keep in mind those people are not my friends. I only met them tonight, just like you."

"Whatever." She crossed her arms tightly across her chest.

The light turned green before Merlin came to a full stop and he pressed on the accelerator again, roaring through the intersection.

Sonya was quiet for a few moments and then she gestured ahead and to the right, "You can stop right there. Beside that bike."

Merlin pulled to a stop next to a white, Suzuki GSX-R600 motorcycle.

Without another word, Sonya Tapper got out, slamming the door shut and stepping to the back of the motorcycle where she picked up a helmet and pulled it over her head. Hiking her black dress up to reveal bare thighs, she straddled the motorcycle and started it. A moment later, the four-stroke, 600cc engine purred loudly and she accelerated into the street, disappeared like an angry rocket into the night.

Merlin was left there, engine idling. He was surprised to find he was intrigued by this woman. How she was able to bound across rooftops with ease, dress elegantly and talk so easily at a formal fundraiser, and then then ride away on a motorcycle, still dressed to the nines. And then his thoughts turned to what she had said and the people they had met tonight. His impression that the Russian and this Henderson were predators was right. But he was surprised at how fast they had worked on her. He knew he shouldn't be surprised but the episode was a reminder to keep his guard up. These men were ruthless, willing to do whatever it took to get what they wanted. The good part? He didn't have to worry about Sonya Tapper and he could get back to his assignment. Stopping Dimitri Starkov.

Chapter 15

MERLIN RETURNED TO the coffee shop where he had talked with the Washington Times freelancer, had a coffee and sandwich as he mulled over what it happened, and then returned to the Ritz-Carlton Hotel. There he paced, trying to figure out how to play this thing out when he next met with Roland Henderson. Would it allow him to get close to the Russian and find out who they had turned into Russian agents? If he snuck back into Starkov's condominium now that he was here, would he find evidence on some laptop or cell phone he had brought with him? There was something else he was wondering about. He grabbed his cell phone, punched in the numbers and listened.

The voice that answered was sleepy and slurry, "Hello?"

"Sammy? It's Merlin."

"Merlin?" There was a pause, then, "What time is it? It's after midnight...what's wrong? Are you okay?"

Running a hand through his sandy hair, Merlin felt bad about not being more aware of the time, "Sorry, I was just thinking and I didn't know what time it was and...."

There was a rustling sounded and then Sammy said, "That's okay. What...what's up?"

It almost sounded like she was going to fall back to sleep again. "I'm sorry, Sammy. Don't worry about it. I'll call you in the morning—"

"No, no, no. You called for a reason. What is it?" Her voice sounded fainter as she talked to someone else. "It's fine. It's okay, you go back to sleep."

"Is that Jigs? That's the main reason I was calling. How is he?"

"He's fine. He was curled up behind me, snoring away."

"That's good. He really trusts you. Thanks for doing this."

"No problem. I've been eating healthier, lots of chicken."

Merlin laughed, "The little con artist."

"Yeah. Now, you said Jigs was the main reason, what else do you need?" Sammy asked.

Scratching the back of his head, Merlin told her, "That article Clevon Stuart did for me in the Washington Post worked really well."

"That's good to hear."

"Yeah. But I was just thinking I need something at Harvard and Goldman Sachs in case someone checks."

"That's part of your background? Harvard and Goldman Sachs?"

"Yeah. I know you're not really in the position to help... but maybe you could reach out to someone...?"

Sammy was silent for a moment and then she said, "I'll see what I can do. I have to read the article first and then...yeah... I can try and get something injected digitally into their records as fast as possible. It won't pass deep scrutiny but it will work on a surface request."

"That sounds right for what I need."

"Okay, good. Anything else?"

"Yeah." He knew he had to open up more so she could give him the help he needed. "I'm working on something that involves Dimitri Starkov, a Russian oligarch."

"A Russian oligarch? Really?"

"Yeah. Try and check out Telekom AG in Stuttgart, Germany. Starkov is supposed to be the owner. And check out Roland K Henderson and his wife Rebecca. They live here in the Washington area. He runs Blackstone Strategies LLC and I need to know about that as well. All of that popped up in what I'm doing. And for some reason, I didn't have any information on any of the companies or the people."

"Okay. Telekom AG. Blackstone Strategies. Roland K Henderson. Rebecca Henderson. Anything else?"

Merlin gave it a thought for a moment and then said, "Yeah, add the name Sonya Tapper to the list. I think it's an alias but...you never know. I'll send you a text message with all of these names."

"Sounds good. Oh, one other thing. A woman showed up at your door."

"A woman?"

"Yeah. I think it's one of your neighbors. Tall, dark hair, blue eyes. She disappeared into one of the apartments down the hallway."

"Oh. That's probably Jaimie Hartman. She works out of her apartment and is usually the one who takes care of Jigs when I have an assignment. I thought she was going to be away longer...it doesn't matter. What did she say?"

"Well," Sammy said slowly, "I don't think she was too happy with seeing me in your apartment."

"Oh."

"When she left she said...tell him I won't be."

"Tell him I won't be? What does that mean? Won't be what?"

"I think...waiting? I'm not really sure." Sammy yawned, "Sorry. I wish I could be more specific but...."

Merlin chewed on his lip, "That's okay. Don't worry about it. I'll talk to her when I get back. And I'll let you get back to sleep and you can get the ball rolling in the morning–"

"No, I'm up. I'll get started on it now. This is too important to let it wait."

The call ended and Merlin stood there, wondering what had happened back home with Jaimie.

Chapter 16

BLACKSTONE STRATEGIES, LLC

IT WAS 10:45 IN THE MORNING and the sun rose warmly in the blue skies. Merlin had called the number on the business card Henderson had given him and was told by a woman—who identified herself as Olivia Van Buren and the Chief Financial Officer of Blackstone—that Roland Henderson would meet him here this morning at 11 AM. He parked the Porsche in a visitor spot in front of the building, turned off the engine and checked his phone for messages from Sammy. There weren't any and he found that unusual. He had hoped she would be able to give him a heads up on any of the companies or the names by now. Or confirmation she had been able to set up some background information for him–

The revving of an engine caught his attention. Merlin looked into the rearview mirror but didn't see anything. The engine noise stopped and Merlin went back to his phone for a moment, double checking for messages. But there was still nothing and so he got out. The Porsche sounded twice as he locked the doors. Slipping the keys into the pocket of his dark suit, Merlin walked toward the entrance, looking over the building. Blackstone Strategies was a thirty-story building featuring black granite, gold trim, and gold windows. There were thirty other vehicles sitting in the parking spots in front of the building this morning, all of them high-end luxury vehicles or costly

European sports cars. It gave Merlin the impression everybody who worked here made a lot of money–

A hand slid around his elbow, something soft settled against his arm and a voice said, "Good morning, sweetie. What are we up to today?"

Merlin was surprised to see Sonya Tapper holding onto his arm, a bright smile on her face. "What are you doing here?" he asked her. "I thought you were finished with everything?"

Sonya gave him a shake of her head. "Oh, no. When I thought over all those richy-rich people at that big do last night, I still want in on whatever scheme you're planning."

"What about Roland Henderson and what he wanted–?"

Giving him a slight shrug, Sonya said, "I'll just have to keep my knees glued together. Unless of course, you have any plans along those lines?" She gave him a wink.

"How about if I give you some rope to tie those knees together?"

"Oh? You like it kinky, do you?"

Merlin shook his head. "I don't think this is a good idea–"

"You're not talking me out of it. And—if my feminine charms appear to give us an advantage—I decided to wear this outfit." She stepped back and held her arms out wide. "What do you think?" She wore a white blouse—and apparently a push-up bra the that added considerable more emphasis to her bust and cleavage—and a red dress that was a few inches above her knees. She turned in a circle to display the outfit. "I think the shorter skirt and heels show my legs off quite well, don't you think?"

Merlin looked at the shoes. The heels had to be four inches high. "How do you walk in those things?"

Sonya put her hands on her hips. "They're not for walking. They're for displaying my wares, if you get my meaning."

"Okay, if you say so." Merlin's thoughts went to the engine he had heard and he glanced around the parking lot. He spotted her white motorcycle, "You drove here on your motorcycle in that dress and those heels?"

"Why? Are you afraid I wasn't being a lady?" She reached down to the hem of her red dress and whipped it right up over her hips.

Merlin nearly went into a panic. Until he realized she was wearing tight, black bicycle shorts that extended halfway down her thighs.

Sonya let the dress dropped back down to cover her legs and put a finger under her nose, giggling. "If you could just see your face." She took his elbow again and turning him and heading to the entrance again, "Now...who are we here to see this morning? And how does it fit in with your scheme?"

Merlin took a breath in and let it out slowly. Having her involved again wasn't good. But what choice did he have? If he tried to push her away too hard, she could ruin everything, maybe even tell the Russian he was in his condo unit. Of course, that would indicate she was there but he had no idea what she was capable of. Then again, maybe it gave him some added cover. There was no way Henderson or Starkov could link her to him and dig deeper. Either way, he had no choice. "Blackstone Strategies is Roland Henderson's firm," he told her. "I'm here because he's going to get me started in politics."

Sonya's brow furrowed. "So you're still going with the politics angle? I read that article they talked about last night. The one in the Washington Post? I still don't see how this all plays out. Are you just trying to gain their trust–?"

"Why don't you just play along and see what happens?"

"All right." She lowered her voice. "If we're partners in this thing, are you going to tell me your real name?"

"Rhett Butler. But no one would believe it."

Sonya laughed as he opened the door for her and she led the way inside. Ten minutes later, they were led from the reception area by Olivia Van Buren herself to the thirtieth floor by means of a plush, fast, and quiet private elevator. Merlin was surprised the Chief Financial Officer would take up that duty. He was equally surprised by her beauty and her youth for such a high position in the organization. He decided she was some amazing whizz with numbers and had risen quickly through the organization.

The elevator stopped and let them out into a hushed hallway. The air had the scent of rosemary. As they walked a hallway lined with expensive art, Merlin spotted the woman with the 'pillows'. She was going into an executive office. What was her name? Merlin shook his head. He could remember the body but not the name–

"Get your eyes off the flotation devices." It was Sonya. She had an amused tilt to her lips, glancing from the woman to Merlin.

"Sorry."

"Don't be. If you're a boobs man, you're a boobs man."

Merlin let out a sigh. Trying to spar with her verbally was going to end up embarrassing him. He gestured ahead, "She's waiting?"

Van Buren was waiting. She had an office door open and was gestured for them to go in.

Sonya led the way again, this time into a large office with rich furnishings and a wall of sparkling windows that overlooked the city.

Roland Henderson sat behind a massive black-and-gold desk and he gave Van Buren a nod and a wink as she closed the door behind them. Then he stood up. "I'm so glad you could come to see us this morning, Rhett." But as he said that, he made a beeline around the desk to Sonya and gave her a tight hug. "And it's so nice to see you again, Miss Tapper."

Sonya looked to Merlin and rolled her eyes.

Merlin was relieved to see whatever had happened between them last night and her withdrawal from his advances hadn't complicated matters in any way.

Breaking off the hug, Henderson shook hands with Merlin, "I'm sorry that Dimitri isn't here. He planned to be but he says something came up suddenly that demanded his attention."

Feeling disappointed at losing contact with his target again, Merlin said, "That's too bad, I was looking forward to talking with him."

"And he was looking forward to talking with you as well. Both of you." Henderson gestured to a pair of plush chairs on this side of the desk, "But why don't you two take a seat and we can talk anyway?" As they took a seat, Henderson walked back around the desk and sat in the massive black-and-gold chair, leaning it back slightly.

As Merlin sat down, he was fully aware Henderson's eyes were on Sonya. And she obviously knew it, sitting down and crossing her legs slowly in a way that caught his eye even more. She was playing a game. He only hoped it didn't burn her. But right now, he had his own assignment that she didn't know anything about and he had to take every advantage given him. "So, Roland, you said you might be able to help *us* get ahead in the political world?"

The *us* comment delighted Sonya and she gave Merlin a wink.

Henderson caught the *us* comment as well. He leaned forward, elbows on his desk as his eyes eagerly ran over her body, "Yes, well, there are a number of steps you can both take to help your advancement in the political world."

Sonya gave him a smile. "I'm willing to do my part. I'm all ears."

"You much more than a pair of ears, Miss Tapper." His eyes caressed her legs. Then he looked to Merlin. "First things first, do you belong to a political party?"

"Uh...no. I thought I could run as an independent–"

"Won't work. Well, it can, but once you do get elected to an office, being independent leaves you outside of the political system in terms of getting appointed to valuable positions. They won't spend political capital on a party outsider."

"I never thought of that."

"That's where Blackstone Strategies comes in. We do the thinking and guide you to success. Now...you take your pick, Democrat or Republican. It doesn't matter to us. We work with politicians on both sides. In fact, we may have two of our clients—one on each side of the aisle—who may be stepping away from politics. Your choice won't matter."

"You make it sound like a job is opening up in a company."

"Something like that."

That comment sobered Merlin. The man felt he had more say over who gets the office than the masses who cast the ballots.

Henderson simply pushed on. "Once you choose a party you can feel comfortable with, you will begin to donate to various candidates. That gives you visibility within the party that you join *and* it strengthens your relationship with those candidates. You never know when you need to call in a favor from one of them in return for that support." He held a finger up. "And then—you choose one prominent candidate to support—and you begin a super PAC."

Sonya leaned forward. "What's a super PAC?"

"That's a political action committee that can raise *unlimited* funds. Now...you can spend the money on pushing for the election of a specific candidate...but you're not supposed to communicate with that candidate in any way shape or form." He tapped the side of his nose. "That's where we come in. We secretly coordinate between you and the candidate."

Sitting back, Sonya said, "And I imagine then you can call in a bigger favor?"

"Yes...it's tit-for-tat." Henderson's eyes dropped to her breasts and then back to her eyes. "I help you, you help me."

Sonya glanced to Merlin, "Sounds reasonable to me."

Merlin wasn't so sure but he asked Henderson an important question, "How much money do I give to each of these candidates to start with?"

Henderson gave him a steel trap smile. "You leave all that to Blackstone. We can donate in your name. And that includes the Super PAC. We can do all the fund raising for you...*and*...Blackstone Strategies will donate $10 million to start off the Super PAC itself. If you're agreeable?"

Sonya emitted a low, breathy whistle and she looked at Merlin. "Isn't that amazing?"

Nodding, Merlin knew it wasn't amazing. It was actually a setup. They supply the money and he was compromised. He gave a slow nod of his head. "Of course. I'm agreeable to whatever you stipulate."

"Excellent. Next...have you ever volunteered for someone's electoral campaign?"

Merlin knew this was leading to something. Henderson had been leaving breadcrumbs from that first meeting he had encouraged his wife to start. Breadcrumbs that would sink his claws deeper into his victim. Merlin shook his head. "No. Never. Is that something I need to do? I mean, if I'm running for election, how do I volunteer for someone else?"

"It's imperative that you learn how campaigns run, Rhett. Every campaign needs volunteers that do the grunt work. They're the boots on the ground, knocking on doors, registering voters, getting a feel for the issues and how voters feel about you as a candidate. It all helps to shape the campaign and drive you to election."

"Okay, I can see that. But...."

Henderson gave him another steel trap smile. "But you're worried that means you've got to put off your own run for Senate beyond two years. No, that doesn't need to happen. Senator Alan Watson has resigned his Senate position to become United States

Secretary of the Interior. A special election is being held next month and we are backing the leading candidate, Quinn Olivares."

Obviously knowing where this was going as well, Sonya interjected herself into the conversation. She looked to Merlin. "Maybe we can help this Quinn Olivares in his campaign? Right?"

"Of course, whatever it takes."

Henderson rubbed his hands together. "Excellent. There's not much time and if you are agreeable, you can meet with him tonight—"

Sonya jumped right in again, "That sounds good to us."

Henderson seemed to like her take charge-attitude. "Excellent, nothing like getting the ball rolling as soon as possible. I'll have my secretary give you his home address and I'll call ahead to make the arrangements."

Slowly uncrossing her legs and standing up, Sonya said, "I'll roll all the balls I have to...Roland."

Chapter 17

ONCE OUTSIDE THE BUILDING, Merlin pulled the keys from his pocket as they headed toward his Porsche. He was making some headway in this assignment, but he had concerns. And those concerns dealt with the woman walking beside him. "Are you sure you aren't biting off more than you can chew? I mean, you're really baiting him–"

"I appreciate your concerns but I can take care of myself." She took a quick step, turned and stopped in front of him, "What I don't get is what you get out of this." Sonya narrowed her eyes. "And don't tell me it's about becoming some Senator. You have a deeper motive. I can feel it." She stood silent, waiting.

Merlin stepped around her, pressing on the unlock button on the key fob. The Porsche sounded twice as the doors unlocked. Opening the door, Merlin got in and inserted the key into the ignition.

Sonya walked to the open door, put her head back and her hands out, pleading, "Oh, come on, I'm dying to know what we're doing. How can I enjoy the thrill of the chase if I don't know what we're chasing."

"Is that what you're in this for? The thrills?"

Bending over and trying a different tactic, she reached out, straightening his tie. "You can't tell me you didn't get a thrill breaking into the Russian's condo. I could see it on your face. You and me aren't so different."

Merlin removed her hands from his tie. "And I'm telling you again, be careful how hard you play Henderson. It could backfire on you."

Sonya remained bent over, hands on her knees as she gave him a mischievous smile. "How *hard* I play him? Is that some kind of pun?"

Merlin let out a sigh. She deftly wasn't listening.

"How do you think he'd want to do me? Bent over his desk? Or does he want me to sit on his desk? Is that how we would do it?"

"Just don't let his wife catch you–"

"Oh, puleese. That one is doing some banging of her own."

"What are you talking about?"

Sonya straightened up, crossing her arms over her chest. "Do you really think she's married to him because he's her soul mate? She is in it for what she can get out of it. I saw her talking to another man just like you. Another guy looking to get ahead in politics. And believe me, she was all over the guy, using her own feminine charms to string him along. Maybe you're the one who doesn't understand what you're getting involved with?"

Merlin felt the information roll roughly through his system. How had he missed that?

Sonya turned and strutted away, calling back over her shoulder. "I'll be at the Ritz-Carlton at six. That should give us enough time to get to this Olivares' place."

Merlin pulled the door shut, started the car...and then sat there, hands on the steering wheel, thinking. This assignment was like wading into a cesspool. And what else was he missing? He heard the motorcycle start, and the engine rev. Glancing in the rearview mirror, he saw a helmeted Sonya, sitting on her motorcycle, pass behind the Porsche, her dress pulled up over her hips and the bike shorts on full display. She was intriguing and maddening at the same time. He wanted her out of his hair but she was proving useful at the same time. Hopefully, she didn't get hurt, or even killed,

The motorcycle's engine purred. She was soon out of sight, and the sound disappeared into the distance.

Chapter 18

SONYA TAPPER SHOWED UP on time, carrying a tote bag. She showed up in her black tracksuit, the black and silver track shoes on her feet, and disappeared into the bathroom to get dressed. Merlin took a Perrier from the suite's mini fridge and sat waiting as she got dressed. His cell phone rang and he moved as far away from the bathroom as he could and answered quickly, "Yeah?"

"Merlin? It's Sammy. Is everything okay? You're talking low."

"I'm with someone but they're in the bathroom. What have you got for me?"

"First of all. I finally managed to get a simple background for you at Harvard and Goldman Sachs. I'm sorry it took so long but I ran into a roadblock."

Merlin's heart beat faster. "A roadblock? What happened?" Did Dimitri Starkov have someone on the inside of Interpol as he had feared?

"It was the same problem I had before. For all intents and purposes, you don't really exist when you're on assignment, remember? I tried on my own, but I had to reach out to a tech for help. But it's hard for me at my level to get someone with the expertise to do it without triggering suspicion *and* blowing your cover."

"Oh yeah, right." It was all part of the plausible deniability his job as The Stopper offered every government and individual in Interpol.

"I had to reach out to the Director at the hospital," Sammy told him, "and he and Evelyn O'Toole did their magic. It just took a little longer."

"I understand. I'm sorry I put you in a difficult position."

"No problem. I just wanted you to understand. I've got a little bit of information on those things you asked about but it's been difficult as well. Fortunately, the Director's put me in direct touch with a team he has working on it and it should go faster."

"Okay, good. What have you got so far?"

Sammy paused and then her tone was very serious. "Like you said, there was absolutely no connection showing between this Dimitri Starkov and Telekom AG in Germany. That caused Evelyn to look into Telekom and its products it and she *may* have found something alarming. Or should I say her techies did when they ran a scan on file pointers on our systems and then started on some of the outside systems. And I say *may* because her tech specialists are digging deeper."

"I take it these pointers showed something was missing?"

"Missing...or *changed*. Remember when those car manufacturers were caught installing software on their vehicles that hid the real output of nitrogen oxide emissions to get around the pollution laws?"

"Vaguely."

"The software was designed to turn on the full emission control systems only when the car was undergoing government testing for those emissions. When the car wasn't hooked up to the computer doing the testing, the emission control systems were turned off, allowing their vehicles to get better miles per gallon ratings. They used those bogus numbers to advertise heavily against their competitors."

"Okay. I take it the techies found something similar?"

"Yes. Telekom AG has sold communications hardware to a number of Interpol countries. That includes Canada and the United States, although it's been limited to us so far. But her specialists have detected the presence of software code embedded inside the individual pieces of hardware. Because Interpol is connected to all these countries, it's possible the hardware's built-in software is monitoring the digital traffic and was picking up any references to, or investigations into, Starkov. The working theory is they also have malware in the code that allows them access to the databases we connect to. They could delete those reports on Starkov but the tech specialists believe it would take too much time to actually overwrite the files and it would be noticed. And they would have to add a special software tool to do the shredding, making it more likely an ordinary inspection would find the embedded code. I have a theory—I suggested this to Evelyn and she agreed it's a viable theory—that Starkov's people simply change his name in any report to Smith or whatever and leave everything else in place. That's less likely to be noticed and he continues to operate under our radar."

"That's ingenious. With all the investigations going on between member countries, someone would have to be focusing on Starkov to ever see it."

"Right. And without an accumulation of suspicious activity, his name never rises to the top to trigger a full-blown investigation. Fortunately, Director Laurent has an instinct for guys like Starkov and he felt the Russian was worth looking into. Now, as for the rest...."

Merlin heard a keyboard clicking away. He wondered if the search they did on Starkov in connection with Telekom AG was the reason why Dimitri didn't show up at his meeting with Henderson. Did his people detect the search? Was the Russian spooked? Would he go into hiding, making it impossible to find out what he was doing and who he had compromised? Merlin pushed it aside—for now—the hardware and code theory was just that. Theory.

"Here we go," Sammy said. "Roland and Rebecca Henderson. They seem legitimate. Henderson was an investment banker who started a political consulting firm, which is that Blackstone Strategies you mentioned. There is no connection to Starkov that we could find. But, like I said, they're digging deeper. What they did find was a Blackstone Strategies' connection to Audrick J Pittman. Henderson is the face of the firm while Pittman is the silent partner who stays behind the scenes."

"I was just at a fundraiser at Pittman's home. That's where I met Starkov and the Hendersons."

"Pittman is a shadowy figure who has a wide range of companies in America, Europe, and Africa. A number of them are fossil fuel related, and the enterprises in Africa are tied to a number of dictators. From what I gather, Pittman backs every politician he can. Not from altruism but as a means to shape government policy to benefit himself."

"Sounds like someone who would be willing to deal with a Russian oligarch for what he can get out of it."

"I agree," Sammy said. "I was given something else that may or not mean anything. A list of Senators that Blackstone Strategies helped."

The door to the bathroom opened and Sonya walked out. She wore a soft, black gown with a plunging neckline, diamond earrings, and a diamond necklace.

Merlin turned away and lowered his voice, "I can't talk now. Send the list of Senators to my phone."

"Okay," Sammy said. "Uh...one other thing...."

"I have to go."

"Yeah, but...you had a large shopping bag left at your apartment door."

"A large shopping bag?"

"Yeah. And it was weird but...inside it was a colorful dress, fancy underwear, and nylon stockings. You know...the sexy kind?"

"Okay."

"It was all...sliced up."

"Sliced up–?" Merlin's heart fell. It had to be the Can-Can outfit he had brought back from France for Jaimie Hartman.

"I don't mean to pry but...you have weird neighbors...or something?"

Merlin ran a hand over his face, "I'll deal with it when I get back."

"Okay." The call ended.

Turning to Sonya, Merlin almost felt like canceling the whole thing and flying back to Ottawa.

Sonya was upbeat and ready to go. She held her arms out wide. "How do I look?"

Managing a faint smile, Merlin said, "You look fine."

"Fine? That's it? I think I clean up pretty good. And look at this." She extended a foot forward. A slit in the gown opened up, revealing a long shapely leg...in a nylon stocking.

"Seriously?"

Sonya shrugged as she kept the leg extended. "If showing off my wares gets these guys hot and bothered and off guard, that helps us. Right?"

Merlin waved his arms. "No way. The slit and the leg are fine. The stockings are a no. A definite no. Take them off. Or we end everything right now."

Frowning, Sonya pulled the leg back and crossed her arms. "You're not my brother or my father or...my protector–"

"No, but I *am* calling the shots."

Scowling, Sonya headed for the bathroom.

Chapter 19

QUINN OLIVARES and his wife Dorothy lived on the top floor of a condominium building that offered twenty-four-hour security personnel and stunning views of the Potomac River, the Kennedy Center, and Washington itself. Dorothy was a blonde knockout, outgoing but sweet. Quinn was outgoing as well. But he was also nakedly ambitious and contemptuous of the constituents he was supposedly going to serve. And Merlin had the feeling that Dorothy was more a trophy wife, or maybe just someone who could help him get where he wanted to go. What happened after that was anyone's guess. And Quinn definitely enjoyed the slit in Sonya's dress. There was no telling how forceful he would've been if she had worn the sexy stockings and they had been alone. Because it didn't take long for Merlin to make one observation about Quinn. The man walked around the apartment with his fists clenched as if he was marching. The thumbs were held parallel to the trouser seams. That clenched fist position was used by the military to denote a readiness to fight. The habit gave Merlin the impression the man was ready to fight at a moment's notice, to be the aggressor in any situation. He was a man who wanted what he wanted. And probably took it, one way or another.

After an excellent meal of mustard-crusted boneless prime rib roast with cream sauce, while the two women went off somewhere to talk, Merlin was taken to an outside balcony for a glass of wine and a cigar.

As Olivares stood at the railing, a glass of wine in one hand, and a Cuban cigar in the other, he looked very much like a man who was overlooking a land he was about to become ruler over.

Merlin played the part of smoking the cigar but only letting the smoke curl from his mouth and drift away on the warm air as he listened to his host's plans. They went on and on.

Blowing out a sharp line of blue smoke, Olivares punctuated his plans with a statement like it was fact. "Senator is just the *first* step for me, Rhett. Once I get appointed to a few key roles like the Senate Judiciary Subcommittee on Oversight, Homeland Security, or Crime and Terrorism, I can make a real name for myself."

Swirling the wine in his glass, Merlin said, "I imagine it's not easy to get one of those roles. Everybody probably wants the same thing."

A wry smile settled on Olivares' lips. "Not when you have the right people behind you."

"The right people?"

"Yeah. The right people." Olivares walked a few feet to set the wine glass down on a small table and then walked back to the railing where he leaned against it, jabbing the cigar at the city the overlooked. "Washington is a place of influence, both seen and unseen. In many ways, my wife and I are an ideal power couple. But–"

"A power couple? Your wife seems too sweet to be a power anything."

"Don't let Dotty fool you. She's not necessarily ambitious but she has some clout in Washington circles. She works for one of the seventeen intelligence agencies in the area—exact one unnamed, of course."

"Of course."

"And her parents are both with the Department of Defense." Olivares held up a finger of emphasis. "*But*...you still need money—if you're ten times richer than the next guy, you're one hundred times more powerful—and you need the ability to gather crowds."

"The ability to gather crowds?"

"Exactly. Think of a television celebrity or a famous movie star, They can influence their fans to buy a product, back a cause, whatever. Blackstone Strategies has developed some unique tactics and methods to gather immense sums of cash, turn people into stars, gather crowds, *and* they have the smash-mouth techniques down pat to destroy your opponents. You've done a smart thing, Rhett, throwing your lot in with Blackstone. You've got the right people behind you."

Pushing down his personal dislike for the man, Merlin kept a neutral face. "I hope you're right. To tell you the truth, it was simply good fortune that I met with Roland Henderson."

Olivares shook his head. "No, it wasn't good fortune. Someone saw enough in you to invite you to the fundraiser in the first place, Rhett. You were there for a reason."

Merlin smiled internally: *If only you knew.* He did the same as his host had done. He walked to the table, set his glass down. Then walked back to the railing, where he drew in some more cigar smoke and then let it drift from his mouth. "I guess you're right. But I'm not sure I have the talent to take on one of those jobs you're talking about. Don't get me wrong, I have all the confidence in the world in my abilities. But those abilities were along the lines of economics–"

"Then you ask for a role in one of those subcommittees that gives you a high profile, like economic policy, housing, or energy and natural resources."

Narrowing his eyes, Merlin looked at his host. "What do you mean ask? Is that how it works once you get in as a Senator? You ask one of the party leaders to–?"

Olivares give him an amused look. "Roland told me you were a political neophyte, but I didn't expect you to be a total virgin."

Merlin raised a hand, feigning irritation. "Fine, forget I asked."

Turning to lean with his side against the railing, and squarely facing Merlin, Olivares took in a drag on the cigar and then blew the smoke out.

A rich, loamy scent swirled around Merlin's head as he looked out over the Potomac.

"No need to get your panties in a wad, Rhett. This is a tough town. You going to need balls to move ahead."

"Having balls and wearing panties don't go together. I would suggest you use another analogy." Merlin was trying to push every button he could, from flattery to anger in order to get information.

"Rolland told me you played hockey. I guess it takes a punch in the face to get you to fight back."

"Yeah, but I won't be getting a fighting major for tossing you over the railing and making you do a face plant in the riverbank. How many stories up are we?"

Olivares emitted a low, arrogant laugh. "It's fifteen stories. But I bet I hit the river instead."

"Let me know when you're ready to try it."

Turning back to face the Potomac, Olivares took another drag on the cigar and blew the smoke out. "All you have to do is ask Henderson for the position. He has a lot of pull in this town. He usually has something on someone who can make it happen—no make that *always*. He always has something on someone. When you talk about pulling the levers of power, Henderson has his hand on the hands pulling the levers."

"What does he have on you?"

Another low laugh.

"I only hope it's that easy."

Olivares was quiet, taking another drag and savoring the cigar before he spoke again. "Why don't you go talk to Scott MacDuff? I worked on his campaign, just like you're going to work on mine.

I was taught the insides and outs of campaigning by Scott. And now he's got the position of chairman of the Senate Armed Services Committee. I can give him a call and set up a meeting for you."

"Yeah, I would appreciate that." Scott MacDuff was on the list of Senators Sammy had sent to his phone—the ones helped to power by Blackstone Strategies. The others were Derrell Hebert, Shermon Best, Torben Flores, Adrian Kazaku, and Dan Herszman.

"Good," Olivares said. "Now you owe me a favor." Another low laugh.

Chapter 20

ON THE DRIVE BACK to the Ritz-Carlton, it was raining lightly, and Sonya Tapper was quiet, arms and legs crossed. If they had been boyfriend-girlfriend, Merlin would have said she was still miffed at him for the stocking episode. After ten minutes of silence, Merlin tried to break the ice. "Did you learn anything we can use?"

Sonya stared straight ahead, the eyebrows raising slightly. "So it's we *now*, is it?"

Okay, there it was. She was miffed at him. "Look," he said gently, "about the stockings–"

Grabbing the dress by the slit, Sonya pulled it right back and draped it open, displaying her legs nearly to the crotch, "I display what I want, when I want, and how I want. Not you."

"I just thought you were playing with fire–"

"Well, these are my fire sticks and I can do what I want," she shot back. Crossing her arms tighter, she glared dead ahead.

Merlin glanced at her bare legs, looked down the road for a bit, then glanced back at her.

Sonya fought back a smile.

He couldn't help himself. "Just how much heat can you generate when you rub your legs together?"

Still fighting to hold back the smile, Sonya released a short, suppressed laugh in her throat. Arms still crossed, she put a hand over her mouth to prevent any more.

Allowing himself a smile, Merlin drove on for a moment. Then he glanced at her legs. "You should cover up. I think I see smoke rising."

Lifting her butt from the seat, Sonya pushed the dress back down and closed the slit as best she could. "Okay, smartass." She pretended anger but there was still an amused look on her face.

Merlin brought the Porsche to a stop at a red light.

Sonya crossed her arms again and looked at the traffic and the pedestrians before she finally said, "What I'm really mad at is the fact you have *another* meeting with *another* Senator and you didn't tell me about it."

"How do you know that?"

She glared at him. "Because our sweet Dorothy told me about it after you and her hubby did your stupid macho thing out on the balcony."

"It wasn't *my* stupid macho thing. It was his idea, not mine."

"Whatever."

Merlin opened his mouth and closed it. An argument over the wine and cigar thing on the balcony wasn't important. Something else was. For the next few moments, the only sound was the soft swish of the wipers every ten seconds or so to wipe away the light rain. The streetlight turned green and Merlin sat there, distracted by his thoughts.

A vehicle behind the Porsche beeped. Then one behind that vehicle beeped impatiently.

Sonya looked at him. "Aren't you going to drive? The light is green."

"Uh...yeah." He pressed down on the gas and pulled through the intersection. As he drove, his speed was only half the limit, and the car behind sounded the horn in anger, pulled out and sped past, the horn continuing to sound displeasure. Another vehicle did the same thing, the horn sounding as it sped away into the distance.

Sonya shifted in her seat. "Are you okay? What's wrong?"

"How did our sweet Dorothy know Quinn was setting up a meeting? We were all together after we left the balcony. I never heard a single word from him to her about it." He glanced at Sonya. "And when did she tell you? I never heard her saying anything." He stared ahead. "At least...I don't remember hearing her say anything...."

Looking down the road a moment, Sonya chewed lightly on her lip, then said, "It was when I had to use the washroom. Remember? She led me there because she wanted to show me something, I think. Yeah, we were talking about Broadway shows. She loves musicals, she even joined a group...what did she call it? The Metro Alliance Theater. It rehearses on Saturdays and puts on plays and musicals. Anyway, she went to the bedroom to get a brochure on some musical she wanted to see...what was it? Oh yea, that Crazy Circus hit on Broadway. Apparently it's coming to the Kennedy Center and she wanted to see it but couldn't get tickets." She cocked her head at Merlin. "Why does it matter when she told me?"

There were a lot of things he couldn't tell her, but Merlin knew something was happening here.

"Rhett?"

It took a split second before he recognized his undercover name and he glanced at her. "Because I think they're playing us while we're playing them."

Sonya was intrigued. "How?"

"I'm not sure. But while *we* are playing at becoming a Senator, *they* are playing at sucking me into some scheme where they compromise me and use me down the road."

Sitting up straighter, Sonya said, "Aha. So you *don't* want to be a Senator. I was right. What I don't get, is why you won't let me in on the whole thing?"

"Because you're as open as that dress of yours is."

Sonya looked down and saw the slit had settled on both sides and her bare legs were on full display again. She gave him a saucy look. "You certainly seem to notice it a lot. Just how much do you want to see?"

Merlin looked away.

"You show me yours and I'll show you mine."

Feeling uncomfortable, Merlin said, "No thanks, my mother said I'll go blind."

A hand on her mouth and snickering, Sonya said, "So what do you want to do about it?"

"Not go blind."

"No, you idiot. I'm talking about the situation with our newfound friends."

"Oh."

There was silence. "You're a real klutz when it comes to women, aren't you?"

"Klutz is such a pejorative word."

"Idiot then."

"That's better." Merlin slowed to turn into the Ritz-Carlton entrance, putting on his blinkers. "When is this circus musical thing at the Kennedy Center?"

"It opens in two nights. Why?"

He turned into the entrance. "What if I can get you tickets to take them?"

"Why–?" Sonya shifted in her seat and her excitement heightened. "You want *me* to take them *both* to the opening? What are you going to do? Break into their condominium?"

"It's better if you don't know–"

Her countenance fell. "And now you're trying to play me. We're in this together, pal. So spill the beans."

Merlin shook his head. "Not going to happen. It's how I work, okay?" He pulled to a stop beside her motorcycle. "Like I said, I call the shots."

Sonya's foot bounced. She shook her head at him. "Okay, fine. But I'm not getting on that motorcycle and riding away. I figured you might try to dump me at some point. So, I checked at reception before I went up to your room. The suite next to yours was empty and I put a reservation on it. *You* are going in there and paying for it. Me and you —we're joined at the hip from now on."

Chapter 21

SONYA TAPPER WENT UPSTAIRS as Merlin paid at the front desk for one week with his debit card. Sonya left carrying a motorcycle tail bag with extra clothing that she had left at the front desk when she first arrived. There was no doubt she had been prepared and one step ahead of Merlin at all times.

The clerk returned Merlin's debit card to him. "Thank you, sir. I hope you both enjoy your stay."

Merlin stayed silent as he slipped the card into his pocket. He simply took in a breath and let it out slowly, contemplating just how difficult things were going to be. He had a job to do and she was going to be tough to shake without creating suspicion. Even if he simply took off and set up in another hotel, she could watch for him around Starkov or the Hendersons—and then something even more unsettling struck him.

"Is something wrong, sir?"

Looking at him, Merlin didn't answer. He knew his face registered unease but that was that was the least of his worries right now. Something unsettling was far more important. "Do you have an extra keycard for my friend's room?"

"An extra keycard? The young lady took both of them—"

"I know. But I need to surprise her. I'm going to need to sneak into her room. Can you give me another one please?"

The clerk seemed reluctant. "It's not something I'm allowed to do...."

Merlin set his voice low, confidential. "I want to ask her to marry me but I need to set it up. You know, really special? I'll pay extra if I have to."

"No need to, Sir. I understand. One moment."

Merlin turned and looked across the lobby to the glass front entrance and the parking lot beyond. As he waited, his concerns began to mount.

"Here you go, Sir."

"Thanks." Merlin took the key card and headed across the marble lobby. Stepping outside into the light rain, Merlin walked along the wet pavement until he reached the area where her motorcycle was parked. And next to the motorcycle was his Porsche. He looked up at the hotel, trying to gauge where the two suites were. If he was oriented right, the windows should be overlooking the street to the left and he was out of her view.

The hum of traffic was steady, interrupted by the beeping of an impatient horn from time to time. The light rain danced and the surrounding lights glistened off the moist pavement.

Merlin stared into the distance, thinking. How did Sonya Tapper know he was going to be at the fundraiser? She had shown up out of the blue and taken him off guard. How did she know?

A car door slammed somewhere and quick footsteps indicated someone was running for the shelter of a building

How did Sonya know he had a meeting with Roland Henderson at Blackstone Strategies? She had shown up, dressed and ready to take part in the meeting. It was possible Henderson had told her—his obvious intentions to get into her pants had been on display every time they had been together and he no doubt wanted her there—but something told Merlin that wasn't the case.

The sounds of cars splashing through shallow puddles echoed off the surrounding buildings.

And then there was the fact she knew he was staying at the Ritz-Carlton. How? It was a spur of the moment decision, made as he was driving. It was right after he had come down from the roof of Starkov's condominium–. Merlin cursed under his breath. The white motorcycle that sat between the two cement pillars near the group of buildings. The sound of the motorcycle he had heard after he had left the bank. She had known he would have to go down through the bank stairs—somehow she had a faster route down—was she that fast and agile? The way she bounded across that roof and disappeared so quickly told him it was possible.

He strode across the wet blacktop to the Porsche. Squatting, he began checking the underside of the vehicle. He found it tucked up under the right wheel well. A small GPS tracker that was magnetic. They were easy to buy now. And it was probably hooked into her cell phone. Once she had followed him here, she planted this sucker and was able to track him wherever he went. Who was she? He rolled the tracker around in his hand for a moment and then replaced it under the wheel well. Wiping off his hands as he headed back for the entrance, Merlin knew he needed to find out who she was. And fast. It was possible he was being played in more ways than one. It was also possible that she *was* tied to the Russian. And Starkov was running a counter-intelligence operation to investigate Merlin and what he was up to.

Chapter 22

MERLIN WENT BACK to his suite and retrieved another bottle of cold Perrier from the mini-fridge. Grabbing a towel from the bathroom, he wiped the bottle down. Leaving the door to his own suite open, Merlin walked down the hallway to Sonya's door, bottle held in the towel, and rapped loudly. It took three more knocks before the door swung open.

"What do you want?" Sonya stood there, one hand on the door handle and the other on her hip. She wore black, silk pajamas. "If you think you're coming in for a nightcap—or a good night quickie—it ain't going to happen."

"Nothing so mundane is that." Holding it by the top with the towel, Merlin held out the bottle of Perrier, "I just wanted to ask you to take this screw top off. I hurt the knuckle on my right-hand and I can't apply enough pressure. And I'm useless with my left."

Sonya narrowed her eyes and grabbed the bottle from his hand, "What do you mean mundane? You wouldn't be able to sit down for a week once I got finished with you." She put the bottle between her knees and twisted on the cap, breaking it free. She thrust the bottle back at him. "Now head back to your own room, wimpy kid."

Using the towel, he took the bottle back from her. "That hurts."

"You'll live."

"So you say."

Her voice was mocking and teasing as he headed back to his own door. "And does the cold, cold bottle also hurt your delicate hands?"

"It's not as cold as you are, sweetheart."

The sound of a raspberry echoed off the walls.

Merlin closed the door hard, sending the signal of being miffed. Setting the bottle on the counter in the bathroom, Merlin bent over, squinting his eyes as he looked over the surface of the bottle. Using the towel on the cap, he turned the bottle slowly until he saw what he needed. The set of fingerprints wasn't perfect but they would be more than adequate. Retrieving his cell phone, he took several pictures, added them to a text message to Sammy and sent them on. Leaving the bathroom, he headed to the bedroom, the furthest room from the door. The bedroom had wood and glass French doors and he closed them as well. He hit speed dial.

"Hello?"

"Sammy? It's Merlin. Sorry if I got you up again."

"No, it's fine. I was just watching an old movie with Jigs."

"How is he doing?"

"He's doing great. After we finished off the remainder of yesterday's meal, we got another chicken dinner for two. What can I do for you?"

"I just sent you a set of fingerprints. They belong to the woman I identified to you as Sonya Tapper."

"That's good," Sammy said, "because we didn't get a single hit on that name. It has to be an alias she made up and/or one she's never used before."

"I can believe that." Merlin paused for a moment, gathering his thoughts. "Sammy... I need you to run the fingerprints ASAP. And I need you to have them back off on any more probing they're doing with the hardware from Telekom AG."

The concern thickened in Sammy's voice. "Why?" What's happened?"

"I'm not sure," Merlin admitted. "But I might be compromised by this woman. My biggest fear is she's working with Starkov. If we're not careful, we could drive him underground and lose our opportunity to counter whatever he's doing to damage our security. And Henderson could destroy any evidence linking Blackstone Strategies to the Russian and any moles they have working in the US, Canada, or Great Britain."

The phone rustled, sounding like Sammy stood up. "I'll contact everyone right now and get them to stand down. We won't do anything more until we hear from you."

"Good. Good." Merlin ran a hand through his damp hair. He couldn't think of anything else to do right now except wait.

"About Blackstone Strategies," Sammy said. "The Director said it's possible Henderson doesn't have any idea about what the Russian is doing."

Merlin paused with his fingers in his hair. "Why would he think that? Hold on...." He glanced through the French doors. It was unlikely Sonya had come inside his suite, but he still felt vulnerable to this woman and couldn't afford to take any chances. Seeing a still-empty hotel room, he put his mind back on the call, "That doesn't make any sense, Sammy."

"That's what I thought. Until he explained it to me. Large Russian companies operating outside of their country typically have a member of Russian intelligence working for the company at the senior level. Some are still active intelligence officers with the FSB, the Federal Security Service, and some are ex-KGB—even though the KGB doesn't exist any more—those guys really don't retire. Anyway, the officer is called a kurátor. Basically they're embedded spies and report back on any contacts they make, or intelligence information they pick up. Sometimes the company itself doesn't even know they have one of these kurátors on staff, although they suspect it. The Russian government spies a lot on its own people, especially oligarchs who try to get active politically and upset the Russian apple cart. Starkov could have one of these kurátors at Blackstone Strategies, feeding him information and coordinating his efforts."

"Okay. I can see that. Henderson and Pittman see it as a business opportunity. And Starkov sees it as both business and intelligence gathering. *And* solidifying his standing back home with the government."

"It's possible."

Merlin's mind went back to the fundraiser. And then the top floor of Blackstone Strategies. "Miss Boobsalichious."

"Pardon?"

"Sorry. I think I know who the kurátor might be at Blackstone Strategies. A woman."

"Well, be careful." Sammy had an amused tone to her voice, "The Director said the kurátor could be a man or a woman. He told me a line a former Russian operative gave him. You ask your men to stand up for your country. In Russia, we ask our women to lie down for our country. The Director called it a honey pot or a honey trap, something like that. Don't do anything I wouldn't do."

"That leaves open a wide range of bad conduct, Powless."

Sammy laughed. There was a pause and then she said, "I've got the images of the fingerprints. I'll call you back."

The call ended. The name came back to Merlin. Oksana Pavlovich. He wondered if an operative like her would have a transmitter in each one.

Chapter 23

MERLIN AWOKE with a start. He sat up in bed, wondering what it was that took him from a fitful sleep. He glanced at the clock on the nightstand. 4:35 AM. There was a ringing sound. His fuzzy brain tried to make sense of it. There was another ring. Finally realizing it was his phone, Merlin scrambled out of bed. He had left the phone in the other room on the coffee table. The hotel room was cold from the air conditioning unit running all night and he felt the chill on his skin as he crossed the luxurious, hand-knotted wool carpet, dressed only in his shorts. His suit, shirt, and socks were draped over a plush chair, his shoes under the coffee table. He didn't even remember getting undressed. Grabbing his phone, he pushed the answer button, "Hello?"

"Hi. Sorry to get you out of bed so early."

It was Sammy. And her own voice sounded heavy from a long night without sleep. "That's okay. What have you got?"

"Something and nothing."

Merlin rubbed his hand over his eyes, wiping the sleep from them, "What exactly does that mean? I'm too tired for riddles." He took a step and dropped to the sofa, putting his head back as he listened.

"Sorry. I guess I'm just too tired to talk properly." Sammy yawned and then cleared her throat. "Sorry. Annnnd I'll stop saying sorry. Anyway. I had to get the Director and Evelyn out of their bed as well.

Not out of bed as in being together... crap... you know what I mean, I had to get their help."

"Yeah, I understand." Merlin felt his eyes closing and he fought to stay awake.

"The fingerprints you sent me triggered a flag in the system."

"A flag? What does that mean?"

"The fingerprints were under seal. The flag was put in place by the United States Marshals Service."

"U.S. Marshals are involved? How?"

"It means whoever this woman is, she's in the witness protection program," Sammy told him. "Interpol received a call that was routed to me. I talked to a US Marshal by the name of Gerald O'Malley. He wanted to know why I was looking for whoever this woman is. I wasn't in a position to authorize an exchange of information...and that's when I got the Director and Evelyn O'Toole involved."

"And what were they able to find out?"

"Nothing.

"Nothing? I don't understand." Merlin sat forward and ran a hand through his hair. This case was frustrating.

"Director Laurent told me the Marshals were very reluctant to share information, despite his position in Interpol. So he told them it was part of a routine investigation being run by the FBI into a stolen car ring in the United States. That they were simply going through all of the fingerprints found inside the cars. And that as a favor to them, he would send a report back on those prints as no identity found."

"I don't get it. Why would he do that?"

"If he went up the ladder of command and got them to share information on their side, he would have to do the same thing on our side. You don't exist, remember?"

"Okay, that makes sense. But...." Merlin felt his frustration rising.

The Director told me to give you the case and file numbers the Marshals Service are using *to you*. And that you would know what to do with it."

"Me?" Merlin sat back again, head up and closed his eyes. Then it came to him and he stood up. "Send me the info right now. Then don't go back to sleep. I'll call you back."

"What do you mean don't go back to sleep. I haven't been to bed–"

Merlin ended the call and looked at his phone, just to make sure. His first conversation with Laurent came back to him. *When you look at your phone, the special features will be unlocked. It's connected to Interpol's I-24/7, our secure global police network. As the name implies, you can access our databases 24 hours a day, 365 days a year. All 190 member countries of Interpol add their information on a constant basis to our databases. You'll be able to search and cross-check information on just about anything in a matter of seconds.* Using the Internet or satellite, Merlin's phone would *connect him automatically, rolling through the connections...breaking passwords as necessary without you needing to do a single thing...all messages and calls one hundred percent secure.*

He waited. The information from Sammy came through. He went to work, tapping away at the screen with his thumbs. The screen rolled through the Interpol connections to the American databases...to the Criminal Intelligence Branch...to the United States Marshals Service. The password cracking application began and Merlin began pacing, waiting it out. Combinations of numbers, symbols, capital letters, and lower-case letters rolled across the screen. They became flashes...faster and faster—the screen paused—and files opened up. He was in. Merlin read eagerly. This was progress. Names, dates, and facts began building a picture. But it was incomplete in some senses. Flipping to another screen, Merlin sent some of the information to Sammy, asking her to do a deep dive into the names and facts, hopefully filling in the gaps and giving them as complete a story as possible. He went back to the files, made copies, storing them in a file folder, and ended the connection. Setting the phone down, Merlin padded to the single serve coffee maker on the table on the far side of the room. He had to stay awake. Choosing a mocha blend from the variety of pods, he made a coffee. Then, hot cup in hand, Merlin went back to the sofa, pulled up the files on his phone and began reading again, solidifying everything in his brain.

Chapter 24

IT WAS A HALF HOUR LATER, two coffees in and he was sitting on the couch, when Merlin's cell phone rang again. "Hello?"

"It's Sammy. I've got some more information on our mystery guest. Well, I guess she's not a mystery guest anymore, just a little mystery is left."

Merlin could tell she was a bit loopy from lack of sleep. "Just fill me in like it's my first time."

There was a hesitation, "That sounds like a birds and bees thing."

"Concentrate, Powless."

"Okay, here goes. Our girl is Lara Nikola Furnari. Nikola with a K. Her father was Constantin Antonio Furnari. Both from Brooklyn, New York. According to newspaper accounts, he was a cat burglar—who knew they existed outside of movies—he was known as Connie the Cat. He specialized in stealing jewelry from high-rise buildings. Specifically from penthouse units, because that's where the highest rewards are for a cat burglar. The higher the better. Most people that live that high up never expect someone to climb the outside the building and break in. But Connie the Cat did."

To Merlin, Brooklyn made sense, given her light Brooklyn accent. "You said newspaper accounts. I take it he was caught?"

"Yes, eventually. But not for the highi-rise stuff. Connie the Cat suffered from arthritis that ended his career as a cat thief at age 35. He had grown up with a kid whose father was connected to the Lucchese crime family. The father, Dante Taccetta—is a *capo*—a made member of the crime family who heads a crew of soldiers in Brooklyn. The son, Frank Taccetta, was one of these soldiers. Frank got his old friend Connie the Cat a job with his father, mainly driving the father around as well as appraising jewelry and the like that they got their hands on. There was a falling out between Frank Taccetta and Connie the Cat. Frank shot and killed Connie. The police had forensics tying Frank to the shooting. But the clinching eyewitness testimony was given by the seventeen-year-old daughter, Lara Nicola Furnari. Frank Taccetta was convicted and sentenced to life in prison."

Merkin could see the rest of the story from there. "And that's when the daughter goes into witness protection."

"Yes. There were the obvious threats against her. But Frank Taccetta was knifed to death two months after the trial. The father is convinced the daughter did it and puts a million dollar bounty on her head. Two million if someone brings her to him alive and breathing."

"And she won't be that way long after he gets his hands on her."

"Or maybe it is long...he could string out the agony," Sammy said.

"True." Merlin focused internally for a moment. "And that explains something else I saw in the files. There was an internal investigation into the Marshals Service. Someone cracked the secrecy on where she was. I guess the thought of two million was tempting to someone on the inside."

Sammy swore under her breath.

"Yeah. She was living in Oregon. I guess she was told she would have to relocate and she ran, deciding she was better on her own. Why she chose Washington is anyone's guess."

"Maybe she sees an opportunity to make a living?" Sammy said.

"What do you mean?"

"Constantin Furnari's wife died in childbirth and he raised her by himself. It turns out, he taught her the same profession."

"You're kidding?"

"Nope. The father called her Nikki the Cat—two Ks—and apparently, she was good. Far more agile and gutsy than he was. I would think a place like Washington offers a lot of rich people living high up with expensive jewelry just waiting for her."

Merlin took a sip of coffee. That explained her ease across the roof. And how she was able to get down so fast. It was second nature to her. And maybe it also explained the expensive jewelry she wore to the fundraiser. The sleek, black tracksuit made sense as well. It was her climbing outfit. And the black and silver shoes were not track shoes—they were molded perfectly around her feet—they were custom-made climbing shoes.

A knock sounded at Merlin's door.

"And get this...that falling out between Frank Taccetta and Connie the Cat...it was over the daughter. Frank was always hitting on her and Connie the Cat didn't like a forty-year-old man lusting after his teenage daughter. And then Frank finds out the daughter is doing these high-rise jobs. Says the old man and his daughter are holding out on the family...one thing leads to another...and bang, the father is dead."

"That makes a teenage girl willing to testify," Merlin surmised. Another knock. He set the coffee cup down with a clunk on the table and stood up.

"I'd do it, that's for sure," Sammy said forcefully.

Another knock. "Hold on." Moving across the wool carpeting, Merlin looked through the peephole.

'Sonya Tapper' stood on the other side of the door. She was dressed in a white blouse and blue jeans.

"She's at my door, I've gotta go."

Sammy's voice took on an urgency, "Don't hang up, don't hang up. Laurent wanted me to pass on something else. Something important."

"Be fast."

"A U.S. naval intelligence officer in Moscow says classified military and intelligence information has been passed along to the Russians by someone in the American CIA. It's going to negatively impact our ability to fight terrorism and organized crime. The intelligence officer is not in a position to dig deeper but it appears to be coming through Starkov. We just don't have enough on him to do anything at this point. They've stopped any searches on the hardware/software from the Russian's company so they don't spook him. But the Director says you have to accelerate what you're doing to expose his network."

Merlin cursed.

"Yeah. "

"Okay, I'll do what I can—"

The next knock was slower but louder.

"Crap. I'm going to lose her if I don't—"

"I hear her," Sammy said, "The Director says you have to clone the cell phone on anyone involved and plant a software bug on their personal computer or laptop."

"Clone the cell phones? How am I supposed to do that?"

Louder.

"I can send you everything you need and the instructions. Plus thumb drives with the software. You get to their computer system, stick the thumb drive in and it does the job for you. Then they can monitor the phones and computers and watch for anything being done through the hardware/software. And especially the kurátor's phone and computer. It should allow us to figure out who the moles are."

"Okay, that sounds like a good plan. I'll send my plane back to Ottawa to pick it up. Someone will contact you," Merlin said. He unlocked the door with one hand.

"Your plane? You must be kidding?"

"No. I gotta let her in."

"Okay. Be careful."

"Yeah." He opened the door.

A visibly irritated Sonya Tapper slipped through. "It's about time."

Closing the door, Merlin spoke low into the phone, "You've done a good job. I want you to get some sleep and then keep digging."

"Okay."

Ending the call, Merlin turned to face 'Sonya', "You're up early."

She stood with her arms crossed, brow furrowed, "The least you could do is put some pants on."

Merlin realized he was still in his shorts.

Chapter 25

STANDING THERE, clad only in his shorts, Merlin felt the cool air from the air conditioning unit again. And he felt the embarrassment of being nearly naked in front of this woman. But he also felt the urgency of the moment. And the need for closure, to get her out of his life once and for all. He felt the softness of the wool carpet under his feet as he headed for his clothes.

"I thought we could go for breakfast and discuss what we do next," she said as she turned slightly to give him some privacy. And yet she kept her eyes on his butt as he passed her.

"I've got some other ideas." Reaching the plush chair and his clothing, Merlin moved aside the pant legs to reveal his conceal holster with the Beretta. There was a soft whisper from the holster as he discreetly pulled the Beretta out.

"When you're dressed like that, I don't want to know any ideas you've got in your head."

Hiding the gun with his body, Merlin stood up straight. As he turned, he slipped the gun around behind his thigh to keep it hidden, and then crossed the carpeting toward the door again.

"Cat got your tongue?"

The comment was said with amusement. And Merlin was reminded of the day she showed up at the fundraiser and caught him off guard. He had trouble getting his words out that time and she had used the same line. *Cat got your tongue?* It was her subtle way of saying she was in charge of the situation. Reaching the door, he turned to face her again.

She raised her eyebrows, looking down at his body, "Excuse me? Did you *still* forget to put your clothes on before we go to breakfast?"

"No. But your question about *cat got your tongue* is very interesting, considering your real name goes along with Nikki the Cat—two Ks." He lifted the Beretta to his shoulder, on full display.

Nikki the Cat turned white, fear etched on her face.

Before Merlin got another word out, he saw the expression on her face change. A fierce, defiant expression was followed by a panther-like growl of words that rolled from her tongue.

"I'm not going down without a fight." Nikki the Cat sprang forward.

Her body slammed into Merlin, legs wrapping tightly around his waist like a boa constrictor, one hand gripping the wrist of his gun hand, while the other reached around behind his head and yanked hard on his hair.

A guttural grunt flew from Merlin's lips as his head was jerked backward.

Nikki's hot words drilled into his ear, "I'll kill you first you son of a—"

Merlin instinctively turned, woman wrapped around him, took a hard step and slammed her body into the door. It banged and shuddered from their combined weight. The breath exploded from her lungs. As her grip on his hair loosened, and the wrap of her legs un-tightened, Merlin took a half step back, grabbed the back of her blouse, and turned hard, propelling her away from him.

Nikki hit the carpet hard and rolled. Coming to rest face down, she groaned, lay still for a second, and then pulled her feet in, struggling to get to her knees. Her face was a mixture of pain, distress, and defiance, as she looked in his direction. She bared her teeth as she tried to get her lungs filled with air and her words out.

Striding across the carpet, Merlin said, "If I wanted you dead, you would already be dead." Grabbing her elbow, he lifted her to her feet, pulled her across the carpet and pushed her to the sofa.

Her body bounced once. And then Nikki the Cat struggled to get to her feet, her face still defiant, and her words choppy as she struggled to regain her breath, "Right...right...two million...two....better than...one–"

"I have no intention of turning you over to Dante Taccetta." He held the gun up for her to see, "I'll put this away so you don't have to worry. I just want you out of my life. All right?" Walking to the still-open French doors to the bedroom, Merlin walked through and tossed the Beretta to the bed. Striding back across the carpet, Merlin went to the plush chair and picked up his pants.

Nikki watched him with eyes still defiant, her chest heaving slightly. Springing from the sofa, she ran hard across the carpeting into the bedroom. Grabbing the gun from the bed, she sprinted back and held the gun on Merlin with two hands.

Merlin looked at her for a moment, then continued putting on his pants. "You can pull up trigger but it won't work."

Narrowing her eyes, Nikki said, "I will shoot. I'm not bluffing."

The sound of his zipper closing carried across the room, "I know you're not bluffing. But it doesn't matter. Just do me a favor and leave–"

Nikki pulled the trigger. And again. Her eyes blinked. Holding the gun in one hand, she looked at it. Holding it with two hands again, she aimed and pulled the trigger.

Merlin picked up his shirt. "What part of *it won't work* don't you understand?" He slipped the shirt on and began doing up the buttons.

Shifting back and forth on her feet, Nikki continued holding the weapon out.

Tucking the shirt into his pants, Merlin shook his head without looking at her.

Turning with a growl, Nikki crossed the carpet again and threw the gun into the bedroom. It bounced on the carpeted floor twice before coming to rest. She stomped back to look at Merlin, "Who are you? And how do you know about me? You're not a Marshall because...." She crossed her arms, half with defiance and half with a feeling of vulnerability, "And you're not with him. So...." She studied him for a moment, "So you're like me. And I want to be in on what you're doing. I *need* to be in."

Merlin looked at her. "What are you talking about?"

Nikki put her hands on her hips. "Your scheme...your scam...whatever you want to call it. I still want in, I can help you."

Pushing a hand through his hair and rubbing his head, Merlin felt the frustration rising again. "There is no scam or scheme. There's nothing here for you–"

"The Olivares' place. You won't be able to get in without me."

Merlin stopped his head rubbing and looked at her.

"It's a secure high-rise building. They have a guard presence twenty-four-seven. You saw them sitting at the security desk when we were let in. More than likely they'll have security cameras. That's true of just about every high-end condominium or apartment complex in this city. That's the nature of the beast with all these politicians and people with big secrets. The only way in is to climb the outside of the building. That's my specialty. I know that's not yours. Whatever you want—you need me to get it."

The truth of what she said struck Merlin hard. Penetrating the high security of the buildings and/or each Senator's office, as well as whoever else was involved, was going to take more planning. And more time. Time he didn't have.

Chapter 26

STILL WITHOUT HIS socks and shoes on, Merlin walked across the carpet to the single serve coffee maker. He needed a shot of caffeine. Not only to stay awake but he was going to need a lot more energy to come up with a revised plan. He chose a French Roast pod and stood cross-armed, watching the dark liquid pour into the cup.

"I'm still here you know? You can't just ignore me."

Merlin didn't bother turning to her. "You can disappear again. I'm not going to tell anyone about you or–"

Nikki's words were hard and bitter. "And how did you find out about me in the first place? The same way Taccetta's men found me?"

"The Marshals Service can relocate you–"

"That's what they were trying to do when the gunmen showed up. I was living off the beaten path in Grant Pass, Oregon when two U.S. Marshals showed up at my door, telling me I had to relocate. I was in the bedroom packing a small suitcase when the gunfire started. The Marshals were cut down by half a dozen men. I knew who they were. I'd seen them around with my father before he was killed. If it wasn't for my ability to climb through the window and down four floors, I would be as dead as those Marshals."

Running a hand over his face, and then back through his hair, Merlin felt everything going sideways. He doctored the coffee with sugar, and creamer from a small fridge, stirring it with a plastic spoon, thinking. He had a job to do. One that was difficult enough without having Nikki the Cat hanging around him. And now he had the possibility of Brooklyn mobsters showing up. He tossed the spoon into the waste basket with some force, then headed back to the sofa.

Nikki watched him closely, silent for a few moments. "I ended up in Washington because I had a cousin here. My mother died when I was born. She wasn't from the neighborhood—she was Finnish and not Italian—and they were only together for a little over a year. My father took me to see her relatives a couple of times when I was a kid. They lived in a small place just outside Washington."

Merlin didn't bother sitting on the sofa. He continued to the window and looked out over the street below. "Why are you telling me all that stuff? It doesn't have anything to do with me."

"Actually, it does."

He looked over his shoulder at her. "What are you talking about?"

"I came to Washington because no one in Brooklyn knows my mother's side of the family. Plus, my cousin Niles runs a security service for high-rise buildings in the area. He knew about what had happened to my father...and about the trial from the newspapers. When I told him what happened with the Marshals, he helped me to go into hiding. He knows when people are away from their apartments or condominiums and he lets me stay in them. He leaves a window or a balcony door open and I climb in and out."

"That's why you were in Starkov's condo?"

"Yeah. Only Niles and I know. Makes it a lot safer for me than relocating with the Marshals. And I can make a living with all the high-rise buildings in Washington. A girl's gotta eat, right? As long as I don't target one of Niles' buildings, he's fine with it."

All that made sense to Merlin. And he couldn't care less about the burglaries. He had more important things to worry about. He took a sip of coffee. "Okay, so you get your cousin to get you another place to stay and—"

"And like I said, I can help you with what you're doing. If it's a big enough score to set me up for a long time, maybe the people you're targeting—I know there have to be more than the ones I've seen you working—maybe some of them live in buildings that my cousin takes care of. Maybe I can talk him into taking a cut that also sets him up—"

Merlin's voice was hard and firm. "Didn't you hear me? There is no scam. There is no big score." He let out a hard breath of frustration. "You should just go." He turned to look back at the window, sipping at the coffee.

Nikki studied him, watching him closely. "Who are you? You're a real klutz with women in a lot of ways. You're a nice, easy going guy...and yet you slammed me up against the wall... most guys would think twice about doing that to a woman—"

"I slammed you against the door, not the wall. There's a difference."

"True. And yet something inside you...makes you do whatever you have to do, no matter what it is. It just shows up—"

"Leave a forwarding address and I'll send you cash for the psychiatric evaluation." Merlin knew she was right. It was a character trait he had never seen in himself until he was hired to be The Stopper.

"I'm not going anywhere. Somebody on the inside gave Taccetta's men my location so they could kill me. And somehow you know all about me as well. That means no matter where I go, I'm not safe. And as long as I have to continue doing high-rise jobs, I run the risk of being caught. Once I'm in jail—"

"Then stop climbing buildings and stealing things."

"And then what? Get a job as a secretary? I don't have any other skills except the ones my father taught me. I'm not going to be able to marry someone and settle down in the suburbs without putting someone else in danger. The Marshals Service couldn't even keep me safe in their witness protection program with a new identity and the whole ball of wax. How the hell am I going to do it on my own? I need one big score and then I can disappear off the grid." Nikki took a few steps to the side, leaning slightly and looking at the side of his face, "I know you have something planned. I know it doesn't have anything to do with becoming a Senator, you've already admitted that. No one goes to this kind of trouble, planting a story in the newspaper–"

Merlin shook his head slowly like she didn't know what she was talking about. "Who said it was planted?"

Nikki pushed on, "You broke into Starkov's condo and the only thing you took was an invitation to that fundraiser."

"I didn't break in. The door was already open, thanks to you."

"A rooftop door. And you had no idea if it was open before you got there. You had every intention of breaking in. And there was no way you broke in just to steal an invitation. You were looking for something. *I was there, remember?*"

Merlin cursed himself—and everything else—under his breath. He should have backed away when he found that rooftop door was unlocked.

"Don't beat yourself up about it," Nikki said. There was a touch of humor in her voice. "It happens to the best. Look at me."

Feeling a smile caress his lips, Merlin glanced at her, "That's very touching—and modest."

Nikki gave him a facial shrug, "When you're the best, you're the best. Nothing wrong with saying it."

Merlin returned to looking out the window—looking at nothing really—and sipping his coffee.

Changing tactics, Nikki's voice became softer, almost pleading, "Look... as long as Taccetta is alive and kicking...he won't stop looking for me. He's known in Brooklyn as Mad Dog Taccetta. Just one big score. That's all I need. And based on the wealth I saw roaming the floor at that fundraiser, there's more than one big score in whatever you're doing. There can be more than enough for both of us. Then we can both get out. Live a good life. Not running forever."

Something stirred in the back of Merlin's thoughts. A new—and maybe totally stupid plan—began to coalesce around this whole fiasco. Desperate times. Desperate men—could he call himself a desperate man? Time *was* running out. He took another sip of hot coffee. Savored it. Swallowed it. He glanced at Nikki, "What about the rest of this Lucchese crime family Taccetta belongs to? What happens if Taccetta is dead? Won't they still come after you?"

Nikki shook her head, "No. This was a personal matter with Taccetta. The boss—Johnny Blue Eyes—he told Taccetta to drop the whole thing. He said it was bringing too much attention to the entire operation and wanted it stopped. But Taccetta wouldn't listen. Some even thought Johnny Blue Eyes would simply make Taccetta disappear. But that never happened. And I doubt it ever will. In a lot of ways—with me in the witness protection program—it kind of died in the eyes of the public. Taccetta could pursue me behind the scenes without bringing heat down on him from the boss. That's why I need to do something *now*, while I have the time. And I'm not sure I'll ever get a better opportunity than here in the Washington area."

Merlin considered her sincerity. "Are you sure you could give up the thrills of a high-rise burglary?" He watched her focus internally, pondering the question herself.

After a moment of reflection, Nikki's eyes refocused on his, "I don't know. It's all I've ever known. From the time I was a kid, it's the only life I've ever known. I'd like the opportunity to try something else. Even if it's only a try—it has to be better than what I have now. Right?"

That was something Merlin could agree with. He just wondered if he had the right plan to give her that opportunity. Or if he could pull it off. Or...if he was jeopardizing everything. Then again—what choice did he have under the circumstances?

Chapter 27

MERLIN WAS VERY much aware of the dangers—for him, for her, for his job—in what he was about to do, *if* he did it. Back tracking through his thinking to look for the flaws in his decision, he took another sip of coffee, concentrating. The scent of the French Roast blend lingered in his nostrils, the taste strong on his tongue–

"Hello? Are you going to let me–?"

"Shhh, I'm thinking." He couldn't afford to be distracted, and maybe swayed by her situation.

Nikki crossed her arms tightly. "Did you just shush me? Seriously?"

"Yeah." He turned and walked to the coffee table where he set his cup down with a clunk of porcelain on glass. "I'm going to make you a deal"

"You are? What kind of deal?"

"I'm going to take a shower."

Nikki scoffed, "I'm *not* taking a shower with you. Try again, pal."

Merlin reached for his suit jacket, found his cars keys in the left pocket and tossed them high to Nikki. "Here."

Nikki barely got her arms unwrapped in time to get her hand out. The keys jangled as they dropped into the palm of her hand. "What is this? You think giving me your car is going to buy me off?"

"No. I want you to pack up your stuff and put it in the Porsche." Dropping the suit coat on the chair again, he headed for the bathroom. "Then I want you to go to that boutique next to the lobby and buy me the outfit on the mannequin It's the one that's my size—the one with the leather jacket, dress jeans, and black T-shirt."

"You're kidding–?"

"No. I need a change of clothing." Reaching the bathroom door, he looked back at her. "Charge it to your room or mine. It doesn't matter. Bring it back here and then we can go have breakfast. We talk things through, and see if we can come to some kind of arrangement."

"Arrangement? What kind of arrangement?"

"You help me. I help you. Take it or leave it."

Nikki looked at him for a moment, thinking. She glanced at the keys in her hands, unsure.

"And while you're at it, take the tracking device from the wheel well." Merlin started unbuttoning the shirt as he went into the bathroom. A moment later, he heard her call out.

"It took you long enough to figure it out, genius."

Chapter 28

AT BREAKFAST—coffee, bacon and, eggs for him, coffee, and blueberry pancakes with syrup for her—Merlin was still quiet and somewhat uncommitted. His plan was still knocking back and forth in his brain. What did he reveal, what did he hide?

Nikki seemed to read his mind and she grew irritated as she ate. "Don't think you're going to con me, pal. I'm not–"

"I said we can talk things through, see if we can come to some kind of arrangement. We haven't reached that point yet. You have a pen? And a notebook or something you can write on?"

Her eyebrows pushed together for a moment. Then she reached into a side pocket of her blue jeans. "I have one of the hotel pens." Then she reached for a napkin. "And I can use this. Why?"

The thin, supple material of the leather jacket whispered as Merlin pulled his cell phone from the left pocket. "Mark these names and places down." He started the list of targets with Roland Henderson and his home. Quinn Olivares was added, along with the information they already knew. As was Dimitri Starkov. And then he revealed the names of the other Senators helped to power by Blackstone Strategies; Scott MacDuff, Derrell Hebert, Shermon Best, Torben Flores, Adrian Kazaku, and Dan Herszman.

"Who are these people?"

"Senators."

One eyebrow raised. "You've got a thing for Senators? Is that your specialty?"

"No." He had her add Blackstone Strategies to the list as a target. And last but not least was the suspected kurátor; Oksana Pavlovich.

Nikki wrote that last name down, smoothed the napkin with the back of her hand, and then looked at him. "Who is that?"

Merlin paused between bites of egg. "Miss Boobsalichious. From the fundraiser? She was the one we also saw at Blackstone Strategies when we went up to see Henderson."

Raising her eyebrows, Nikki looked at him for a heartbeat, and then said, "Do you want me to break in and steal her brassiere for you as a souvenir? I can use that as a parachute to get back down."

Chewing on a piece of bacon, Merlin smiled at her. "Jealous much?"

"Hah. Give me the money and I can buy a pair bigger than hers. I could knock your eyes out. Literally from here across the table." She jabbed two fingers towards his face, "I'm pretty sure my nipples would knock your eyes out."

"That I would like to see."

"How are you going to see if I knock your eyes out with my inflated nipples?"

"Extended, not inflated." There was no doubt she was much more upbeat with the promise of working together. Merlin still had his doubts and worries but his tentative plan still seemed like a viable option. He just needed more facts to solidify it. "I want you to do a search on your phone for each name and place and tell me what you can do."

Nikki glanced at his cell. "Can I borrow your phone to do a search?" She shrugged. "My cell phone is a burner. And pretty limited in its functions. Staying hidden and difficult to track by a team of mobster goons is easier if you stay off the grid. I usually case a building in person and then use a public computer to do any Internet stuff."

"Makes sense." He slid the phone across the table, "We don't have time to do the in-person thing right now. Just check on the building or home for each one of those names and guesstimate what you can and can't do."

Nikki snatched the phone from the table, "There isn't anything I can't do, buster."

"Except knock my eyes out in your present condition."

With a thin smile on her lips, she went to work on the phone. "*That* is just cruel." She began tapping away on the screen. "Then again, maybe I wouldn't have to climb if I had a couple of dirigibles on my chest."

For the next half hour, she worked away on the phone, sipping on her coffee as she called up each building on the Internet or on Google Earth, determining what could be done in each case. When she was finally finished, she slid the phone back to Merlin, picked up her fresh coffee and looked over the notes she had made on the napkin.

Merlin watched her for a few moments. "So what's the verdict?"

It took a couple more sips of coffee before she began talking. "All of them are in high-rise buildings. All of them are using Goldstone Securities for wireless intruder security services–"

"Why would they all use the same service?"

"They're the biggest in the area, and the most cost-effective because their size allows them to get special deals from the manufacturing companies, so it makes sense. My cousin works with them as well. Let's see...only Macduff and Flores don't have penthouse units but they are near the top. I'm looking at 20 to 40 story buildings–"

"Doable?"

"Yes, no problem. I used the map's street view to take a quick look at each building to make sure there are ways to get started on the climb. My cousin's security company deals with all but two of the names. Olivares is one. We can work together on that one. And the other one is Shermon Best." Nikki looked at Merlin. "I could ask Niles to let me into the buildings he does operate instead of climbing. Like a said, if we made it worth his while–"

Merlin shook his head. "No. Your cousin can let you know when the places are empty, just like he does for you now. But anything else would involve his employees, one way or another. We have to keep this tight. Me, you, and Niles, nothing beyond that."

Nikki nodded in understanding and chewed on her lip. "Is it okay if I get him to turn off an external camera? It's what we do now. He makes it look like there's a malfunction and gets his staff to turn it off until he can have it fixed."

"That sounds good."

She looked back at her notes on the napkin. "We could make another visit to Olivares and his wife. Work on some kind of distraction... maybe I go to the bathroom while you keep them occupied. Shermon Best... that one will take some planning."

"But still doable, right?"

"Yeah. It won't be any different than what my father and I used to do. No risk, no reward." She clenched her hand, glancing at the gold and black onyx ring.

"Did that ring belong to your father?"

There was a flicker of pain in her eyes. No words came for a moment. "He always wore it. I don't even know where he got it. It was always there from the time I was a kid. He said it identified him and his profession." She drifted off into her thoughts again.

Merlin felt some discomfort at broaching the subject, and he brought the conversation back on point. "Okay then, we have a basic plan. We can work out something with the Olivares...and the same with Blackstone Strategies. We can find a reason to pay Henderson a visit again." He tapped his fingers against his coffee cup. "I'll have to find some way to get into Pavlovich's office at Blackstone Strategies."

"Just don't do her over the desk as a distraction. That one will still basically be standing up no matter how much she tries to lie face down."

Merlin laughed. "You're an idiot."

"But *not* incorrect."

"True." Merlin made a critical decision to go ahead with his overall plan. Taking his phone in hand, he prepared two text messages and sent them both. "Okay. Let's pay for breakfast and then we have to hit the road."

"Where are we going?"

Merlin pushed his chair back. "You know what they say, if I tell you that, I'd have to kill you."

"Uh-huh. Keep in mind I have the strength *and* agility to carry you up fifty-floors and drop you on your head."

Chapter 29

PULLING THE PORSCHE TO A STOP on the tarmac in front of the Bombardier Global 8000, Merlin turned the car off and got out. He opened the back door and grabbed his go-bag as Nikki got out of the passenger side. He closed the back door as she opened the back door on her side to grab her motorcycle tail bag. But she reached in twice, missing the handle both times because her eyes were on the ultra-long-range business jet. The airstairs were down and waiting and Merlin headed for them, glancing back at her. "I suggest you concentrate on your tail bag or we're never going to get onboard."

Nikki looked at him, looked at the jet and then cleared her throat, "Right." She snagged the handle, slammed the door shut and jogged across the tarmac to walk beside him. "Why are we here? And who does this jet belong to?"

Remaining silent, Merlin gestured to the stairs. "You first."

Looking up at the open doorway, then at the stairs, Nikki looked back at Merlin. "Why?"

"You don't trust anybody do you?"

"It's how I stayed alive. You first."

Merlin took the stairs two at a time. He didn't hear her behind him until he was near the top, and then he heard her footsteps climbing the metal stairs. Waiting at the top, he then led the way into the cabin.

Sherrell and Saab were standing and waiting on the other side. They both gave him a nod and a 'sir', then turned their attention to the woman with him.

Nikki's eyes opened wide when she saw the luxurious interior. She took in the plush seats and then the long sofa, the television, and the minibar. Her head jerked to look at Merlin, whispering, "They called you sir? Who are you?"

Merlin directed her attention to the others, "This is Captain Charity Sherrell and her co-pilot, Captain Faith Saab. This is our guest, Lara Nikola Furnari. They call her Nikki the Cat—two Ks."

Saab gave her a nod of greeting. "Ma'am."

Sherrell did the same, "Ma'am. Or do we call you Nikki...wIth two Ks?"

Nikki opened her mouth, unsure of what was happening, then said woodenly, "Yeah...you can do that...two Ks."

Turning her attention to Merlin, Saab said, "We take off in five." She glanced at Nikki and then back to Merlin. "Powless has arranged for everything to be delivered to the airport by the time we arrive. Is there anything else?"

Merlin shook his head, "No. That sounds good." He looked back at Nikki, considering her continued reactions to the luxury jet and the two pilots. He looked back to Saab. "Why don't you give us fifteen? I want to make sure everything is good to go. Is there any coffee on?"

The pilot looked to Nikki and understood. "Yes, sir. We'll get everything ready for takeoff, you just let us know when you're ready to go." Turning with her copilot, they headed for the flight deck.

Nikki watched them for a moment, then she looked at Merlin, her voice low, "Those two are military." It was more statement than question.

Merlin didn't answer. He dropped his go-bag on one of the plush chairs. "Why don't you put your bag down and let's go have a coffee." He headed for the doorway to the galley.

It took a moment more for Nikki to respond. She put her tail bag on the other seat and followed Merlin into the galley.

He was already had coffee pouring into a cup. "Cream and sugar? I think that's what you took at breakfast."

"Uh...yeah, yeah."

Finishing it off, Merlin passed it to her and made his own.

Cup in hand, Nikki wandered a few feet away, stretching her neck and looking through the next doorway.

"Back there is a suite with two single beds, a private washroom, and a stand-up shower. Plus a few other things."

Nikki swung around, "Who exactly are you? A rich tycoon—? No, rich tycoon's don't climb to a roof and break into someone else's place. Are you a spy?"

"If I told you I was like James Bond, would you sleep with me?"

Shaking her head, Nikki said, "Nope. I'd rather swallow one of those pills you keep in your tooth that kills you."

"In that case, I'm not like James Bond and you don't have to kill yourself."

"You're a weird dude. You can joke with a woman all day long, but as soon as things turned to a serious nature, your nuts tighten up."

Merlin laughed. "I wouldn't quite describe it that way but I get your point. Let's go and sit down." He led her back to the main cabin area and sat in one of the chairs with a table.

Nikki sat in the other.

Sipping at his coffee, Merlin knew it was time to open up. Time to find out if she was really in or out. There was no doubt he needed her help if he was going to get his job done before too much damage was done to the free world. "My name is Merlin Dragon. That's as much as I can tell you on that part."

"Merlin Dragon? Really? Rhett Summers sounds more plausible."

"What can I tell you? My full name is Merlin Arthur Dragon. My mother loved King Arthur and the Knights of the round table, and all that stuff."

"For real? Wow."

"There is no scam...or scheme...or plan...to take any money, valuables, or property from any of the people we talked about."

Nikki took a sip of coffee, considering what he had just said. "So...we're talking information? Like blackmail or–?"

"No." Merlin paused for a moment. "On the surface...Dimitri Starkov is a wealthy Russian businessman. He is wealthy, but he didn't make it the honest way. He's actually ex-KGB–"

"That's a Russian spy, right?"

"You could say that. They were responsible for everything from foreign intelligence, to counter-intelligence, border security, guarding the leadership of the Communist Party, basically whatever it took. It was replaced by an agency that does the same thing when the Soviet Union collapsed. That's when a bunch of guys like Starkov made their money. But you could say—once a spy—always a spy. In fact, that's what I'm working to uncover. He's just one of these Russian oligarchs using their immense wealth to influence politics in the free world, to compromise and blackmail people–"

"Are you saying all those Senators are being blackmailed?"

"Right now, I'm not sure. All I know is Starkov is working with Blackstone Strategies to help get people like them elected to government. He works through Henderson and his company to provide the money needed—sometimes millions of dollars—to run a political campaign for office. Once they're in there–"

"He's got them by the nuts."

Merlin laughed. "I guess you could say that. I'm not even sure Henderson knows what's going on. He has his own agenda." Merlin shifted in his seat, feeling the warmth from the cup in his hands. "Right now, secret intelligence information from the American government is being passed by someone under Starkov's control to Russia. It's also possible the same thing is happening in Canada and Great Britain."

"So how do I fit in? Why would you want me to climb a building? How does that help?"

"Because I need to—*we* need to get close enough to clone the sim cards on their phones—and to plant special software on their personal computers so we can monitor what they're doing. And we have to do it fast if were going to prevent any more valuable information—information that can destroy our security—from being passed to the Russians. I can do it on my own, but it's going to take a lot of planning and time. Time we don't have. With your help, we can do it much faster."

Nikki sipped her coffee for a moment, thinking. Then she asked an important question, "So what's in it for me? Once I help you with all this spy crap, I'm back to slinking and hiding in the dark."

Merlin shook his head. "No. You help me...and I'll help you."

"No offense, but that's what the Marshals told me. And I've been running ever since."

"True. But I can do what the Marshals can't do—or won't do. You said it yourself—I do whatever I have to do, no matter what it is. And the less you know the better."

Chapter 30

OTTAWA, CANADA

TWO HOURS LATER, the Bombardier Global 8000 descended through the fluffy white clouds, landed and taxied to the private and secure area at the Ottawa Macdonald–Cartier International Airport that served as the home base for the business jet and its crew.

Nikki was glued to one of the cabin windows, watching with great interest as a large camouflage Humvee pulled to a stop not far from the plane at the same time.

Merlin unbuckled his seatbelt. "Time to go." He rose from the seat, grabbed his leather jacket from another one and slipped it on.

Her seatbelt rattling as she unbuckled it, Nikki stood up. "Where are we? And where are we going?"

Captain Faith Saab appeared almost immediately. The stairs began lowering, the hydraulic whine whispering softly through the cabin.

Nikki watched her for a moment, bending at the knees to look through the window again. "Does somebody want to tell me what's going on?"

Locking the airstairs in place, Saab stepped outside.

Merlin headed for the now-open door. Reaching it, he looked back and gestured to Nikki who stood rooted to the spot. "Don't worry, nothing bad is going to happen to you."

Working her jaw for a moment, Nikki finally headed for the open door. "Yeah. And that's what they say to the girl in the movies before the monster or the serial killer gets her."

"True. But the girl is usually just in her panties and bra. Do you want to take your clothes off now?"

"Hah. You'd like that wouldn't you?"

"Not really." Merlin stepped outside and moved down the stairs to the tarmac.

Nikki stepped outside and stood beside Saab. "Did he just say he *didn't* want to see me in my underwear?"

"Yeah," Saab said, "he's shy that way."

"More like a moron." She called out to Merlin who was striding across the tarmac. "I'm hot stuff in my underwear, pal."

Merlin simply gestured over his shoulder for her to follow him.

Nikki took the stairs two at a time and jogged across the tarmac to catch up to him as he reached the camouflage Humvee

Merlin opened the back door and gestured for her to climb inside.

"You first, pal."

Shaking his head, Merlin climbed into the Humvee and moved across to the other seat.

Nikki stuck her head in, glanced at the two soldiers sitting in the front, their eyes straight ahead, then decided to climb in and pull the door shut. She leaned toward Merlin and whispered, "Who are they?"

The Humvee took off, pressing them back in their seats as Merlin answered. "They're with the Intelligence Branch of the Canadian Armed Forces."

"Canadian Armed Forces? What are they doing in the US?"

"They're not. You're in Canada."

"Canada?" Nikki shifted in her seat looking around. "Canada. How come we didn't go though customs?"

"Why? Do you miss a security pat-down or something?"

Shrugging, Nikki said, "It depends on how good looking the guy is. I've been on the run for a while and I haven't had a good cavity search in a long time."

Merlin laughed. "Like I said, you're an idiot."

Nikki leaned closer. "Do you have someone you play customs with? What's she like—?"

Merlin held a hand up. "Let's just concentrate on the task at hand."

"I was just being friendly." Nikki's jaw worked away as the Humvee traversed the tarmac to a low, brick building, where it pulled to a stop.

Merlin opened his door and climbed out, "Let's go."

As the door slammed shut, Nikki leaned over and looked over the building for a moment. Then she opened her door, got out, slammed it shut and jogged around to join Merlin just as he was walking through a door into an open room.

The only thing in the entire room was a single table in the center with four chairs, two on this side and one each on the left and right side. An open laptop and a cardboard box sat on the table.

Two soldiers in uniform—a man and a woman—made a quick, formal salute, then relaxed.

Merlin returned a quick salute, and then gestured to Nikki. "Take a seat and they can get started."

The soldiers went to work, one of them producing a thumb drive from a box on the table, the other sitting on a side and tapping on the laptop's keyboard to wake it.

Nikki approached the chair cautiously. Her eyes took in the badge on their caps—scarlet, dark green, and white, with a North Star symbol in the center. "More intelligence people?"

"Yeah." Merlin sat down, waiting for her to do the same.

It took a moment before she did. Then Nikki leaned slightly toward Merlin, her voice low and her gaze on the male officer. "He's cute."

"Concentrate."

"I am. On what he could do for me. I missed my cavity search, remember?"

Merlin put a finger to his lips.

Nikki crossed her arms, waiting.

The male officer started, holding up a thumb drive, "It's pretty simple as far as the thumb drive goes. All you have to do is slip it into the USB port on any computer and the software goes to work automatically, planting a program that allows our people to monitor all communications." He plugged it into the side of the laptop and the thumb drive began flashing. "As simple as that."

Nikki tightened her crossed arms. "Oh, yeah, pretty simple. Except for the part of getting near a bad guy's computer without them seeing me...*and* me getting killed."

Merlin leaned his head slightly toward her, "I think we all understand your concern. You can quit any time you want."

With a slight sniff, Nikki said, "No. I just wanted you to know how incredibly brave I am."

"Of course. Along with beautiful and–"

"You forgot sexy." She looked at the male officer she obviously found attractive. "Right? He forgot to tell *you* how sexy I am."

The officer nodded, a slight smile on his lips. "Of course, ma'am."

Nikki looked at Merlin, mock distress on her face. "He called me ma'am. You can't be called a ma'am and be sexy."

"Did you tell him you're called Nikki the Cat?"

Looking back at the officer, she said, "You hear that? I'm a slinky, sexy, feline woman and I can climb a fifty story building in my sleep."

"Yes, ma'am."

She pretended to throw her hands up, "I give up. All you military types are alike. No romance." She glanced to the female officer, "Do you get the same treatment?"

The female officer smiled, "Yes, ma'am."

Nikki held her hands up in mock surrender, "Now I really give up."

Merlin could tell there was a real nervousness and concern beneath the joking exterior. There was no doubt—once the men and women from the Canadian Security Intelligence Agency, and the Armed Forces began to go through what she had to do —it all became real. She was understanding the seriousness of the situation and it no doubt scared her at some level. The good part of her willingness to testify at trial—going into witness protection—and fighting to stay alive with mobsters hunting her—was the fact she had continued to do whatever was necessary, and could perform her high-rise feats while under extreme pressure, including facing her own death.

The male officer gestured to the box on the table. "We've supplied a dozen thumb drives in case one gets lost —or dropped when you're climbing a fifty-story building...ma'am."

Nikki clucked her tongue. "I don't drop anything on the way up or the way down, pal."

"No, ma'am."

Merlin spoke up. "What if someone *does* get their hands on one of these?"

"If anyone tries to access the thumb drive, it's programmed to wipe everything clean." He pulled two cell phones from the box, gave one to Merlin, and passed the other over to Nikki. "Lacroix will explain the situation with these. We've moved away from the suggestion on the sim card cloning."

Merlin took the phone in hand. "Why the change? Not that I care either way." He placed a thumb on the screen and it lit up, showing three icons in the center of the screen; red, green, and black. At the bottom were the typical phone and message icons.

Lacroix pulled her chair around to sit almost next to Nikki. "The sim card cloning is too difficult... or should I say too dangerous...with all the phones you're going to have to deal with."

Nikki watched what Merlin was doing and did the same, looking closely at the screen. "I'm all for lessening the danger, "

"Here's how they work," Lacroix said as she pointed at Nikki's screen. "The icons on the bottom show you can make a phone call or send a message, just like any normal cell phone. That's to avoid suspicion if someone should happen to see the screen when you're using it."

"Okay, makes sense. What are the other icons for?"

"I'll explain that in one moment, ma'am. But first, it's imperative that you press the icons in the exact sequence required to operate the internal software."

"Okay."

"Got it," Merlin said.

"First, you press the red icon on the left. Second, you press the black icon on the right. Third, you will press the green icon in the center. Any other sequence will cause the internal security to wipe the phone clean."

Nikki looked at her. "That's in case someone gets their hands on the phone? Like a Mission Impossible thing—it self-destructs."

Lacroix smiled, "It doesn't self-destruct, it doesn't burn up or melt or anything like that. It simply wipes the phone clean."

"Okay. Still cool. So... I press left - right - center."

"Correct. When you get near a target phone, you press the left icon to initialize the internal software–"

"And basically tell the cell phone I'm the good guy," Nikki added.

"Correct. Next, when you press on the right icon, the cell phone will now act like an IMSI-catcher."

Nikki looked at her, "What's an... what did you call it?"

Speaking slower, Lacroix said, "An IMSI-catcher. It's a telephone eavesdropping device used by law enforcement to intercept mobile phone traffic. The letters I-M-S-I refer to the international mobile subscriber identity on each phone. It's a 64 bit field sent by the phone to the network."

"If you say so."

"I saw an IMSI-catcher used before," Merlin said, "it was a lot bigger than these cell phones."

"You're right," Lacroxi said. "And that's the problem with using a standard IMSI-catcher. We'd need you to place one within a half a mile of each building or workplace. That would be difficult with the Senate office and the counterintelligence efforts protecting them. And then we'd need people on the ground with you to sort out all the cell phone traffic the devices would capture. Since we know the people you're dealing with, tech specialists are already putting together all their cell phone numbers. The government phone numbers are easy to find out. We're hacking and cracking the cell phone providers to find out about any personal phones the targets have."

Nikki looked at her, "Is all that legal?"

"That's above my pay grade, ma'am. I just do what I'm told." She exchanged a slight grin with Nikki but managed to maintain a professional exterior. "And all we need you to do is get near the target cell phones by visiting their home or office. Once we intercept the data we need, we can do the rest remotely. We can even turn on the internal GPS on their phones and track them."

"Do they have to make a phone call when we're with them? Or send a text message?"

"No, ma'am. The cell phones basically are in constant communication with the cell towers so a phone call can be made easily. These cell phone act like a cell tower, intercepting the signal."

"Okay." Nikki pointed at the screen, "What is the center icon for?"

"Once you press the right icon to activate the internal IMSI-catcher, you press the center icon to activate a connection from the target phone to our intelligence command. Once we get a fix on the signal, the software on your phone shuts down."

"And I go onto to the next target phone. Sounds easy." Nikki touched the phone and message icons lightly, "And I can make calls if I need to?"

The male officer spoke up, a light smile on his lips, "Yes, ma'am. And if you double-tap the phone icon, it acts like a direct speed dial to me. In case you have a problem."

Nikki raised an eyebrow, "Like needing a pizza at 1 o'clock in the morning?"

"I'm afraid it would be cold by the time I got there, ma'am."

"But I wouldn't be."

Chapter 31

AFTER AN HOUR OF PRACTICE, and going through all types of scenarios they could encounter, Merlin and Nikki were driven back to the jet. Each of them had six thumb drives, and two the IMSI-catcher cell phones. A large panel van with the words AirTec Products sat next to the global 8000. Merlin followed Nikki up the airstairs and into the cabin.

A man in a set of dark-green coveralls with an AirTec Products logo on the chest stood next to Saab, talking.

Saab gestured with her head to Merlin, "There he is now."

The man reached down to the top handle of a large green-colored metal container that looked like a large toolbox, "Yes, sir. Where would you like me to put this?"

Merlin gestured to the doorway to the galley, "You can take it through there."

Nodding, the AirTec man turned and headed through the doorway.

As Merlin followed him, Saab gestured to one of the seats, "A courier delivered those items just after you left."

Two black duffel bags sat on the floor next to the seat. In between the duffel bags was a manila envelope.

"Okay, I'll take care of that when I get back. Once I talk to this gentleman we can head back to Washington."

"All right, I'll let the Captain know."

Inside the galley, Merlin had the man set the green box down on the small counter. Once they had a conversation on how to use the contents, he led the man back to the main cabin area and the exit. Nikki was sitting in one of the chairs. looking to be deep in thought, but her eyes followed them with interest. Merlin put a hand on the man's shoulder, "Just remember that this is all a hush-hush, right?"

The AirTec man nodded solemnly, "Oh yes, sir. You don't have to worry about me, sir. I'm bonded. And I also have a security clearance. I've been on Canadian Forces Station Leitrim a number of times. I even had to fly up to CFS Alert in Nunavut. Yes, sir, I'm the man they send on these types of jobs." He made a gesture of zipping his lips shut. "I know how to stay quiet, sir."

Merlin clapped him on the shoulder again, "Okay, thanks." He turned away before the man could say any more, walked to one of the chairs and hit an intercom button, "Our friend is off and we can leave anytime." He then turned his attention to the manila envelope between the two black duffel bags. Inside he found a passport, a New York driver's license, and an American Express credit card, all in the name of Rhett Summers. Tossing the envelope to a table, he pocketed the identification, picked up the bags by the padded handles and headed back to the galley. As he checked their contents, he heard the hydraulic whine of the air stairs closing. Satisfied everything was as needed, Merlin closed the duffel bags, he stowed one in the electronic locker in the suite, along with the green box and his Interpol passport and credentials, and then carried one black duffel bag back to the cabin area.

Saab was already headed towards the flight deck and she glanced over her shoulder, "Take off is in ten. Please buckle up."

"Will do." He looked at Nikki. She was sitting there, leaning and looking out the window, but it was apparent she wasn't really looking at anything. "Are you okay? Second thoughts?"

It took a moment before Nikki glanced in his direction, "No. No second thoughts. I was just thinking, is all."

"As long as you're sure."

There was a nod, but she looked back out the window, staring at nothing.

"You should buckle up."

It took another moment. Then she said yeah, and stirred, buckling herself in for takeoff.

Merlin looked at her for another moment and then placed the duffel bag on her lap. "Maybe that can be a start to making you feel better." He sat in the next seat and buckled up as she looked at him, at the duffel bag, and then back at him.

"What is it?"

"Open it and see."

Nikki used one of the padded handles to move it a bit, testing the weight, "It's...it's got something in it."

"Do you think I'd give you an empty duffel bag?"

"With you, you never know." Nikki undid the top zipper and looked inside. She blinked. Looked at Merlin. Looked back inside...and then reached a hand inside. She pulled out a thick, banded wad of money. Glancing at Merlin, back at the money, and then looking back inside the duffel bag, her voice was faint, "What...is this?"

"Two million dollars. Unmarked, non-sequential serial numbers. You can start a new life."

"But–"

"You let me take care of your friends in Brooklyn. You just do your part."

Nikki looked at the money. "Aren't you afraid I'll just take off–?"

"If you do, then I just have to do everything by myself. Either way...I just need one thing from you."

"What?"

Merlin told her.

Nikki wasn't sure she could do it.

Chapter 32

BROOKLYN, NEW YORK

IT WAS LATE IN THE DAY. The sun hadn't been set yet and the air was hot and sticky. Traffic in the street to his left moved slowly, with a lot of honking and anger, as Merlin approached Club Lavender cautiously on foot. He had left his weapon a block away in the vehicle he rented when the Global 8000 landed at LaGuardia Airport sixteen miles from here. He had no idea which way this was going to go. These weren't 'businessmen' in the typical sense of the word. They were just as likely to kill him, take what they wanted, and keep what they had. It would be a few hours before the hot night-spot became a hub of activity and Merlin wanted to get in and out long before the crowds hit. Two hard-core bodybuilders stood guard at the main entrance, obviously bouncers or security, dressed in tank tops that showed off their massive arms. The one on the left spoke up as he approached, "Sorry, sir but the club won't be open until–"

"I'm not here to party, I'm here to talk to Dante Taccetta." Merlin held his right hand out, fist closed, palm down.

The second security guard glanced at his partner. Then he looked back at Merlin, unsure. A moment later—muscles tense and ready to react—he held his open hand out below the closed fist.

Merlin dropped the item into the man's palm. "Tell Taccetta that's my calling card."

Looking at the item in his palm, the security guard said to his partner, "Keep an eye on him. I'll go show this to the boss."

The Mr. Muscles who remained, crossed his arms, highlighting the massive guns.

"Impressive," Merlin said, "kind of reminds me of myself when I was younger."

The security guard's eyes moved up and down Merlin's body. He wasn't impressed.

Merlin was dressed in the leather jacket, black T-shirt, and blue jeans. He lifted his arms out to his sides. "Do you want to frisk me now so we can get this moving?"

It took a moment before the security guard unwound his massive pythons and did a thorough search of Merlin. He was just finishing up when the other security guard appeared back at the door.

"Okay. The boss wants to see him."

"Already did a pat down. He's clean."

Merlin stepped through the doorway and followed the security guard. Glancing over his shoulder, he saw the door pulled shut as the other security guard remained outside. Relieved he didn't have to worry about being shot or stabbed in the back, Merlin concentrated on the dangers ahead. He then realized he couldn't really see because the security guard was so wide across the shoulders and lats—until the guy stepped aside.

Sitting behind a long booth table, leaning back against a foam padded backrest, was a tough looking guy in his 50s. He was dressed in a black, open-neck shirt, no tie, and a tweed jacket. He was bracketed by two women who reminded Merlin of Miss

Boobsalichious back in Washington. The only difference was the four dirigibles he was looking at were far more exposed, if that was possible. There were three hard-core men on the left of the table and two more on the right. All wore suits with bulges that indicated handguns in shoulder holsters.

The man in the middle spoke. "I'm Dante Taccetta." His voice was gravelly, thick from years of whiskey, cigarettes, and who knew what else. He set the object Merlin had sent to him on the table. It clicked on the glass. "And where did you get this?"

Merlin looked down at the object he had sent in to the mobster; the gold ring with the black onyx stone and green jade cat—Connie the Cat's ring.

"I got it from the daughter." That's all Merlin said. He waited.

Taccetta looked at the ring, considered it for a moment, then looked up at Merlin again. "And where is this daughter?"

"I have her on ice with my men."

"I see. And why should I believe you?"

Merlin considered the gangster for a moment and then gave him a half shrug, "Fine. You want to dick me around, then I guess we can't do business." He leaned over and reached for the ring, "I'll just dump the bitch in the East River and cut my losses–"

Taccetta slammed his hand down over the ring.

The other men went on alert, a hand inside their jacket, ready to pull iron and fill Merlin with lead.

Slowly straightening up, lifting his hands to his shoulders, Merlin said, "Fine. You can keep the ring. I'll just be on my way–"

"Is she alive?"

"Yeah." Merlin slowly lowered his hands. "I'm a good businessman. When I hear two million, I think that's better than one million."

"Bring her to me. And the two million is yours."

Merlin shook his head. "No. I don't think. You got too many guys here. That puts me at a great disadvantage. I have her in an old warehouse at the Brooklyn Navy yard." He gestured toward his side pocket, "Can I...?"

Taccetta nodded.

Slowly reaching into his pocket, Merlin pulled out a folded piece of paper, reached forward and placed it on the table. "That's a diagram where I have her. It's right on the river. Midnight tonight—you bring *two* men with you. And the cash. That way it's basically even. I leave with my guys, and you do what you need to do."

There was no movement, Taccetta simply sat there. As did his men. The two women looked bored with the whole thing. The sounds of bottles and glasses clinking carried across the nightclub as the staff got ready to open.

Merlin was very much aware he would be overpowered quickly by the superior numbers on the gangster side. He concentrated on relaxing, to send a message he still had everything under control despite the odds. "Look," he said. "If I don't walk out of here in a few minutes with a deal in place, my guys won't storm the place trying to rescue me. They'll cut their losses. It's not that we're disloyal to each other, we're bounty hunters. It's the nature of the beast. We win more than we lose, but there are losses–"

"Where did you find her?"

The test Merlin had expected. "California. We'd picked up someone else who burned her in exchange for their freedom. They had been doing some jobs together. We found her holed-up in a high-rise loft that was vacant. Nearly lost her climbing out a window. She had an Oregon driver's license on her. Bogus name." He gave Taccetta a devious smile. "Of course, we kept tabs on the first guy who burned her and turned him in for the bounty. A guy's gotta make money, right?"

There was silence. Then, "We have a deal." Taccetta raised a finger, his words slow but firm, "But if you are lying...or if you are screwing with me...."

"Midnight tonight. Sharp. Don't be late." Merlin turned on his heels and walked away, half expecting a bullet in the back. Of course, they would probably wait and try to put one in the front somewhere around ten minutes after midnight.

Chapter 33

WASHINGTON. DC

NIKKI THE CAT prepared herself mentally. It was one AM and she was in the shadows of several trees, not far from the oval, thirty-story, glass-and-steel high-rise condominium where Senator Shermon Best had the top penthouse. She had started her part by following Best in the Porsche Merlin had left for her to use. Best was going to be the toughest job. Her cousin couldn't help her with this one. She followed the Senator and his wife, wanting to get an understanding of his daily schedule, hoping to find a time frame she could use to enter his home. To her surprise, ten minutes after she followed Best from his Senate office to his home—he parked in the circular driveway out front which meant he was going somewhere else—he came back down with his wife, and she had followed the couple to the airport. There she watched them at the check-in, presenting tickets to somewhere, and then fly off into the Washington skies. Leaving the Porsche at the Ritz-Carlton Hotel, she got ready and then switched to her motorcycle to get back here.

Pulling a black balaclava over her head, she rolled her shoulders. She wore a tight, black climbing suit, climbing shoes, a black pouch over her left hip, and black Nike Vapor gloves, similar to those worn by wide receivers in professional football. They allowed an incredible 'sticky' grip while remaining flexible and giving her a full feel under her fingertips. Of course, she always felt her natural climbing ability was the real reason she could do what she could do. Sprinting from the shadows and across the six feet of space illuminated by soft lights, Nikki the Cat leaped and grabbed onto a thin seam in the facing of the building and pulled herself up.

The architecture of the building gave each floor a balcony that sat in front of a glass wall of windows and a glass door access. These balconies wrapped around the building, broken only at the four rounded corners. And that's where Nikki headed for as she climbed across the face of the building. It would give her a direct climb to the top but it was also more in the shadows than the basic four sides. Once she reached the curved glass-and-steel corner, she used the thin seams to climb. The adrenaline coursed through her veins as she felt those seems under her fingers and toes. The cool night air touched her nose and her eyes, making her feel alive as she climbed. No one else could do this. Not even her father had been able to climb a building like this. She was special, she felt it in her bones.

The climb only took her fifteen minutes. Reaching the top floor, Nikki moved across to the glass-and steel-balcony railing of the penthouse. Adding to the thrill, she pulled up on the last seam with her fingers and vaulted over the railing, landing softly on the other side. The feeling of danger was exhilarating. Moving quickly across to the double glass doors, Nikki reached into her pouch, pulled out a cell phone and a small antenna that she inserted into the top of the phone. An antenna was normally used as a signal booster for communications. In this case, she was using it to boost the signal from illegal software on the cell phone used to offset wireless burglar alarms. It served as a jamming device to prevent the signal of an intruder being sent over the wireless system. Clipping that to the belt for her pouch—the range was limited but would work to shield her as she moved around inside—Nikki then pulled out a set of lock picks and was inside within seconds.

She had memorized the layout as best as she could from the floor plan and images she had seen on the Internet, placed there by the real estate company when the building was first opened up three years ago. There was little changed and most of the main area was a wide open space. The penthouse furniture was eclectic, the air smelled of peppermint, and the soft cork floor was comfortable underfoot.

A library and a den on the far side of the penthouse were the most likely spots for computers. It didn't take her long to determine there was no computer in the library. Moving quickly and softly into the den, she found a desktop computer as well as a laptop. Senator Best and his wife only had one large suitcase with them, no briefcase or laptop bag, so she assumed this was his personal laptop. It didn't really matter. As long as she began the task of getting all those intelligence and/or military types into his system, one way or the other. She fired up both computers. Pulling the special thumb drive from her pouch, she inserted it into the desktop. It flashed and went to work automatically, just like she had been told it would. A few moments later, she stuck it into the USB port on the laptop and watched it go to work as she shut down the desktop. This was all easy-peasy, in and out–

A sound.

Nikki went on alert. She strained to listen as the thumb drive stopped flashing, indicating it had finished its job. She pulled the thumb drive and dropped it into her pouch, turned off the laptop and closed the lid. It made a slight clicking sound–

That was followed by another sound somewhere in the penthouse.

Moving to the still-open door of the study, Nikki listened.

The faint sounds of footsteps.

The offset sounds of those footsteps told her there were two people, at least, in the penthouse unit with her. And Nikki knew instinctively that they were not the footsteps of people coming home—those were the sounds of footsteps moving cautiously. Searching footsteps. Were they searching for her? Did they know she was here? Her mind went to Merlin Dragon. This was similar to what it happened when she was in that Russian's condo—only she was sleeping when she heard his footsteps. The odds of it being Dragon—or another burglar—were slim, none, and zero as far as she was concerned. Was this a setup?

She would have to figure that out later. Right now, extricating herself from this situation was imperative. The footsteps were to the left. If she was oriented properly, that was the front entrance. And that would cut her off from the way she came in. If her research was right, she had another escape route, through another set of balcony doors, off to the right. Slipping out of the den and closing the door softly behind her, Nikki moved low in that direction.

As she neared the wall of windows she could see the balcony doors–

Footsteps to the right. The spear of a flashlight beam lit her up. "Freeze! Police."

Nikki cursed under her breath. Without Niles to cut off the outside cameras—or maybe it was someone from a surrounding building—she had been spotted climbing the building. There had been no time to do a proper surveillance of the surroundings to discover and counter all the problems. But at the same time as she cursed, and with all those thoughts oursing through her brain, she sprang forward and did a somersault over a long sofa, landing low on her feet on the other side.

The sound of surprise came from behind the spear of light. "It's a woman. She's running."

Moving low and quick, Nikki reached the balcony door, unlocked it, sprinted outside and across to the railing. Planting her hands on the metal top of the railing, Nikki was up and over, dropped to catch the bottom railing—it stuck out barely half an inch—whipped her feet out and then in to gain momentum—and dropped to her feet on the balcony below.

The sounds of cursing and "How did she do that?" came from above.

Nikki ran hard along the balcony, heading for the far corner of the building.

The hiss, static, and conversations over a police radio could be heard from above.

Reaching the curved steel-and-glass corner, Nikki climbed from the balcony and began a rapid descent. As she moved downward from seam to seam, she tried to orient herself, imagining how she had entered the penthouse...moved through it...and had to run...if she was right, once on the ground, she would find her motorcycle parked on the street off to the left. She only had two floors to go now—

"Police. Don't move."

Nikki stopped and looked down. A police officer was below her, gun drawn and pointed up at her. Don't move? What the hell was he going to do, climb up and handcuff her? She began climbing again, figuring out another escape route.

"Don't move or I'll shoot!"

She was near a third-floor balcony and moved laterally. Why would he shoot? She was just a burglar who wasn't threatening him—

A gunshot.

Nikki felt the impact. The side of her lower back burned with pain. Her right hand let go of the seam.

Chapter 34

BROOKLYN, NEW YORK

THE BROOKLYN NAVY YARD was three hundred acres of yesterday, filled with old, abandoned factories, vacant piers, and row upon row of abandoned warehouses. A fog was rolling through the dingy alleyways, making the outside look like an apocalyptic wasteland as Merlin prepared himself inside a large, open warehouse that smelled musty and sharply metallic. He had taken one of the guided tours with forty other tourists and chose this building next to the waterfront. He stole a motorboat and came back in later through the pier out back, making sure there was still electricity to the place and that the layout would work. There was a long, poorly lit, open area that the gangster and his men would have to walk through, allowing him to make sure they weren't going to overwhelm him. He had no doubt Taccetta wanted Nikki, but he was greedy—no, make that treacherous enough—to want to keep the two million dollars as well. The building also had office space with a lunchroom. He was now in the lunchroom's kitchen area, wearing a pair of tactical shooting gloves and getting ready. A courier had delivered two black duffel bags to the Global 8000. One had contained the money for

Nikki. The other contained items Merlin needed for this part of his plan.

He had a small infra-red wireless-camera sitting on the wide inner frame of a green, leaded-glass window, aimed through a broken pane and overlooking the area out front. He watched the image on his phone as he set to work under the few lights that hadn't been knocked out by vandals. From the duffel bag, he pulled out a six cavity aluminum bullet mold and set it on the counter next to the sink. Next came a large thermos of water that he set on the counter. He had boiled the water on the jet, a simple method of deaerating the water to remove dissolved oxygen. That would prevent tiny bubbles from forming when he worked with the water. After the boiling, he had worn gloves and used sterilized scissors to cut off minute pieces of cotton, adding them to the water.

He placed the green box that had been delivered by the man from AirTec Products into the sink and opened it. It contained liquid nitrogen.

Taking the thermos in hand, Merlin shook it vigorously to evenly distribute the cotton fibers. Unscrewing the top, he poured the water into each one of the six bullet molds. Working quickly, he set the bullet mold into the liquid nitrogen. White mist swirled and a moment later, Merlin pulled out the mold that now held six ice bullets.

Actually, Merlin had created six Pykrete bullets. Ice was too weak—in part because of the bubbles and hollows created by the dissolved oxygen—to resist being shattered when fired from a gun. The ice would even begin to melt from the friction of the gun barrel. Pykrete was a frozen composite material that would work better for this task. It has been invented during World War II as a candidate material for a super-sized aircraft carrier for the British Royal Navy when steel was scarce—it was up to 14 times stronger than regular ice. Or concrete for that matter.

Freeing the first six ice bullets, Merlin set four more in the liquid nitrogen, then set to work using a small hand press to ready his 'ammunition'. In ten minutes he had loaded a ten round magazine–

A flash of light on the cell phone screen caught his attention and Merlin cursed under his breath. A black SUV pulled to a stop in front of the building. Was it Taccetta? It only took a few seconds to determine that it was. Taccetta and the two muscle man in tank tops emerged from the vehicle. Two more vehicles came to a stop and parked about ten feet behind the first one.

Merlin had expected the gangster to arrive early, just not this early. He went to work even faster. Keeping half his attention on the screen, he pulled the parts for a Vanquish modular sniper rifle from the duffel bag—the high-tech weapon was designed to be assembled in seconds with no tools. Disassembled, the longest part was the barrel at 20 inches—assembled, the weapon was only 39 inches. Slapping the magazine in place, Merlin grabbed his cell phone as well as the scope and headed for the catwalk that overlooked the open space. He reached the spot he had set up behind empty cardboard boxes as the front door swung open.

The first muscleman entered, cautious but with a muscle-man walk that tried to send a different message.

Merlin clicked the scope in place. He only needed it from this distance to make sure he nailed his target with a death shot on the first pull of the trigger—although he hoped to get off a double-tap kill shot. But after that first shot with an ice bullet, all hell would break lose and there were no guarantees.

Taccetta entered next, carrying a duffel bag in his left hand, leaving his right hand free to pull a weapon.

The second muscleman entered behind his boss, pulling the door closed.

All three men stood side-by-side, looking across the open space to the chair thirty feet away...and the person in the black hoodie tied to the chair, back to them.

Merlin had used pillows inside clothing to create a 'body' that he had tied to the chair. A smaller square pillow inside the hood created the head. It was crude but effective for a gangster determined to gain revenge for his son.

And Merlin only needed a moment.

Not seeing anyone else in the open space, the two musclemen went on alert, each one reaching behind their back and pulling a weapon they had stuffed in their belt.

Taccetta remained motionless, staring at the 'person' in the chair, his jaw set hard. He was far more interested in getting his hands on Nikki the Cat.

From his cell phone screen, Merlin could see eight other men gathering around Taccetta's vehicle, ready to come inside at a moment's notice as well. Merlin had no doubt the gangster was ready to take everything once he knew he had Lara Nicola Furnari in his grasp. But he had other plans. Lifting the rifle to his shoulder, Merlin took aim at the gangster through the scope—and pulled the trigger—twice.

Two cracks of gunfire.

Two ice bullets crashed into the skull of Dante Taccetta.

As Taccetta's body was dropping to the concrete floor, Merlin fired a shot into the muscle man on the left.

As he was dropping, his partner fired off shots wildly, unsure of where the echoing shots had come from.

Merlin dropped him with a shot to the skull.

Pocketing his cell phone, Merlin sprinted across the catwalk toward the large, opaque green-leaded glass window facing the front of the building. Reaching the window—he had already knocked out two other panes of the leaded glass to give him a field of fire—he spotted the rest of the men heading for the door. Lifting the rifle to his shoulder, he pulled the trigger twice, taking out two men in the lead. The others began scattering for cover. He fired off another shot, taking down one more man with an ice bullet in the back. Grabbing the wireless camera and pocketing it, Merlin sprinted away from the window, slipped under the railing and dropped from the catwalk to the floor below.

His boots hit the worn concrete floor echoing across the open space..

Gunfire sounded from outside and the green-leaded glass window above exploded inward.

Sprinting across the floor to the front door, Merlin slammed the corroded bolt in place, locking it. He put his remaining ice bullets into Taccetta and grabbed the briefcase. Before he took another step, Merlin saw Taccetta was wearing the gold ring with the black onyx stone on his middle finger, like some vulgar winning trophy. Pulling the ring off and slipping it into a pocket, Merlin sprinted across to the chair and the fake Nikki the Cat. The setup wasn't heavy and he dragged it into the lunchroom, where he took it apart.

The gunfire stopped.

Tossing the items he had used to create the body into a corner, Merlin figured it would simply look like someone had been sleeping here. He wasn't really concerned about much of an investigation being done. A gangster was dead. He had created the ice bullets to simply prevent any forensics taking place that would tie the ammunition to any particular weapon and create problems down the road. The ice would be melted in no time, the remaining cotton particles wouldn't mean much to anyone, and it was doubtful anyone would perform DNA testing on any 'water' around the wounds. Even if they did, he had been cautious about leaving any traces.

Disassembling the rifle—he could hear faint banging at the locked door, along with voices—Merlin put everything back into the duffel bag, carried it, the green box, and the gangster's duffel bag out back to the pier, where he loaded it all into the motorboat. Firing up the outboard motor, Merlin twisted the throttle and drove the boat in an arc away from the pier.

Voices shouted at the buzzing sound coming from the river.

Angling back to the shore, and using the next pier for cover, Merlin stayed low in the motorboat.

Gunshots.

Merlin glanced back to see flashes of gunfire from the pier. They were shooting in the direction of the sound. In a few moments, he could hear the shots but no longer see the flashes. He felt relief course through his body. His plan had worked much better than he thought it would. If Nikki's part went this easy, it wouldn't be long before they took down the Russian's efforts to infiltrate the politics of the free world and shatter his growing spy network.

Chapter 35

WASHINGTON. DC

NIKKI THE CAT hung precariously by her left hand—her weaker hand—the one with the weaker grip. She remembered working so hard to make both sides equally strong, but there was no doubt she was in trouble. *And* she had been stupid. Of course, they would shoot. She had just been caught red-handed inside the home of a United States Senator. She could've been a terrorist—domestic or foreign—it didn't matter, and maybe planting a bomb. Or she was a foreign spy and had taken some secret documents for all they knew. Either way, they weren't taking any chances with her. She pushed all that from her brain. Failure by giving up wasn't an option right now. There was too much at stake.

Steeling herself against the pain she knew was about to come, Nikki reached up with her right hand and grasped the seam. She shut her eyes tight, tears streaming under the balaclava as her lower back screamed for her to let go again.

"Don't move."

Nikki grit her teeth and grumbled, "Oh, shut up will you? I'm trying to concentrate here."

161

Whether the cop heard her or not, he yelled again, "Stay still. Don't try anything–"

Propelling herself sideways across the curved corner of the building, Nikki went hand over hand as she fast as she could toward the balcony. She was a foot away–

A gunshot.

A bullet struck the building near her head, causing an explosion of glass and metal. Nikki felt the pain of tiny, sharp fragments striking the mask and the skin around the edge of her eye. Her right hand lost its grip. She held on with her left again, refusing to drop to the ground. With a cry of rage, She lifted her right hand to the seam, pulled hard with both hands and vaulted upward. Grabbing the upper railing, Nikki struggled to get a foot up.

Another gunshot.

There was a sound of a ricochet off the metal railing.

Getting the foot over the railing, Nikki lifted her body up and over, landing hard on her back. Her breath shot from her lungs in a squeak. She heard the static of a police radio below as she struggled to her feet. Running close to the building, Nikki reached the patio door, took several seconds to get it open and then ran into the condo unit. An alarm sounded and she promptly took a tumble over a low object in the dark. She cursed herself, the furniture, the pain in her back, the stinging around her eye. But she struggled to her feet amid the noise and moved on, looking for a way out of this nightmare.

The sound of voices came from behind a door to the right.

It sounded like a man and woman and the words 'get the gun' or something like that sent a chill of fear through her. Getting shot by the police *and* the homeowner wasn't a great outcome. She moved away from the area of the door that she assumed was a bedroom and tried to figure out where the front door was. Moving down a long hallway, she emerged into a large open space that appeared to be a living area and entertaining space all rolled into one. A large piano sat against the glass wall on the far side. The front door was off to the left. Her best bet was to get back outside on a balcony and see if she could climb down. Without getting shot.

A man's voice sounded from the other end of the hallway. "Whoever you are, I'm armed."

The voice sounded strained, filled with fear. Nikki doubted he would confront her but she couldn't take the chance. She moved on through the darkness, passing a land-line telephone—an idea came to her. Picking up the phone, she dialed 911.

"911. What is your emergency?"

Nikki talked low, just enough to be heard over the alarm system, and she gave out the address. "I heard shots and a woman in black just came into our place from the balcony. I'm on the third floor and I'm armed."

"Ma'am, please don't confront–"

"She ran out the front door. I'm sure she's headed downstairs to the main lobby–" She cut herself off, hanging up. That 'I'm armed' comment should keep the cops moving slow and cautious as they eventually climbed the stairs, looking for her.

Doing her best to sprint across to the front door, Nikki pulled it open. She left it that way as she took off in the opposite direction, hoping she wouldn't run into the armed homeowner. Moving along the glass wall, Nikki found another door and moved out onto the balcony. Stepping cautiously to the far edge, she peered over to the ground below. There were two dark forms and the beams of flashlights below. She could see flashing police lights on the street. Her breathing was raspy, and the pain was sharp and intense in her lower back as she waited. The sounds of police static carried across the night air and all the lights began heading towards the front of the building. Nikki didn't wait. She couldn't wait. Her strength was beginning to run out. She was running on pure adrenaline now. Climbing over—and nearly slipping off—Nikki took a deep breath—steeled herself from the pain that was about to come—dropped and caught the lower railing. She did the same thing to the next, and the next, finally dropping to the ground below. Laying on the grass for a brief moment, fighting back the intense pain her entire body now felt, Nikki then rose to her feet and began a limping run through the trees to the street beyond. She couldn't afford to just slink away. It wouldn't take long before they realized she wasn't coming out the front. Crossing the street, she did her best to stay in whatever shadows she could find as she moved on shaky legs—she spotted her motorcycle half a block ahead. Reaching it. her hands were shaking now as she straddled the white Suzuki. Getting it started, Nikki pulled the balaclava off her head and stuffed it in her pocket. The pain from the skin around her right eye was sharp and her eyes blurred with tears. Pulling away from the curb, Nikki did a U-turn in the street and roared away. Running two red lights at first, she slowed to the speed limit and did her best to look normal. There was a warm dampness on her right butt cheek and the back of her thigh. She wondered how long it would take for her to bleed to death.

Chapter 36

THE RITZ-CARLTON HOTEL
Washington, DC

THE ELEVATOR WASN'T moving fast enough. Merlin was anxious to see Nikki. On the way back from Brooklyn, he had received confirmation that she had been able to plant bugs on a computer and laptop belonging to Senator Shermon Best. The intelligence team hadn't talked to her or received word from her since then. He found that strange, positive she would have used the opportunity—just making sure she had done it right of course—to at least call and flirt with the intelligence officer she had taken a liking to. The software 'had phoned home' the moment she planted it, so that was great news. But now he wondered where she was. And what she was doing. She wasn't answering her cell phone or her room phone. Her motorcycle was parked downstairs next to the Porsche. Maybe she was out having a late breakfast?

The elevator doors finally rumbled open and Merlin hustled down the hallway. The only sound was a vacuum cleaner operating in the distance. He could smell cleaning products in the air, which told him the cleaning staff had been cleaning this area not long ago.

As he approached their two rooms, he noticed a 'do not disturb' sign on Nikki's door handle. She was sleeping in? That didn't make sense. Unless she had been out all night planning another high-rise job? Merlin rapped his knuckles against her door. He listened. There was no sound from inside. He rapped again. Ear against the door, he closed his eyes and tried to shut out the vacuum cleaner in the distance. Silence from inside her room.

Pulling his cell phone, he tried calling hers again. Nothing. She was using a burner phone and kept it off most of the time out of habit. He slipped the cell phone back into his pocket and pulled out the extra key card for her room. The lock turned green and he opened the door a crack, "Nikki? It's me."

No answer.

"I'm coming in." He slowly opened the door and stepped inside, "Nikki?" He closed the door behind him, "Nikki? It's Merlin. Are you home? Where are you?"

Nothing looked out of place. There was no indication she was even here.

Merlin moved through the suite slowly, not wanting to startle her, or maybe come across her in a state of undress. "Nikki? It's Merlin. Are you here?"

The bed was made. Since there was a 'do not disturb' sign in the door, he had to assume it was made up yesterday. Where was she?

The bathroom door was partly open. The light was on.

Merlin couldn't hear a shower running. Or a bathtub filling. He approached carefully, listening, rapping his knuckles against the door, "Nikki? Nikki? It's Merlin. Are you decent? I'm coming in."

The door swung in slowly from his push. "Nikki–?"

A foot in a black climbing shoe was propped up on the edge of the tub. The door to the medicine cabinet was wide open. Items were scattered across the bathroom vanity and in the sink.

Merlin's heart jumped into his throat. A bloody towel lay on the floor next to the tub. He rushed forward.

Nikki lay face up in the tub. She was dressed in her black climbing outfit. Her eyes were closed, her skin was ashen.

His knees on the edge of the tub, Merlin touched her face. She felt cold. He checked for a pulse–

Nikki's eyes shot open. Her mouth opened in a gasp of fear. She fought feebly against his arms.

"It's me. It's me, Nikki. It's Merlin. It's okay."

Her eyes didn't fully register on his but she stopped fighting. There was a croak in her throat as she tried to say something.

"What happened? What's wrong?"

Nikki's eyes closed slowly. Her body slowly began to settle in the tub again.

Merlin reached out, placing his arms under her arms and around her back, lifting her body. "Come on, let's get you out of there–"

A cry of pain shot from her ashen lips, agony registered on her face.

Letting her body settled back in the tub, Merlin leaned closer, "What's wrong? Nikki? What's wrong?" He gently slid his hand along her arms, looking over the front of her body, looking for a broken bone or something that was causing her all this pain. Her body was angled slightly and he did his best to check her upper back, then lower–

There was a soft lump of something in the small of her back, under her black pullover. Gently pulling the garment up, he felt a criss-cross array of adhesive tape, and adhesive bandages holding a soft lump in place. Placing one foot into the tub, Merlin got close enough to see she had stuffed a couple of large, square sterile gauze pads and—was that the end of a washcloth stocking out from underneath the tape and plasters as well? He glanced to the medicine cabinet and the array of items on the vanity. There was a small pair of scissors, several used antiseptic wipes, an empty box of adhesive bandages, what was left of a roll of adhesive tape, and other scattered contents from the first aid kit he saw in the trunk of the Porsche. She had used the contents to dress a wound.

Merlin touched her face, "Nikki? What happened?"

No answer.

"Nikki?" He tapped her face gently. "Nikki, what happened to your back?"

Her eyelids fluttered. Her lips moved just slightly. "Shot."

"Shot? Who shot you? Nikki?"

It took a moment. "Police. They caught me...but... I did the job. No worries... I did the job."

"Why didn't you go to a hospital emergency room?" He put his hands on her arms again. "We have to get you to the hospital–"

Nikki fought back weakly, "No. No hospital. Can't. They report gunshot...wounds... We can't afford that."

"We can't worry about that now. We have to get you some help."

She shook her head. "No. Name and picture will be in the paper. The Russian will know."

That struck Merlin hard. She was right. Merlin ran a hand through his hair. No, he could play with his own life, but not hers. He touched her arm again. "Let's get you out of there and then figure it out–"

"No. That's why I'm in here...so I don't get blood on the bed...then...then someone will know."

"You let me worry about that–"

"No, please. I shoved a washcloth into the wound to stop the bleeding. It's working. Don't make what I did go for nothing. I tried. I really tried."

"You did more than try. You succeeded. The intelligence people have access to the two computers you got to."

Through the agony, Nikki looked relieved, "Good. I tried."

Merlin made a decision. "Look, I'll meet you halfway. I won't take you to a doctor but I will get you some help."

"Don't bring someone here—"

"I won't. Can you walk? If you can walk, I'll take you somewhere to get you help. Just trust me. I won't compromise what you did. I'll come back and clean up this bathroom later. But right now we need to get you some help. I can't climb those buildings without you, right?"

Nikki nodded, "That's true. Okay. I'll...try...." Her agony was apparent and vocal as she struggled to get up. Her feet and hands slipped on the tub's smooth surface.

Merlin found it difficult to help her without putting a hand somewhere for support that put some tension on her lower back.

An agonized grin on her lips, Nikki could sense his difficulty and spoke through clenched teeth. "You might have to hold onto my boobs and drag me backwards."

"You're not giving me much to work with there."

A guttural, agonized laugh came from her throat. "If I were Miss Boobsalichious, you could just tie a string to my leg and float me out."

"Yeah, right. Then you'd probably fracture your skull against the ceiling."

A half laugh-half groan.

Merlin slipped one hand around her upper back, and then one under her knees, scooping her from the tub. He carried her from the bathroom and across the suite towards the door.

Nikki's teeth were clenched in agony. "You can't carry me downstairs like this. It's not exactly a subtle move, Dragon."

"We don't need to be subtle. Trust me, it will work better this way." He struggled to get the handle down and the door open, Sticking his foot in the door when he finally cracked it open, Merlin checked the hallway. The sound of young laughter echoed off the walls. There was a couple with three kids at the far end but they were going in the other direction. Slipping out and letting the door close behind him, Merlin headed down the hallway to the elevator. "Press the down button."

"But–"

"Just do it. Then just rest your head against me. If anybody asks, you hurt your back and I'm taking you to a chiropractor. Understand?"

Nikki nodded and pressed the button. The doors rumbled open.

There was no one in the elevator and Merlin moved inside. Jabbing the lobby button with an elbow, he stayed just to the right of the door, ready to get out as soon as he reached the bottom floor. The long, slow ride down was interrupted only one floor from their destination. The elevator stopped and let an elderly couple on.

The elderly woman looked both surprised and concerned. "Oh dear, is she all right?"

"She hurt her back," Merlin told her, "the front desk gave me an address for a chiropractor and I'm taking her there now." He looked to the elderly gentleman. "If you could press the button for the lobby...?"

The elderly man tore his eyes from the dark figure in Merlin's arms and pressed the button. "Yes, sir, I'm sorry."

As the doors closed, the elderly women stretched her neck to look at Nikki's face. "The poor dear."

Nikki only moved her eyes slightly as she looked at the older woman. Her voice was rough with agony. "We're newlyweds. I told him to take it easy in the sack. But you know men."

The elderly woman expressed surprised and then smiled. A slight giggle followed as she looked at her husband.

He was embarrassed and looked away.

A moment later, the elevator came to rest and the doors opened.

Merlin looked to the elderly woman, deciding to use her as more cover. "Would you mind holding the elevator doors open? And then maybe you could help me with the front doors to get her outside? I can take it from there."

The elderly couple went into action, holding the door open and then walking with them across the lobby to the front doors. A few people showed interest, with the elderly lady mentioning that the young woman had hurt her back and they were taking her to the chiropractor. Holding the doors open, the couple waved and called out 'good luck'.

Finally getting Nikki into the Porsche, Merlin strapped her into the passenger seat and was on the road in a few moments. He pulled his cell phone, hit speed dial and speaker before sitting it on the console. It rang twice. He heard the connection made.

"Mr. Dragon?" It was Saab.

"Yeah. I found Nikki. She's with me now in the passenger seat."

"That's good.

"It is except she was shot."

"Shot? Any idea who did it?"

"I'll explain everything when I get there. It looks like she's passed out. She patched herself up without going to emergency and I think she's lost a lot of blood. I need you to get ready to fly back home. Call ahead and get a team of military paramedics ready to help her. I'd try and take her to an emergency room, but if she wakes up, she'll fight me tooth and nail. She's already in bad shape and needs all her strength."

"Understood. I'll get everything started. We can contact the tower now to get clearance and take off as soon as she's aboard." The call ended.

It was difficult but Merlin stayed at the speed limit. He couldn't afford to get pulled over with a gunshot victim and having to explain everything. As he drove, he wondered how he was going to continue on with his assignment without her help.

Chapter 37

MERLIN KEPT HIS WORD to Nikki, cleaning up the bathroom in her room at The Ritz-Carlton Hotel. It was like creating good karma, to offset the bad karma that had collided with her trying to help—if there was such a thing as karma in the first place. Right now it didn't matter. It made him feel he was helping her in some way. Stuffing the bloodied towel and all the items from the first-aid kit and bandage box into a garbage bag he had gotten from a member of the cleaning staff, Merlin cleaned up streaks of blood, removed the 'do not disturb' sign from her door, and deposited the garbage bag into a garbage bin behind the hotel.

All through his task, Merlin's mind whirled through all kinds of pros and cons on what he could and couldn't do to push forward with his assignment. And climbing buildings the way Nikki the Cat could, was definitely something he couldn't do. Which meant he had to find another way to access the personal computers—desktop or laptop—of the remaining Senators. And he still had to get close to their cell phones in order to get the internal IMSI-catcher thing going. Without Nikki helping, the mountain seemed higher than before. And with classified military and intelligence information already being passed along to the Russians by someone in the CIA, the stakes were mounting as well. It probably wouldn't be long before they detected the same thing coming from somewhere inside Canada and England.

As he headed for the Porsche, an idea floated in his mind. One he had basically rejected in his discussions with Nikki. He pressed the key fob and the trunk sprang open. The briefcase he had taken from Dante Taccetta was still sitting there. He picked it up, closed the trunk, got in the front seat of the Porsche and set the briefcase on the passenger seat. He sat for a moment, considering and reconsidering the idea. He didn't have much choice. Taking out his cell phone, he did a search, running through company websites until he found the address he needed, programmed it into the car's navigation system and headed off.

It took forty-five minutes before Merlin was inside the reception area of the two-thousand square foot office of Guaranteed Security LLC. It was an hour before closing time. The phones rang incessantly and the smell of stale coffee bounced off the fake plants. A tall man in his early forties, with round glasses, sandy hair, and a ruddy complexion was headed his way. Merlin hoped it was Nikki's cousin, Niles. She had mentioned her mother was Finnish and a search had only turned up one name that sounded Finnish, and someone with the same first name, Niles Tikkanen.

The man gave Merlin an open smile, and extended his hand, "I'm Niles Tikkanen, how can I help you today?"

Merlin shook his hand, "Thank you for seeing me." Then he gestured with a thumb over his shoulder, "Could I talk to you outside? In private?"

His eyebrows pushing together, Tikkanen glanced to the glass door behind Merlin, puzzled. "What's this all about?"

Extending his hand, Merlin held the gold and onyx ring in his fingers. "Just a moment of your time. Please." He assumed the cousin would recognize the ring. If not....

Hesitating for a moment, the man took the ring from Merlin's fingers. "Where...where did you get this?"

Merlin simply turned, stepped outside, and waited.

It took a moment, but Tikkanen stepped out behind him. He didn't say anything, holding the ring, looking around the parking lot like he wasn't sure where this was going.

"There's no need to be nervous. I'm aware of you letting Nikki stay in some of the condominiums–"

Tikkanen's jaw clenched. "If this is a shakedown–"

"It's not." He paused for a moment. "Nikki is fine... but she was helping me with something and...she was shot yesterday."

His eyes narrowing, Tikkanen said, "That was Nikki?"

"What do you mean?"

"It was in the newspaper this morning. The cops said they shot someone breaking into a Senator's home." A deep scowl creased Tikkanen's face. "I should have figured it out. It was a high-rise building. If you've gotten her into some kind of scheme–"

"Dante Taccetta—the mobster who wanted Nikki the Cat dead? And the reason you were helping Nikki? He was shot to death last night."

"He was?"

"Yeah. Let's just say I was helping Nikki...and she was helping me. You can check that out in the newspapers as well."

Tikkanen looked at the ring, rolling it around in his fingers. "That's good. But...I'm not sure what that has to do with me." He looked into Merlin's eyes, waiting for the answer.

Merlin had parked the Porsche a few feet away in front of the building. Pulling the keys from his jacket's pocket, he extended a hand and pressed the key fob. The trunk popped open. Merlin walked to the back of the car and waited for Tikkanen to join him.

It took a few moments before the security company owner did that.

Bending over, Merlin opened the briefcase, stepping back to leave the lid up and the money inside very apparent.

Tikkanen glanced at the banded bills inside. "I don't understand."

"That's the two million dollars Dante Taccetta was offering for Nikki the Cat. He doesn't need it anymore. Nikki has what she needs to restart her life. That's yours for helping her. And for helping me to finish–"

Waving his hands and stepping back, Tikkanen said, "No way. I'm not getting involved in anything. I helped Nikki and that's it. If you say she's set, she's set. I don't need to get involved in anything shady that screws up my life."

Merlin felt the disappointment course through his veins. It'd been a gamble and he had lost. "I understand. I won't bother you again."

"No, you won't." Tikkanen tossed the ring to Merlin. "Say hello to Nikki for me. And goodbye."

Catching the ring against his chest, the keys jangled, and Merlin watched his chance to infiltrate the homes of those Senators disappear back inside the building. Things just kept getting worse.

Chapter 38

IT WAS BRIGHT AND EARLY as Merlin drove the Porsche slowly through rush-hour traffic. It looked like a great start to a new day for the others around him, but Merlin couldn't feel any of that. Even the rich scent of a new coffee in the cup holder beside him didn't make him feel any better. For all intents and purposes, he was in limbo. It wasn't just going forward or backwards, it seemed every direction was a problem. In order to root out whoever was leaking intelligence information from the US government, he had to go up against the intelligence apparatus that was designed to protect anyone—like these Senators—behind the shield of that government. It was as if the Russian was using American intelligence and law enforcement against Merlin's efforts to take down his network. And he doubted it would be any different if the leaks started coming from Canada or Great Britain—and he had no doubt they would—he would always be fighting against his own side in the battle.

Merlin made a decision, taking a right at the next corner. He decided to head for the nexus of the problem, Blackstone Strategies. He had lost contact with Dimitri Starkov and there was no sense going to his home here. If he just showed up without a reason, it could raise suspicions. Merlin's 'political ambitions' were being routed through Blackstone Strategies, just like anyone else who was eventually ensnared—willingly or unwillingly—in the Russian's plans. It made more sense to try and establish a plan through Roland

Henderson, and maybe bug his phones and computers. That thought made his mind turn to Nikki. She had started the task of tracking the goings-on of the Russian's network and he wondered how she was doing. Saab told him she would call if something bad happened and he had to presume things were going well. He reached out and tapped his cell phone to make a call, refraining from calling the jet.

"Blackstone Strategies. How may I direct your call?"

"Roland Henderson, please. You can tell him it's Rhett Summers."

"One moment."

Henderson's voice came on the line. He sounded pissed. "Mr. Summers. What happened? I lost track of you. And Quinn Olivares has been trying to reach you. He said you asked for a meeting with Senator MacDuff and he never heard from you again."

Merlin had anticipated something like this. "I'm sorry, Roland. Sonja rented a stupid motorbike to do some sightseeing and she had an accident."

"Oh dear. Is she all right?"

"Yes and no. She broke her hip and is in a lot of pain."

"I'm sorry to hear that. Mrs. Henderson and I will have to pay her a visit."

"That's nice of you but she isn't in a local hospital. The doctor was afraid of complications and he wanted her to stay in the hospital for a couple of weeks. She chose instead to fly to Boston to stay with a cousin who is a nurse. I sent her off first class last night."

"I see. Well, we can visit with her when she gets back. I was concerned when I saw her on that motorcycle on the surveillance cameras that first day you came here."

That comment sent a chill through Merlin. Security cameras weren't unusual, but how much did they see? 'Sonya Tapper' had shown up and surprised him that first day here. Did Henderson see that surprise? And was Henderson watching in real-time? Or did he go back through the footage later–?

"Rhett? Are you still there?"

"Uh...yeah. Sorry, I was just navigating around a slow car." He noted Henderson had changed to using his first name instead of the last. That was good. The anger—or suspicion—had passed. "Anyway, I was just heading your way. I'm about half-an-hour away and I was hoping you could give me some more ideas on what I can do to advance my political career."

"I'm sorry, Rhett. You caught me at a bad time. I was just heading out to the airport. I'm flying to California for a couple of days to meet with a client out there."

Merlin felt the disappointment. "I understand. No problem. I can give you a call again in a few days." He considered asking Henderson if his wife was going with him—maybe it was a chance to get into their home—but that would be too suspicious. Maybe if he trailed Henderson to the airport –?

"I tell you what." Henderson paused for a moment as if he was considering his options.

Merlin waited, wondering.

"If you're already headed this way...why don't you come in and meet with Oksana?

"Oksana?" Merlin knew exactly who that was. The suspected kurátor. But Merlin wanted to draw as much information as he could from Henderson. "That name sounds familiar for some reason."

"It does? I don't remember introducing her to you. Oksana Pavlovich is our Chief Technology Officer."

"Pavlovich? Ah...okay. I think she introduced herself at that fundraiser when I first met you and your wife. She is...how do I say it...she's a well-endowed woman...?"

Henderson laughed, "That's our Oksana. And yes, she's not exactly the shy, retiring type. Oksana isn't just responsible for keeping our company up to date as far as technology trends go. She's also our expert on social media platforms. Oksana can help you to get started, or she can refine whatever social media platforms you're already into. These platforms are essential to shaping your image with the public. And to put yourself in direct communication with them, to share your ideas with them."

All that made sense to Merlin. As the CTO of Blackstone Strategies, she was easily at the center of the company's computer systems, which included all messages, emails, or phone calls coming and going. A perfect spot to coordinate a network behind the scenes. "That's probably a really good idea, Roland. I really don't have any idea about these social platforms."

"Well, she can help you with all that. I'll let her know you're coming. Say hello to Sonya the next time you talk to her and tell her we're thinking about her."

"I will. Thank you, Roland." The call ended. This was good. He'd be able to get inside Blackstone Strategies. Now all he had to do was find a way to bug a few phones and computers.

Chapter 39

ONCE INSIDE Blackstone Strategies, Merlin was led by a young lady to the hushed thirtieth floor. But this time he was taken up by an elevator that wasn't private and he wasn't sure where he was exactly when they got out. The air had the scent of rosemary, like before, and the walls were lined with expensive art, but he didn't recognize any of them. He had no way of knowing if he was anywhere near Henderson's office—no, take that back. As the young woman stopped in front of a door to an office and knocked once, he saw several paintings up ahead that looked familiar. If he was right, Henderson's office was just a few doors down. Maybe–

"Sir?"

The young woman had pushed the door open and was gesturing for him to go in.

Merlin gave her a quick smile of thanks and stepped into the office that had a pine scent. A large window looked out over the city, One wall consisted of a warm, wooden bookcase filled with books from end to end.

The gorgeous woman behind the desk didn't stand up. She simply sat there, an amused look in her blue eyes as he took in his surroundings. "I am Oksana Pavlovich. I do hope you remember your name this time?"

The husky voice was teasing, but Merlin sensed a steel strength in the tone. He returned the smile, "Of course. Rhett Summers.

Roland suggested I come and talk with you about my social media platforms."

"Of course. Why wouldn't I know why you're here?" She raised her chest slightly.

Merlin felt his eyes drop to her chest—her red blouse barely contained the contents—and he pulled them back up, feeling himself slipping into some kind of disadvantage. She was flirting with him already, very much aware of her physical effect on men—and on him. He had to remember she was the possible kurátor and dangerous—but he also remembered the words honey pot and honey trap, another kind of danger. One he wasn't sure he was equipped to handle.

Pavlovich extended a hand, "Why don't you sit down...Rhett. And we can talk."

Merlin took a seat. The oak desk had a desktop computer on the left, as well as a square, brushed and polished brass object he assumed was a clock. A laptop sat on a credenza behind Pavlovich. He also saw a cell phone. He had his chance. Slipping a hand into his pocket, he pulled out one of the cell phones. "Sorry, bad habit. It vibrates and I look at my cell phone. A Pavlov's dog thing, I guess." He realized the comment as possible Freudian—and maybe telling. "Sorry."

A smile flickered on Pavlovich's lips. "No problems...Rhett. You will find I don't require a vibrator."

His mouth opened but no words came out. The feelings of being at a disadvantage deepened. He pressed the left icon. Then the icon on the right.

Pavlovich's eyes flicked to the clock. "Can we proceed with the reason for your being here? Or do you need to answer a message?"

'Sorry."

"You have already expressed that sentiment."

Merlin also sensed a change in her demeanor. Was she bored with him already? He had to stay close to get at the computers.

Tapping the center icon, Merlin slipped the phone back in his pocket. He shifted in his seat. "Roland said you could help me with my social media platform? Not that I have one, which means I need all the help I can get."

"We will need to get to know each other much better before I can know how to present you in the best way to the public."

"Don't you mean you have to know *me* much better–"

A devious smile creased Pavlovich's full lips. "Yes, of course. What is it you are suggesting we should do in order to fill that need?"

The slippery slope was getting slipperier—and tilting against him. Merlin also sensed an opening. "Sorry, but is there a washroom I could use? I drank a coffee on the way over here and..."

Pursing her lips for a moment, Pavlovich said, "Yes, of course. Four doors to the right outside my door. Please hurry back."

"Of course. Thanks." Merlin headed for the door, closing it softly behind him as he looked to the right. He could see two doors with the appropriate male and female signs. Heading in that direction first, listened for the sounds of anybody nearby. Cracking open the door for the men's washroom, he checked to make sure it was unoccupied and that he didn't need a key. Something about the way Pavlovich pursed her lips made him cautious. Feeling better about the whole thing, Merlin moved swiftly back down the hallway, treading as lightly as possible. Reaching Henderson's door, he turned the knob as gently as possible and cracked the door open. The office was empty. Slipping inside while he pulled out one of the thumb drives from a pocket, Merlin headed for the desktop computer. He fired it up quickly, inserted the thumb drive and watched it flash, going to work. As it planted the software, Merlin checked the drawers. All of them were locked. There was no other evidence of a laptop or cell phone in the room. Pocketing the flash drive, Merlin shut the desktop computer down and headed for the door again. Cracking it open, he checked the hallway. Still empty. He moved back down the hallway, passing Pavlovich's door and heading for the washroom again. He went inside, turned the lights on, moved to the sink, pumped some soap from the dispenser, and washed his hands. Drying them lightly with a paper towel, Merlin tossed it in the wastebasket and headed back to Pavlovich's office.

Oksana Pavlovich was standing at the window, looking out over the city. She turned smoothly on her red high heel shoes to face him. "Are you ready to go?"

"Go?" Merlin realized she had a purse, the strap slung over her shoulder. Her black slacks highlighted a shapely body on the lower half and gave her a panther-like look as she walked towards him.

"Yes." The blue eyes under the blonde fringe appraised the length of Merlin's body. "You are taking me for a brunch."

"I am?" Merlin could see her take in the dampness of his hands and the smell of the cedar-like scent of the washroom soap on his hands.

Placing a well-manicured hand on his left elbow, Pavlovich turned Merlin, slipped her arm through his, and walking him to the door. "I know just the place. Very nice food. And very intimate atmosphere. Unless you prefer a boring business lunch...Rhett?"

Merlin could feel her press her right breast against his body, not that it took much to do that. "Uh...no that's sounds fine." How much trouble was he in now?

Chapter 40

MERLIN DROVE the Porsche to the southeast. The more he told himself not to think about her bust, the more he noticed it move and jiggle as the luxury car bounced or turned. Or both. He was conscious of a heady vanilla musk cologne drifting across from her. For her part, Pavlovich kept a lingering smile on her face. She discussed the need for a number of different social media platforms and how they worked. But all her words were background noise to his thoughts about—he realized she had said something. "Pardon?"

Oksana Pavlovich's blue eyes were looking directly at him. "I said...you could turn into the next parking lot on the left."

Looking ahead and to the left, Merlin realized they were nearing the far entrance of a parking lot that fronted the Shoreline Restaurant—a building that looked like an old galleon overlooking the Anacostia River. And for the first time, he realized he had been so distracted that he didn't notice they had driven into a very sketchy area of the city. The surrounding buildings looked more like the places where illicit drug deals would go down. He slowed but looked at her. "Are you serious? Why here?"

She smiled, "Because they have the best seafood here. Just trust me...Rhett."

Taking a tight left, Merlin drove the Porsche into the parking lot and across to the front of the restaurant. Coming to a stop, he looked around. "I don't see a lot of cars. Or people—"

"It's brunch time remember? Roland and I come here quite often." She got it out without another word and closed the door behind her.

Merlin watched her walk—actually saunter in a slinky manner—to the door of the restaurant. She glanced back over her shoulder and beckoned him with her finger. Getting out, Merlin pressed the key fob as he looked around. The Porsche locked, beeping twice, making him feel like he would be better off locked on the inside of the vehicle than the outside. He watched Pavlovich shake her head, a slight smile on her face, and disappear inside the restaurant. The sunlight flickered off the glass as the door closed slowly behind her. Taking a deep breath, and not sure if he felt foolish about looking concerned or actually being concerned, he followed her inside.

Pavlovich stood twenty feet away, next to a small podium, right hand digging into her purse, waiting for a server to appear. She didn't bother looking back at him.

As Merlin approached her, she whirled on her high heels, lifting a hand. He wondered what she was holding—a spray hit him in the face. A split-second later, he was bent over, hands clutching at his burning eyes. Pepper spray–?

Footsteps pounded from different directions.

The scent of the vanilla musk cologne was pushed aside by stale coffee and herring.

A rough bag was slammed down over his head.

Light disappeared.

Merlin felt his hands jerked away from his eyes, pulled roughly behind his back and secured. Merlin rolled to his side, pulling his knees up and trying to get his hands free so he could wipe away the agony he felt in his eyes. The stab of a needle in his neck sent a chill through his body. What was going on? He heard voices—Russian accents—as consciousness began to fade.

"Who is he?"

"I don't know. But I detected a signal when he used his cell phone in my office."

Hands searched Merlin's body as he lay there, finding his phones, money, and wallet. *I detected a signal?* He realized the brass clock she had on her desk—she had glanced at it when he pressed the icons on the phone—was some kind of detection device. She was obviously well trained in technology. He admonished himself with another thought—Pavlovich is obviously better at her job than I am. The next time he heard Pavlovich's voice, his mind was fading to black, but he was sure she had switched to Russian.

"Vy dolzhny doprosit' yego. Uznayte, kto yest'. I na kogo on rabotayet."

"Da."

Chapter 41

MERLIN FELT his body floating. It was moving in undulations on the air. Or was it? He could smell salt... and fish. That made sense, he was in a seafood restaurant. But why was it moving? The had injected him with a drug... Was he having hallucinations? None of this made any sense—until he realized he could open his eyes. Wherever he was, it wasn't the restaurant. At least...he didn't think so. He was in a large, dimly lit space, without furniture—actually, there was one piece of furniture. It was a chair in the middle of the room. And he was tied to it. A rope ran around his chest, his hands were zip-tied behind the back of the chair—at first, he thought it was a rope but he could feel the long nylon end brushing his forearm—and each leg was tied to a chair leg. He wore the shirt, blue jeans, dress boots, and bracelet, but no leather jacket. He could tell his conceal holster was gone. As was his weapon, special cell phone, and every item he had on him. He still had his 'escape belt'—which was good but of little use right now.

There was a creaking sound.

Merlin closed his eyes and listened.

Another creaking sound. It was rhythmic, going along with the motion underfoot.

His eyes snapped open and Merlin looked straight ahead at the door. It wasn't a door like he had back home in his apartment. Dead ahead was a bulkhead door. A watertight door on a ship. The restaurant had been close to the Anacostia River. They had taken him from the restaurant to a boat on the river? From the inflections in her voice, he could tell Oksana Pavlovich had issued some instructions in Russian. And a man's voice had answered *da*—'yes' in Russian.

Sounds of a hollow, metallic banging echoed around the room.

Merlin listened carefully. The banging disappeared. The hollow metallic sound was there again—the rhythm was different and briefer. More than likely somebody was working on something on the ship. He returned to his thoughts. The fact he wasn't dead—yet—meant they wanted something from him. Probably information. Which meant an interrogation and maybe torture. Not looking forward to *any* kind of interrogation, he began to examine the space he was in, looking for a way out of his predicament. Turning his head as far as he could in either direction, Merlin looked to see if there was another door. Or cameras keeping an eye on him. Or other furniture. He couldn't see anything, not even another chair.

Next, he turned his attention to his bonds, looking for a way to get free. He had the American Liberty nickel in his back right pocket. But even if he was able to get it out using his fingers, the way his hands were bound by the zip-tie, he couldn't see any way to use the internal blade to cut away the bindings. He experimented with twisting his hands, visualizing if he could get the tiny blade turned enough to–

The bulkhead door clanged with a hollow metallic ring that echoed off the walls. The long handle moved downward and the door swung out. Three men stepped into the room, one behind the other. The first man wore a light camouflage jacket with a hood, black pants, and black boots. The other two wore a black pullover, black pants, and black boots. The second man carried a camouflage duffel bag, the third man carried a chair like the one he was sitting in. He stepped past the other two and placed the chair in front of Merlin. The second man set the duffel bag down beside the chair.

The first man sat down, looking into Merlin's eyes, "I am Sergei. Do you want to tell us who you are?"

Staying silent, Merlin noted the Russian accent. And for some reason, the man looked familiar, but he couldn't place him.

Sergei reached down into the duffel bag, rooted around, and pulled out several items. Sergei then opened a passport, "It says here...you are Mr. Rhett Summers. This driver's license says you are from New York. And you have an American Express credit card."

Merlin watched the Russian closely as he listened. The man didn't have a military bearing, but he did have the presence of someone used to getting what he wanted. Even if he had to beat it out of you. He glanced at the other two men. They stood there passively but gave off the same impression of willing violence. He was definitely in deep trouble.

Sergei looked up from the items in his hand, "You do have some indications of attending an American university...and of employment with Goldman Sachs. And we did find a newspaper article about you, *saying* these things were true. But beyond that...you do not appear to exist. Or should I say Mr. Rhett Summers does not exist?" He dropped the items back into the duffel bag, then paused for effect. "So...who - are - you?"

The second man shifted on his feet, his eyes boring into Merlin, sending the message he was ready to pounce at the slightest sign from Sergei to beat the answers out of him.

Merlin ignored the not-so-subtle message and gave Sergei a slight shrug, "Maybe I'm just shy? I don't like all that social media stuff, and the intrusiveness of the Internet in my daily life–"

"A very nice cover story," Sergei said. He reached into the duffel bag and pulled out some other items, "But a Harvard man...or a Goldman Sachs man...does not carry a cell phone...actually, several cell phones like this one... that wipe themselves clean as soon as someone touches it."

"Maybe I just like my privacy."

"Or these thumb drives that do the same thing when you try to access them."

"What can I tell you? Goldman Sachs taught me well. There is such a thing as corporate spying as well. The need to protect proprietary information is also important in the business world–"

Sergei waved his hand in the air, "Yes, yes, all a very nice cover story." He dropped the items back into the duffel bag, then looked into Merlin's eyes. "Tell me where the woman is."

"Woman?"

Turning his head, Sergei said, "Kakoye imya?"

The third man said, "Sonja Tapper."

"Ah, yes. Miss Sonja Tapper." Sergei gestured to the duffel bag, "You had key cards at the Ritz-Carlton Hotel for both you and for this woman. And we found another similar cell phone as well as a number of the thumb drives in her room. This Sonya Tapper is another person who does not exist. In fact, this woman exists far less than you do, Mr. Rhett Summers." He leaned forward, his voice lowering, "You see? We have everything. And we will find this woman. And she will suffer if you do not tell me what I want to know. So...I ask again...who are you?"

Merlin stayed silent this time.

"All right. Tell me what you were attempting to do at Blackstone Strategies? What was your goal?"

"I was told by Roland Henderson to see Oksana Pavlovich. She was going to help me with my social media platforms–"

"And again, a very nice cover story. But we both know you were there for another purpose. What we want to know is...what is that purpose? We also want to know who you are working for?"

Merlin shook his head, "I'm not working for anybody. I'm trying to get ahead in politics and–"

Sergei turned his head and spoke decisively, "Prinesi v portfel."

The third man quickly moved back to the bulkhead door and opened it a crack. Reaching through to the other side, he picked up something before marching back and placing a briefcase on Sergei's lap.

Merlin recognized the briefcase. It was the one from the New York mobster.

Sergei kept his eyes on Merlin as he opened the briefcase and then turned it to Merlin. "And what of this?"

Looking down at the stack of cash in the briefcase, Merlin said nothing.

"Very, very few people carry around two million dollars in the trunk of their rental vehicle." Sergei leaned his head forward slightly, "Is this a payment for what you were supposed to do at Blackstone Strategies?"

Silence.

"Or is it merely a down payment? The fact you proceeded with your activities tells me there must be more money in it for you. Or you would have run." Sergei used his thumb to flip through a banded stack of bills, "We can pay you much, much more than this. All you need to do is work with us."

That tactic took Merlin by surprise. And then he reminded himself he was here in part because he was investigating the use of dark money to influence and corrupt individuals. It was obviously a method that worked.

Sergei waited for a moment, looking for the possibility of Merlin to turn. "All right then. Who paid you this money? Your accent is Canadian, yes? But I doubt the Canadians would have you spying on an American company. Perhaps you are working with British Intelligence? Are you being paid by the British? Or are you a British intelligence agent with MI6, ready to use this money to bribe someone? Perhaps you betrayed your country and are working for the Chinese? Are you working with the Germans–?"

"That's a lot of people you have me working with, Sergei. The truth is... I'm working a scam. The idea is to get some proprietary business information and sell it to the highest bidder. As for the money...you're right...you never know when you need to bribe someone inside a company to give you access."

"I see." Closing the briefcase, Sergei passed it back to the third man. Then he reached into a jacket pocket and held up Merlin's Beretta, "A man running a scam does not have such a special weapon." He pulled the special cell phone from another pocket, "And this phone that *seems* to have little on it. We will see what we can find but...it all tells me you are very clearly an agent."

Merlin watched the man drop the items into the camouflage duffel bag one by one like he was finished with one tactic and getting ready to move on to another.

Sergei pulled his feet in and stood up. He looked down at Merlin, pausing for effect. "We will leave you for a few moments of reflection. And then will come the answers we want...or the pain you don't want, Mr. Rhett Summers."

Chapter 42

NOT PARTICULARLY looking forward to the pain Sergei was threatening to inflict—and he believed him—Merlin turned his attention back to getting free. The zip-tie binding his wrists was his first problem. It limited his ability to use the American Liberty nickel effectively. He looked around again. Whatever was directly behind him was hidden. Pressing his feet against the metal floor, Merlin jerked his body sideways. The bottom of the chair legs scraped against the floor. They had only moved a quarter of an inch but it was progress. He did that several more times, becoming more adept at the technique each time and had the chair swiveled at least a foot. The problem was the additional view behind him only revealed part of a solid wall. He rested for a minute, thinking. Turning his attention back to the bulkhead door, he decided it was his only chance and he couldn't waste time on anything else–

There was that creaking sound again.

Merlin felt his heart thumping in his chest. It was only the creaking of the ship but he was so hyper right now, every sound was like a hammer blow. He returned his attention to moving the chair. There had to be a better way. He tried pressing forward on his toes, wondering if he could use his weight to tip the chair forward and then creep across the floor. After a moment of experimenting, he realized it could be done. But he also realized if he jerked his weight forward too much, he could crash face-down to the floor and getting up might be impossible. He switched tactics, trying to use his heels, pressing them against the floor and twisting his weight like before. That technique worked better and he got a couple of inches of movement. It wasn't much but it was better than nothing. After five minutes, he got the technique down, actually using the rise and fall of the floor underneath him to get more rotation on the chair. He nearly lost it a couple of times near the end on the downward movement of the floor as his feet and leg muscles began to cramp from the awkward movement, but he was finally able to get his back to the left edge of the bulkhead door. His target wasn't the door handle. It was too high. His target was the hinges and the structural members that had right angle edges. Using his fingers, he found a right angle edge, pressed the plastic zip tie against it and began sawing it up and down as best as he could. It was long, slow and his arm muscles cramped from the awkward angle. But the tie finally snapped.

Slipping his fingers into his back right pocket, Merlin pulled out the American Liberty nickel. Feeling for the heads-up side, he slid a fingernail clockwise along the edge and the small blade of hardened stainless steel rotated out. Shifting his body and arms back and forth under the ropes around his chest, Merlin was able to get his right arm forward enough that when he bent it at the elbow, it brought his hand up and the steel blade held firmly between his fingers rested on one loop of the rope. Not wanting to lose his grip on the coin, he began cutting carefully. It was working. Increasing the pressure bit by bit, he was soon cutting through the individual strands–

As the cut loop fell away, and the bonds around his body loosened, Merlin felt a sharp pain in his chest. He closed his eyes and felt tears running down his cheek. Opening his eyes, he looked down. The steel blade of the coin was partly buried in his flesh. The good part: he hadn't lost the coin. The bad part: it hurt like hell. Gritting his teeth, he pulled the coin free, worked to shuck the rope off, and then cut away the ropes tying his legs to the chair. Standing up, he first concentrated on relaxing his cramped muscles as much as possible. He massaged his arms and legs—and then gave up on that. He didn't have enough time to try and be one hundred percent ready for anything. Sergei could come back at any time.

Still holding the coin with the bloodied blade as his only weapon, Merlin pressed down on the bulkhead door's handle.

The movement of the metal handle and the internal mechanisms boomed and echoed. At least, that's how Merlin heard the sound. The door cracked open, and he held his breath, the tiny blade at the ready.

There was no one rushing to see what he was doing. The only sound was the rhythmic creak of the ship under the movement of the water.

Opening the door and stepping halfway out, Merlin looked up and down the outside passageway that ran left to right. It was empty. There was an open doorway twenty feet to the left, on the other side of the passageway. He could hear low voices speaking Russian and he was sure one of the voices was this Sergei character. Slipping out and closing the bulkhead door behind him, Merlin moved to the right, away from the voices. Fifty feet ahead, he took another right turn down a cross-passageway. It didn't take him long to come to the feeling that he was on a freighter. Which surprised him. What was a freighter doing on a river near Washington DC? It made more sense to him to use an airfreight service to fly cargo to the ocean than have ships come up the river. Then again, what did he know about it?

He came to another cross passageway and he leaned against the right wall, peering around the corner. Still empty. The only thing he could hear was the creaking of the ship–

A hollow shout sounded somewhere behind him.

Merlin turned, back against the wall and listened carefully. It sounded like the alarm had gone up that he was missing. He turned back, looking up and down the passageway, wondering which way he should move—and he promptly cursed himself. The wound in his chest had left a blood mark on the wall where he was leaning. He also realized he had blood on his right hand. He wiped it on the back of his pants as he looked back. He could see he had left several more blood marks on the wall. He was leaving a trail right to himself. Quickly moving around the corner, Merlin rushed ten feet down the passageway, leaned against the wall and made another mark. Then he made a blood smear another fifteen feet away from that one.

Spinning around on his heels, he then jogged back and headed in the other direction. The jogging was a bad mistake and he soon lost his balance under the movement of the ship and slammed against the metal wall. Righting himself, he was at least happy to see he hadn't left another blood trail in this direction.

He moved on, staying closer to the wall and using his hand to stay upright as he tried to move faster. A set of stairs appeared dead ahead. Looking back to make sure he hadn't been spotted, he began to climb the stairs to the next level. He swayed back and forth under the movement of the ship as he climbed. It seemed to him the movement was increasing and he wondered if a storm was coming up. Reaching the next deck, he heard some voices and decided to keep climbing. Coming out on the next deck, he was surprised at the difference. It didn't look so much like a freighter, more like a luxury passenger ship—

Static sounded and a voice echoed over a communication system; "Bud'te nacheku. Zaklyuchennyy sbezhal."

Whatever was being said was repeated three times. And from the urgency in the voice, Merlin had to presume it was about him. Moving along the passageway, Merlin heard some voices coming from up ahead. And then running feet. He considered turning and running and then checked a few of the doors. Most of them were locked. One opened and he looked inside. It was a small passenger cabin with a single bed and a small open wardrobe with several shirts and pants on hangers. He slipped inside, locking the door and listening. Feet went pounding by, apparently heading to the stairways he had just come up. When the sound disappeared, he moved to the small bathroom area, where he first washed the blood off the coin's blade, making sure it wouldn't coagulate and prevent the blade from coming back out of the coin when he needed it again. Putting the blade back inside the coin, he began looking for a bandage. All he found was a bottle of aspirins, some toothpaste, and a toothbrush. Moving back to the small bunk, he looked underneath. There was a cardboard box and he pulled it out. Inside was a pair of smelly sandals, a small pair of scissors, a deck of cards, a small framed picture of a young woman, a couple of letters that looked to be written in Russian, and a roll of duct tape. Nothing he could really use. He turned his attention to the wardrobe and the clothing. They were all dark blue, flame resistant cotton. They looked to be work clothing but the sharp crease in the pants made him think military. He looked over the shirts but didn't see any logos or lettering that would confirm that. But right now, it didn't matter. He disrobed, pulled off his escape belt, and stuffed his clothing under the bed. Then he cut off two lengths of duct tape with the scissors and crisscrossed them over the wound to stop the bleeding. Dressing again in a dark blue shirt and pants, along with his escape belt—he found the shirt and pants a little big and long in the arms and legs—but at least now he would fit in. He palmed the scissors as a weapon as he listened at the door. Silence. Unlocking it again, he slipped into the passageway and headed in the direction the running footsteps had come from.

He found another set of stairs and climbed to the next deck where he found a number of people dressed just like him moving back and forth along the passageway that ran left and right. There was no doubt he fit in clothing-wise. But he still held his breath, hoping no one asked him a question as he started walking. Several minutes later, he passed an open doorway on the left that made him stop...and back up to take a second look.

The room he could see was large, with a number of large-screen monitors on the far wall. The room was filled with dozens of men, dressed in similar blue clothing, all working at computer workstations. Who needed all those computer workstations on a freighter? Or a passenger ship?

He moved on, eventually finding himself in a passageway that ran the length of the ship—and he stared out the windows. He was on the main deck. There was a door twenty feet to the right and he headed for it—still looking at what he was seeing. Stepping out onto the outside deck, he realized he was near the stern of the ship. His mind was whirling as he walked to the rear of the ship. He wasn't on a river. When he woke up he had smelled salt and fish—what he actually was smelling was seawater. As he stood there, moving up and down with the waves, Merlin realized he was on a ship somewhere on the ocean.

Chapter 43

HE PRESUMED he was on the Atlantic ocean, but he couldn't be positive. He ran a hand through his hair, trying to visualize how long he had been unconscious. The truth was there was no way of knowing. The sun was low in the sky but he doubted it was the same day. But he also doubted they would keep him on ice for more than a day or two without interrogating him. But why here, on this ship?

Still palming the scissors, Merlin turned and leaned against the railing, trying to figure this out. The large area on the deck to the left look familiar. It took him a moment...and then he realized it was a helicopter sling loading set up. Helicopter sling load operations were used in a variety of military scenarios like the ship-to-shore movement of cargo, equipment—and sometimes troops—during amphibious operations or the replenishment of a ship's supplies. Is that how they got him here? But even if that was true, it still didn't answer the why. He looked up and got a partial answer.

A massive cross-like structure loomed overhead. The right arm was an ELINT antenna. The center was a COMINT antenna. He couldn't see the left arm. But it didn't matter. The ELINT was an electronic intelligence antenna, intercepting electronic signals related to an opponent's defense network such as radars, surface-to-air missile systems, and aircraft positions. The COMINT section was a communications intelligence antenna—intercepting communications between people. He could see the edges of a large round ball beyond the cross-like structure. It was used for eavesdropping on satellite signals. The realization struck hard; he was on SIGINT ship. A signals intelligence ship designed to perform intelligence-gathering by the interception of signals. He was on a Russian spy ship. They could sit out here—and here was probably somewhere off Delaware or New Jersey—get supplies replenished and be on a constant lookout for new information to steal–

It came to him. Who Sergei was. He had been one of the two bodyguards with Dimitri Starkov at the black-tie fundraiser in Washington. Starkov was ex-KGB. The fact they were on this ship had to mean Sergei was with today's Russian intelligence service—the GRU. Starkov's growing network of compromised politicians would no doubt add to this ship's ability to follow the threads of various intelligence breadcrumbs they picked up. And to be able to drill down through those compromised people deeper into the American intelligence system. He imagined the same thing being done outside Canada and Great Britain. And right now that's why they had him here—Rhett Summers was a possible threat to their growing spy network.

So what could he do about it? The answer right now was not much. Not as long as he was on this ship. He considered his options, which were slim. He considered using one of the 150-person closed lifeboats hanging from a cantilevered platform davit system that would lower them to the sea. They would have an inboard diesel engine. But it was a loser's long-shot bet he could get one lowered without anybody noticing. And even if he waited until it was dark, he still doubted it would be easy to do it without someone raising the alarm. And if he did get in the water, he doubted he would get very far. It was too large and easy to find, even in the dark. The more likely possibility would be in the large barrels along the railing. They contained inflatable lifeboats. If they didn't have a small outboard motor, they would usually have a paddle. It would be easier to disappear into the darkness on one of those. But even if he got one into the sea, and he had a motor or a paddle, which direction did he go in? Once the sun set—he looked up—the sky was overcast and he doubted he would be able to find the North Star. Maybe he could find a GPS device in one of the bigger lifeboats? That brought to mind his special cell phone. That would work, except for the fact Sergei had it. Looking up at the signals towers, Merlin realized he couldn't leave without his cell phone. Its special features were tied into Interpol and all the databases—and these guys could have the technical expertise and equipment to break into it. Adding that to what Starkov was already doing was unacceptable. He had to work his way back down and find it. Of course, Sergei might be expecting that. He had to make the Russian think differently.

Chapter 44

HE WOULD HAVE TO CREATE HAVOC. Merlin headed back inside the ship with purpose, working his way back to the stairs and down to the deck with the small passenger cabins. The first three doors on the left were unlocked. The crew quarters behind each door held a single bed, a wardrobe, and a tiny bathroom. Each one had a similar smell of salt water mixed with sweat, disinfectant, and soap. Merlin assumed everyone in this section was on a shift somewhere. The trouble was he had no idea how long that would last. He would have to work fast. Listening first for footsteps or voices—getting trapped inside would put him back in a locked room—he decided he had to chance it. Slipping into the third room, he closed the door. Moving to the bed, he pulled off the blankets and sheet to reveal the mattress. Jabbing at the mattress with the scissors, he cut into the cotton covering and the foam material, creating jagged tuffs. Unsnapping the Pyro-Band bracelet from his wrist, he scraped the scissors against the internal ferrocerium rod, creating a shower of sparks. On the second scrape, the mattress material ignited. Grabbing the blankets, he set them on the bed next to the flame. Twisting the sheet rope-like, he set it over the flame, letting it ignite. Carefully moving with it to the door, he checked outside again. Still quiet. Moving to the room next door, he set the burning sheet on the bed, pulling the blankets up around it to start a nice bonfire. By the time he left for the next room, the bed was on fire, and smoke was beginning to curl–

The ship's fire alarm sounded.

The sprinkler heads erupted.

The first room had obviously erupted into a full-blown fire faster than he expected. There was no more time. Slipping the scissors and bracelet in a pocket, Merlin took off at a run for the stairs, taking them two at a time to the next deck. He moved to the right of the passageway, keeping his head down. Men began to emerge from doorways, looking for where the danger was. The overhead sprinklers were not on here which meant the system was compartmentalized. Which was good and bad. Water raining from the ceilings would offer some cover–

A voice came over the p.a. system, speaking urgently in Russian.

Men immediately began running for the stairs to the lower deck, shouts of *pozhar* echoing off the walls.

Keeping his head down, Merlin moved slowly, avoiding the men running by, watching for Sergei. He hoped the Russian would assume his escaped prisoner might be responsible for the chaos and come looking. After several minutes, he knew his inaction while everybody else was doing something would stand out. He needed more chaos. And apparently, another way to draw Sergei out from wherever he was. Heading outside, Merlin worked his way forward. The smell of the sea was strong and his legs worked to keep himself upright against the up and down motion of the ship. Reaching the control panel for one of the cantilevered platform davit systems, he cracked open the cabinet and slammed the palm of his hand against the 'start' button. Turning on his heels, Merlin headed back along the deck as the sound of the hydraulic system resonated behind him. He was already back inside when he heard another announcement.

"Vnimaniye! Kto-to aktiviroval sistemu spasatel'noy shlyupki."

The announcement was repeated twice more and then some other words, probably indicating exactly which lifeboat system was in operation. It didn't matter. Once again, Merlin kept his head down as others began running—there he was.

Sergei was rushing in this direction behind another group of men.

Merlin turned with his head down and moved back to a door. Placing a hand on the handle, he pretended he was going to go inside. His shoulder was jostled by someone and he wondered if he was caught.

Men rushed by, two others bumping into him.

Sergei went running by, followed a moment later by his two henchmen in black.

Turning on his heels again, Merlin moved in the other direction, struggling to move against a tide of running men from time to time. Now that he knew Sergei and his men were up here, looking for him, he could do what he needed to do. Reaching the stairway, he headed down. Smoke curled around his legs and then his body. He cursed under his breath, wondering if he had cut his route off with the fire. He wasn't sure about another way to get where he needed to go. Putting an elbow over his nose and mouth against the acrid smell, he took the last step down and saw a number of men standing in the passageway, some of them coughing from the smoke. But they weren't in a panic.

Merlin kept moving. The doors to the fires he had set were open and he saw heavy smoke inside as he passed—but no hint of flames. The sprinklers had been turned off but he kicked up some water as he moved through the crowd and began working his way back down into the bowels of the ship. He made one wrong turn, corrected himself, and finally found his own blood trail. It led him beyond the space where he was held prisoner to the door where he had heard Sergei and his men talking. Holding his only weapon in one hand, the scissors, Merlin opened the door. The room was empty—except for the black duffel bag and the briefcase. The briefcase was open and empty. Unzipping the top of the duffel bag, he looked inside. The two million had been transferred to this bag and it held everything, including his Beretta and his special cell phone. Not bothering to empty the money out, Merlin left the bag un-zipped and dropped the scissors in beside the Beretta. Pulling out the cell phone, he headed back into the passageway. So far, so good. But he had to assume that by now Sergei suspected his prisoner was dressed like the rest of the crew. There was no other way he could be moving around without suspicion. Merlin needed more havoc and chaos.

Chapter 45

WORKING HIS WAY across the ship until he found the next stairway heading down, Merlin turned his special cell phone on and let it do its magic—breaking passwords and working its way through the ships communications systems to an overhead satellite—as he continued to head deeper into the ship. When he saw he could get a search engine, he quickly looked up the information he needed—a generic schematic of a ship this size and two specific Russian words that he cut and paste into a note—then he shut the phone down. Moving on, he watched the signs on the walls for those Russian words. He passed several men who only gave him a nod. But he was sure the longer it took to do what he needed to do, the more likely someone would start to ask something in Russian, maybe even asking that he identify himself.

A sign led him to another set of stairs that took him down to a lower deck and he found himself headed for his general destination: the engine room. The sound of machinery intensified as he looked for his next Russian word. The air smelled of oil and grease. His worry began to deepen until he saw the Russian word he needed and an arrow. It led him to a door that he pulled open and cautiously stuck his head inside—a series of panels lined the inside walls of a small room. And the room was empty. No crew. Which was good. Letting the door close, he double-checked his surroundings. He could see and hear men working but no one was close. For now. He would have to work fast.

Heading inside the room, it only took a few moments to find the panel he needed. Opening the panel door, he looked over all the dials and switches. He cursed under his breath. Which switch and which way to turn it? Using his cell phone again, he looked up the series of words in front of him. It was slow and frustrating because the signal was weak, no doubt because of all the metal around him deeper in the ship—but he finally identified the one he wanted. There was also another possibility that could be used to create more havoc. He shut the phone down quickly, dropping it back into the bag. Grabbing a nearby soda acid fire extinguisher, he set it at his feet and went to work on two specific switches in the control panel. He activated and reversed the bilge pumps. That would suck water into the ship instead of expelling it. There was also a backup cooling system, pulling seawater in to cool the engine components when and if the main system failed. He activated that system, imagining it would create a problem—and chaos—with both systems running.

Pulling his Beretta from the duffel bag, Merlin quickly pounded away at all the switches, breaking them away. He set the Beretta in the back of his pants, grabbed the fire extinguisher, moved the bag away, and stepped back.

The sound of a warning klaxon echoed around the room.

Activating the extinguisher, he sprayed the foam over the face of the entire panel. It would add to the confusion and slow down anyone trying to find and reverse the switches. More than likely they would have to take the panel apart. Which gave him more time. And time was what he needed.

Carrying the empty extinguisher and the bag back to the door, Merlin quickly exited. He set the bag down, turned and bashed away with the empty metal cylinder at the door handle. He bent it over, effectively locking the door and slowing anyone down. Tossing the spent cylinder aside, Merlin grabbed the duffel bag and headed for the stairs, ready to pull the gun if confronted.

Panicked voices sounded in the passageway behind him as he began climbing to the next deck.

A Russian voice boomed over the p.a. system, trying to cut through the noise of the loud klaxon. Whatever the voice said was tinged with urgency.

Merlin continued working his way up through the ship, heading for the bow and starboard side.

Men passed him in full flight.

Footsteps pounded along the passageways in front and behind.

By the time he reached the main deck and headed outside, the sun was setting–

The ship let out a metallic creak. The deck tilted slightly.

Merlin grabbed for the railing. Crap. He hadn't expected that. Creating chaos in order to get away had been his purpose. Going down with the ship wasn't part of the plan.

Another loud creak was followed by a hollow, metallic boom.

The ship tilted again slightly to the left—then the stern seemed to slant downward just enough to be felt.

The darkness of night began to creep over the ship.

As lights began snapping on here and there, Merlin abandoned plans to get further to the bow. He went to work instead on getting an inflatable lifeboat free from a barrel container. He was surprised—and not surprised—to find an inflatable Zodiac boat—the kind used by the military for sea assaults—as well as a motor. Dropping to the sea from this height would probably kill him so he did the only other thing he could do. He hurried to get everything over to the deck beside another cantilevered platform davit system for a large lifeboat. He initiated the system. As the hydraulics went into operation, Merlin scrambled to get the duffel bag, the zodiac, and the motor into the 150-person lifeboat. Getting inside himself, he pulled his weapon and watched for anyone trying to stop him. Fortunately, the chaos on the ship was keeping everyone busy–

The ship tilted and Merlin fell to the floor inside the massive lifeboat. His gun clattered away along the floor. He scrambled to get it and then found himself grabbing the duffel bag as well to keep it from sliding away inside the lifeboat as well. The Zodiac and motor slid a few feet and banged against a long seat. The floor was tilted and Merlin used the seats to pull himself back to the opening.

A metallic moan from the ship echoed inside the lifeboat.

The lowering system jerked. It dropped another couple of feet and banged to a stop.

Merlin looked out to see he was still three or four feet above the top of the three-foot swells. Dropping the gun inside the duffel bag, he worked to get the Zodiac outside the larger lifeboat, where he triggered the gas.

There was a loud hiss as the Zodiac began to inflate. It dropped to the sea. Merlin dropped the bag and the motor to the inflating boat, then jumped, falling on his back. He quickly scrambled around, pulled out an oar that was strapped to the inside and began paddling away from the ship. It was a struggle in the up and down of the sea but he began to make some headway into the darkness–

A gunshot sounded. Followed by several more.

Merlin's heart beat in his chest, hoping they didn't puncture the inflatable.

More gunshots.

The sounds of thuds twenty feet away in the darkness told Merlin they were shooting at the larger lifeboat, not him.

There were shouts in Russian from above.

Paddling harder, Merlin moved his escape craft away from the ship and further into the darkness. After ten minutes of hard paddling, Merlin stopped, his chest heaving from the exertion as he looked back at the lights of the intelligence ship. They were at a 45° angle now and low in the water. He sat there, dumbfounded as the lights began slowly sliding beneath the waves. Loud hisses of escaping air made it sound like a wounded beast dying. There were some dark shapes bobbing on the water, probably the larger lifeboats. He had tried to create chaos, not sink a Russian spy ship. Not that it mattered.

He turned his attention to getting further away from the lifeboats and began paddling again. Sergei and his men might be on one of them and the Russian wouldn't hesitate to continue shooting at his escaping prisoner. He glanced back from time to time, making sure he was moving away from the bobbing shadows on the sea.

After another ten minutes, he decided he was far enough away. For now. Digging out his cell phone from the duffel bag, Merlin turned it on. It took a minute or so before it connected to a satellite again. Using the internal GPS, he checked to see where he was. He was something like 250 nautical miles from Washington, DC. A speedboat running at 20 knots would have taken ten or twelve hours to cover the distance to where the spy ship had been. That was presuming it didn't stop to refuel. He concluded Sergei had used a helicopter. Not that it mattered. He was here. Setting the phone down, he worked to get the motor in place, started it up, and used the GPS system to set a course for shore. Keeping the Beretta close and still watching to make sure no one was chasing him, Merlin made a phone call. He kept the purr of the engine low as he listened for someone to answer. The low purr was joined by the sound of the Zodiac slapping against the waves.

The phone on the other end rang twice before it was answered. "Mr. Dragon, what can we do for you?" It was Captain Charity Sherrell.

"Hi, Captain–"

"What's that sound?"

"Uh...yeah, about that, I need some help. You won't believe this but...."

Chapter 46

STRINGS WERE PULLED through Director Aubrey Laurent and a wet and cold Merlin was picked up as a 'courtesy' by a United States Coast Guard cutter three hours later. Specifically, a Legend-class, National Security cutter under the command of Captain Lopez. Once he was onboard, Lopez told Merlin they had been working with two other ships to keep an eye on a Russian signals intelligence ship named Kop'ye—The Spear in Russian. But they were returning to port immediately because the U.S. satellite system had detected the sinking of the ship *for some reason*. Merlin stayed silent but he was treated like royalty by the crew—he realized why when he saw them pull the Zodiac from the sea like a trophy—the name on the bow was Kop'ye. Merlin decided not to tell Lopez that the 'reason' had been accidental—they were enjoying the blow against the 'enemy' too much and their morale was soaring. Instead, he gratefully accepted a much-needed hot meal, a soft bunk, and a dry US Coast Guard fleece hoodie and sweatpants as they sailed happily to port.

Merlin was surprised when they took him all the way to a coast guard station in Washington, D.C. Joint Base Anacostia–Bolling was a 905-acre military installation that turned out to be a Naval Support Facility and Bolling Air Force Base. And the Bombardier Global 8000 was waiting for him on a tarmac. He climbed the airstairs, bone weary and surprised to find he had trouble finding his land legs after the short but constant up and down on the Atlantic.

Captain Charity Sherrell and the co-pilot, Captain Faith Saab, were waiting for him. Saab held out a hot coffee and offered a suggestion with a smile, "You might want to take a quick shower. You smell like seaweed."

Yawning, Merlin said, "Nice to see you too."

"And once you take that quick shower, there are subway sandwiches in the galley," Sherrell added. "And FYI, Nikki came out of surgery weak but fighting. The doctors said it was touch and go but it looks like she'll make a full recovery."

Merlin took the hot coffee in hand and felt a weary smile settle on his lips, "That's good news. I was worried about her."

"And once you shower, let us know." Sherrell turned and headed for the flight deck, "We're going to fly across to Washington Dulles International Airport."

"Why there and not Reagan?"

"Not sure. Your contact in Ottawa might know. We just do what we're told."

"I think it's above our pay grade," Saab told him. She winked, then headed to close the door.

With the hydraulic whine of the airstairs closing, Merlin sipped at the hot coffee as he headed for the back suite. Taking a quick shower, he grabbed a subway sandwich, made another fresh coffee, and took a seat in the main cabin. After alerting Sherrell that he was buckled in, Merlin set his coffee in a cup holder. He grabbed his cell phone and made a call.

"Hello?"

"Hi, Sammy. It's Merlin."

"Hi. Sounds like you've been having some fun."

"If you consider fun having your cruise ship sink underneath you because you left the shower on, yeah."

Sammy laughed, "First things first. Jigs and I have been playing ball. Although the way he slaps at it and sends it across the room, then watches me—I think he wants me to do the fetching."

"Are you?"

"Uh...yeah. Smart cat."

The jet's TechX high bypass turbofan engines came to life in a deep, buzz-saw moan, sending the sense of immense power surging through the cabin.

Yawning, Merlin took a quick sip of his coffee, "I'm surprised we're not flying back home. The entire operation has been compromised. They'll have to try to send someone else–"

"Not necessarily," Sammy said. "We have some good news and some bad news."

"You can actually have *more* bad news?"

"Yep. Your last attempt to intercept a target's phone signal failed. The tech specialists say the software operated properly and showed an interception. But it was like the person had some device to intercept the interception, if that makes sense."

"That's possible," Merlin admitted. "The last target was Oksana Pavlovich, the suspected kurátor. She's also pretty savvy with technology. I was in her office in Blackstone Strategies and she had what I thought was a clock on her desk. But when I think back to her reactions when I activated the software, I'm pretty sure that *clock* had software that detected my attempt to intercept her phone signal. However she did it, she made me, had me take her for an early lunch, and had me kidnapped."

"Sounds like a lunch date gone bad."

"Something like that." Merlin ran a hand over his hair, thinking. "I was able to put some of our software on Roland Henderson's computers before that happened though. Did we get anything implicating the guy?"

The jet began moving to a runway.

"Nope. Someone removed the software several hours after you installed it."

Merlin cursed. "That had to be Pavlovich. She went back after her men took me." He cursed again.

"Don't be so hard on yourself," Sammy said. "Remember there's also good news. The software bug on Henderson's computer was there long enough to allow our intelligence people to burrow into the computer system of Blackstone Strategies."

That surprised Merlin and he straightened up in his seat. "They did?"

"Yeah. It was tricky, but so far our intrusion has gone undetected. And here's the good, good news. The software bug your Nikki put on Senator Shermon Best's laptop and desktop computer was there long enough for the intelligence people to use his passwords to get into his office computers."

"His Senate office?"

"Yep. And with those two points—his Senate office computers and Blackstone's computers—our intelligence people are building out the Russian's network. And most of the people we were targeting are using a cloud service to connect their personal cell phones and their personal computers—their passwords are pretty weak or they even have them stored in a note we could access. We've been able to access their personal text messages, emails, and even voice messages."

Merlin rubbed at his stubble. "Anything we can use?"

The jet rumbled onto a runway and slowly turned into position for takeoff.

"Yes and no." Sammy paused. "Other than being able to get into Senator Best's system because he was sloppy with protecting his passwords—the official government computers the other Senators use are proving to be difficult to crack. But there's a silver lining."

The turbofan engines growled deeply against gravity and Merlin was pressed back in his seat by the 16,500 lb thrust from the engines as the jet began its run. "And what would that silver lining be?"

"We detected the network is using a foldering system to trade messages."

Merlin's seat vibrated as the jet picked up speed. "What's a foldering system? I've heard of it but I'm not...."

"Telekom AG bought dot com domain names and set up three generic websites on American politics. They had Whois privacy initiated but we were able to penetrate the shield and confirm it was the Russian's company. The hosting service they're using includes an email package that allowed them to set up three private email accounts or systems. Everyone involved in the network has the password to these accounts. A person creates an email in one of the email systems but leaves it in the draft folder. It's never sent. Never. A coded message—probably a text message—is sent to a person they want to read the email. The coded message tells them which of the three systems to look at. The person reads the draft email and then deletes it. That person could then draft an email to reply or pass a message on to someone else. Again—the email is *never* sent. Only a coded message is sent to the person the message is intended for."

"That's slick," Merlin said. The Global 8000 left the ground and soared into the skies. "From what I understand, you do that because emails that are *sent* usually pass through a series of computers before it gets to the end. And you can track or find them, right?"

"Technically, several communicating entities called e-mail nodes—essentially software units working on the application layer of the TCP/IP model—are involved in the process of e-mail delivery through networks around the world."

"Uh...okay. Good to know."

"Anyway, those networks or computers actually make a copy and send it on, in case the final receiving computer is down for one reason or another. That's how investigators are able to trace and gather sent emails long after the fact. But here's the thing...." Sammy paused. "Even if they delete the email from the draft folder, it's still in the system."

"I take it you found something?"

"We did. But it's another good and bad news thing."

Merlin mumbled under his breath. "Of course, it would have to be."

"The Russian's are either spooked by your run-in with the kurátor or something else had happened. Either way, it looks like they're going to clean up their network. We saw a message appear in a folder. It read: I Direct accident. The I and D are capitalized but not the A in accident."

"I Direct accident? What does that mean? And why does the capitalization matter?"

"The intelligence analysts wondered the same thing. It could've been an accident. But considering we're dealing with a covert Russian operation they ran it though a cryptanalytic computer on the presumption it was a coded message."

"That makes sense."

"They ran multiple trial decryptions using combinations of the phrase against all the names we have presently associated with the Russian network. They added their biographies, news articles, anything they could find. The phrase 'I Direct' popped up in connection with Senator Dan Herszman."

Merlin narrowed his eyes, trying to visualize the information. "I don't get it. How does 'I Direct' match with Herszman?"

"The state motto of Maine is the Latin word Dirigo. It appears on Maine's coat of arms, and that coat of arms is featured on both the state seal and the state flag. Dirigo in English means 'I Direct'. One of the two senators from Maine...is Dan Herszman."

Straightening up in his seat, Merlin said, "That definitely sounds like Herszman has been targeted for elimination through an accident."

"That's the conclusion of the analysts. And I agree it's possible."

"Any idea who the message was for, who was supposed to do the job?"

"No. At least, not yet. We're still searching for clues. But Herszman is returning from his cottage in Maine and is going to be flying into Dulles International Airport in less than an hour. That assumes his plane makes it."

Chapter 47

THE DULLES ARRIVAL TERMINAL was crowded and noisy, the noise coming from the mass of humanity coming and going as well as the major renovation going on inside and outside the building. Still dressed in the US Coast Guard fleece hoodie and sweatpants, the hammering, sawing, and drilling pounded against his skull as Merlin moved with purpose, around or through groups of people, ignoring the shouts of protest over his 'rudeness'. The Global 8000 had been given permission to land before other planes—Saab had to go through Sammy and Interpol's National Central Bureau here in Washington to force the issue—but that also meant they ended up at Gate C2, which was at the farthest end of this terminal. And this place was huge, his growing sense of urgency making it seem like it was one-thousand-acres larger than it really. Pulling his cell phone, Merlin brought up the image of Senator Dan Herszman. The Senator was coming in on flight DL1099—and coming through Gate D32—and he was close to it now. Merlin's chest was heaving when he finally reached the arrival gate. The hallway on the other side of the glass was empty and he assumed he had made it before the passengers came through–

His cell phone vibrated in his hand. There was a text message and Merlin brought it up as he kept one eye on the hallway

Sherrell and Saab had been talking with the tower, asking for the information on flight DL1099 when he left them. They had ended up frustrated with the tower, who were in turn frustrated with all the renovations creating bottlenecks and wanting them to move the jet immediately to another part of the airport before they worried about getting them the information. They had finally gotten an answer; Flight DL1099 landed twenty-five minutes ago. Tailwind.

Merlin swore under his breath as he turned on his heels and took off at a jog. "Stupid red tape. Stupid construction. And a stupid tailwind." He followed the signs indicating the route and number for the baggage claim carousel. Hopefully, he could catch up with the Senator and let him know what was happening. He rejected heading for one of the shuttles, fearing he would have to wait for one to show up. But he regretted that decision when the crowds and sounds enveloped him again as he headed for the pedestrian walkway. Even though they were all moving in the same direction, it was like trying to swim downstream in the middle of a million salmon.

His breathing was raspy by the time he reached the baggage claim area. The carousel he needed—number 15—was off to the far left and he struggled at cross purposes with the crowds who had claimed their baggage at carousels 8 to 14 and were headed for the exit doors leading to the parking level and the ground level. The noise of conveyor machinery, mixed with the echo of bags dropping to the carousels, and the rumble of baggage wheels rolling on the floor behind passengers who were headed for those exits. There were still people collecting their luggage. That was good. The problem was there weren't many. He turned in a circle, looking—he spotted the Senator—he was nearing exit door two. Merlin cursed again and took off at a run., realizing he had actually passed him in the crowd.

Herszman disappeared through the exit for the ground level.

Struggling to thread his way through the crowd and ignoring more comments at his 'rudeness', Merlin finally reached the exit and stepped outside. The sounds of construction was even heavier out here. Workmen were busy on the building and the three lanes of terminal roadway as other construction personnel were getting concrete barriers in place to control the traffic as they worked. The walkway was busy with passengers coming and going and Merlin desperately looked for Herszman.

The Senator was headed for a stretch limousine sitting at the curb. A man had the back door open, waiting. He wore a chauffeur's outfit, dark sunglasses, and a cap pulled low over his eyes.

Merlin rushed in the Senator's direction, lifting a hand and calling out, "Senator Herszman! Hey, Senator? Hold up–"

Two large secret security men in dark suits, sunglasses, and earpieces stepped in front of Merlin.

Merlin stepped to go around them.

One of the agents stepped with him, blocking his path, "Stop right there, sir."

The other agent spoke sternly, "Don't make us arrest you."

Merlin shook his head, "No, no, no. You don't understand." He leaned and looked past the large agent. "I need to talk to the Senator."

Herszman slipped into the back seat and the back door to the stretch limousine closed.

The driver headed for the front door.

Merlin let a curse out. "He's in danger–"

The two agents reacted with the curse and the sound of the word *danger*. Their hands moved to their jackets, as if ready to pull their weapons, their eyes fixed intently on Merlin.

Holding his hands up to convey no action was coming on his part, Merlin indicated his top pocket with a subtle movement of his fingers, "Can I?"

The large agent nodded once, "Just use two fingers. And no sudden moves."

Nodding his understanding, Merlin slowly pulled out his Interpol passport. He had taken it so he could get back through airport security once he was finished catching up and alerting the Senator. He hadn't planned on using it like this.

The agent took the passport and glanced at it.

Looking past the agent again, Merlin muttered another obscenity under his breath as the limousine drove ahead. "The Senator is leaving?"

The stretch limousine stopped after traveling only fifty feet along the curb.

The agent glanced over his shoulder. A moment later, he looked back at Merlin, his eyebrows clearly knitting together, "Uh...no. He's waiting for us." He glanced back at the passport, "Can you tell me why you need to talk to the Senator?"

Merlin sensed the agent was clearly confused and concerned with the movement of the vehicle. "I just need two minutes with the Senator," he told the agent.

Glancing over his shoulder again for a brief moment, the agent then set his tone harder, "Sir. I'll ask you again...what do you want with the Senator?"

"Just give me *one* minute–" Merlin was distracted by more movement from the direction of the Senator's vehicle.

The driver of the stretch limousine was getting out. He closed the door behind him.

"Sir? Can you answer me?"

Watching the driver closely, Merlin could see the man wore gloves. The problem was... they didn't look like leather driving gloves. More like...fingerless tactical gloves with a velcro wrist strap. Had he done something to Herszman?

The driver marched away from the stretch limousine.

"Sir?"

Merlin watched the driver, looking to see if he had a detonator in hand as he marched across the walkway, headed for the entrance to the terminal. The fists were clenched, the thumbs parallel to the trouser seams but there didn't seem to be anything held...or was that a thin device with a button at the top in the left hand–?

The agent bent sideways in front of Merlin, trying to catch his attention. "Sir? Can you tell me what this is all about?" He glanced at the passport, "Mr–?"

Merlin felt frustrated and angry. He snatched the passport away, "Look. You can see I'm with Interpol. I need to–" His attention was caught by something hanging thirty feet over the top of the stretch limousine—a chill went through him when he realized what was happening.

A large construction crane held a massive section of concrete barrier in a sling.

Swearing, Merlin moved to go around the agent.

The agent stuck out an arm bar, preventing him from going past him.

"No, no, no. You don't understand–"

The sling released its load.

A loud boom echoed off the walls of the terminal as the massive chunk—tons of concrete and steel rebar—dropped onto the stretch limousine, crushing its roof like a light tin can and compacting everything inside nearly to the bottom frame. The air in the tires exploded with ferocity, sending chunks of high-tech rubber and steel cords in every direction.

The screams of the people standing, walking or rushing to their own cars followed quickly and echoed over the fading echo of deadly concrete.

The two agents whirled around at the sound. They took off running for the stretch limousine—now a crushed coffin of modern day automotive components.

Chapter 48

THE SUN HAD cracked the sky the next morning and was now burning away more precious time. Merlin sat on the jet, drinking a coffee and thinking. It had all happened so fast yesterday. And yet he still felt conflicted in so many ways. There was the sense of failure at not getting to the Senator in time. But at the same time, the man had set the events that led to his death in motion by dealing with Starkov in the first place. What did he think was going to happen? Merlin concluded the Senator probably didn't think beyond the power he had gained. Merlin was broken from his thoughts by Captain Saab.

"Once we finish refueling, the tower wants to know what we want to do." She yawned. "Sorry. The tower says they're going to need this spot near the gate. They have a number of commercial airliners coming in within the hour. They can arrange for a hanger if we're going to stay here longer."

Merlin scratched at the stubble on his chin as he gave it some thought. The trouble was, he had no real answer. "Give me a few more minutes and I'll let you know."

"Yes, sir. I'm going to make a couple more coffees for us on the flight deck. Do you want another one?"

"Uh...no, thanks." As she headed for the galley, Merlin also felt his frustration flaring again. At this point, he didn't know whether they should leave or stay. Right now, he had no real plan that would move his assignment ahead. And time was rapidly running out. If

Starkov *was* cleaning up his network and eliminated all the Senators they knew about—it was also possible the Russian would leave in place any deep cover agents or sleeper agents they didn't know about—unknown subjects he had recruited or compromised through those Senators. And if Starkov left the United States for good–

Merlin's cell phone rang. He answered quickly, "Yes?"

"Morning. It's Sammy. We saw another message drop into the foldering system before the sun was up. It says; the ministry of transportation needs to be eliminated."

"The ministry of transportation needs to be eliminated? That's it?"

"Yeah. Everything is small letters. Not a single capital letter anywhere."

"The intelligence analysts have any idea on what it means?"

"No."

Sammy sounded as frustrated as Merlin felt. He closed his eyes and tried to visualize the message. "Any idea who was supposed to get this message?"

"That would be another no." Sammy paused for a moment. "It's *possible* it's just a political message. But...."

"Yeah. But why would they put any political messaging in a secret communication system? That can be done out of the open."

I agree. And the analysts feel the same way. This has to be another message like the last one. Especially since it has the word eliminated in it. But it doesn't follow any similar pattern to the previous coded message."

Merlin took a sip of coffee, thinking. "There has to be a pattern we're just not seeing."

"Again," Sammy said, "I agree. And so do the analysts. But we're missing some kind of information that would help us to figure it out. We know all the names of the people involved, but when they run the message through their computer systems, nothing pops up like the last time. Even though we don't have any capital letters, they've programmed them into their computers in every combination possible. In fact, they're still doing. But so far, we've got zip."

"Okay." Merlin mulled over the situation. "How about the department of transportation in the United States? Does it have any specific name?"

"Not really. They simply use the Department of Transportation. We even thought about the other countries involved in this thing. The UK uses the designation Department for Transportation. Canada uses Transport Canada. We even tried the acronyms they use—like the D-O-T, the acronym the United States uses, or the F-y-T Great Britain uses. Nothing fits."

Merlin set his coffee down, closed his eyes and rubbed the top of his head in frustration. There had to be something there—his eyes popped open. "Say that again?"

"I said nothing fits."

Sitting up straighter, Merlin said, "No, no, no. Before that. You said D-O-T."

"Right. It probably sounds familiar because you see letters like that labeled on a lot of trucks. A US DOT number identifies carriers operating in interstate commerce. It would be a designation like...United States DOT 123456."

"You're right. I've seen them on trucks. But...I think...in this case...it means a lot more than that."

Chapter 49

THE TWIN-TURBO ENGINE ROARED as Merlin pushed all those horses under the hood of the Maserati Quattroporte GTS. He roared through the streets in the rental, determined to reach the condominium building overlooking the Potomac River before it was too late. Quinn Olivares had referred to his wife Dorothy as Dotty. The name Dot was a short form (hypocorism) of Dorothy—D-O-T. Quinn had said she worked for one of the seventeen intelligence agencies in the area. Whether she was working with her husband, or had been compromised by Starkov on her own, didn't matter. She was perfectly positioned to feed some kind of raw intelligence through the Russian's network. Of course, if Merlin was wrong, someone else was going to die as he ran down his theory. But right now he had no other possibilities. Merlin cursed when he had to pull to a stop at a red light. His hands were fidgety on the steering wheel, and his thoughts were antsy to get moving again.

A large group of kids dressed in baseball uniforms, baseball spikes over their shoulders, were crossing in front of him. The edge of a green and brown, fenced-in baseball field was off to the left.

Merlin felt his anxiety rising. The light had changed to green and the kids were still crossing. They were laughing and talking like they didn't have a care in the world. The problem was, Merlin had every care in the world on his shoulders–

One of the last stragglers turned and waved to another group walking on the sidewalk to the right, calling out, "Hurry up, guys. We're already up nine nothing over you and the game hasn't even started."

The other kids took off at a run for the crosswalk, laughing and razzing the kid who had now taken off at a run.

Merlin watched the second group crossing against the light. *Why weren't these kids in school–? Crap! What day is this?* His thoughts whirled as he dug into a pocket for his cell phone. Crap. His phone wasn't there. What did he do with it?

A car behind him beeped its horn.

Merlin's frustration mounted. He had bought and changed into a sunwashed canvas shirt, dress chinos, and a light cotton jacket in the terminal and—it came to him—he had slipped it into the top pocket. Pulling it out, Merlin looked at the screen.

As he feared. It was Saturday. With everything that was happening, he had lost track of time. Nikki had told him Dorothy Olivares was part of a group...The Metro Alliance Theater...it rehearsed and put on plays and musicals...*on Saturdays.*

Swiping away at his phone, did a search on the theater group in Washington–

There was another beep behind him—this one longer and more insistent—and then a whole chorus of beep, filling the air like angry church bells.

Merlin looked up to see the walkway was clear now and the light was still green. Mumbling an obscenity, he put the car in drive and pressed down hard on the gas. The tires squealed under the power and he rocketed across the intersection. Half a block down, he pulled to the curb to continue his search.

The cars that had been behind him roared by, sounding the horns loudly to express their continued annoyance at being held up for a few extra seconds.

Returning to his search on the theater group, it didn't take long for Merlin to realize he wasn't just driving to the wrong place, he was driving in the wrong direction. Banging his fist on the steering wheel, Merlin set the phone in the cup holder, then programmed the Maserati's navigation system with the address. Stomping down on the gas pedal, he did a U-turn, cutting off several cars and receiving another symphony of protest. Heading for the nearest highway, he began weaving in and out of traffic, taking chances. It took him ten minutes to get to that highway and twenty-five long agonizing minutes of fast driving to get to the exit he needed.

His cell phone sitting in a cup holder rang.

With a need to keep his hands on the wheel as he drove, Merlin ignored it.

It continued ringing.

Chastising himself for not hooking his phone into the Maserati's Bluetooth system so he could have answered by voice, Merlin half considered reaching for it and answering. But his weaving in and out of traffic made that too dangerous.

It stopped ringing.

Wondering who had been calling him, Merlin darted around a delivery truck and pushed down on the gas pedal, pushing the Maserati harder as the light up ahead turned from yellow to green.

There were no pedestrians but cars started moving.

Merlin leaned on his horn to warn the drivers he was coming hard and fast.

Tires screeched in agony. Cars came to a rocking stop.

The Maserati shot between the stopped vehicles in the intersection.

Horns blared their disapproval.

Muttering 'sorry', Merlin pushed on. It took twenty minutes of hard driving before the navigation system indicated he was just two hundred yards from his destination. Things were looking up.

The cell phone rang again.

Nearing a brown, two-tone brick building, Merlin slowed the vehicle. He spotted Dorothy Olivares emerging from the glass doors underneath the Metro Alliance Theater sign.

The cell phone kept ringing.

Sliding the Maserati to a stop next to the curb, Merlin grabbed the phone. "What?"

"It's Sammy. Why didn't you answer me? I was getting worried–"

Merlin glanced back at the traffic and opened the driver door, "Because I'm busy trying to save someone's life."

"That's what I'm calling about. We were able to figure out who looked at that message in the foldering system and then deleted it."

Slamming the door shut, Merlin headed around the front of the Maserati. Dorothy Olivares was only thirty feet away, looking down at her own cell phone as she walked slowly. "Who was it?"

"Quinn Olivares."

Merlin stopped dead in his tracks. "The husband?"

Chapter 50

MERLIN BARELY HEARD the traffic and chatter of the people around him. The warm air actually felt much colder as he considered the implications. Why would Quinn Olivares be the one to see that message in the foldering system they were using? If it was a coded message for some type of assassination, why would he be seeing it? Merlin mumbled again to himself, "The husband?"

"Or someone using his computer," Sammy added. "That's all we know for sure."

Merlin looked around slowly, considering the possibility of the ambitious Olivares being somewhere nearby. "Okay. I could buy that. Maybe. Unless he has someone working for him that I haven't met.""

"The background information the analyst dug up doesn't indicate any specific individuals working for him. Obviously, it *could* be someone we don't know about."

"Of course, nothing is going to make this easy." Merlin took in the surrounding buildings, even looking higher for a shooter's perch. "Does that background information by the analysts give me anything about Quinn Olivares that might prove useful in this situation?"

"Probably the information you want to know about is his military activity."

"Oh, great. Give it to me."

"He was an Army Ranger. Served four years on active duty."

"Good to know. And not so good."

"It looks to me like being a Ranger was a plan for his career," Sammy added. "His father pulled some strings after he had the prerequisite college football experience to put on his resume. Quinn Olivares never served in any combat zone, despite the fact his unit was deployed on three occasions."

Merlin looked back at Dorothy Olivares. She started walking in the other direction, still half-looking at her cell phone. He began walking after her, "How did he get away with that?"

"Like I said. There were complaints of strings being pulled. The father is a private military contractor, specializing in the special operations and protective industry. Their website says the company has protected a lot of high-profile individuals, including a number of prime ministers and presidents over the last forty years."

"That would mean he has a lot of pull. And getting a son into a Senate position would open up a lot of new business opportunities."

"And that would also make Quinn Olivares a great person to take over the business in the future, with a lot of new and lucrative contacts in the bank."

"True." Merlin hurried after the wife. "It makes me wonder if he accidentally fell under the influence of the Russian...or if he sees more opportunity on a worldwide scale. I gotta go." Slipping the phone into his pocket, Merlin reached out and tapped Dorothy Olivares on the shoulder.

The blonde woman turned, her eyes startled. She backed up a step, her eyes narrowing. "Yes?"

"I guess you don't recognize me. Rhett Summers. I was with Sonya Tapper at your place having a nice dinner...?"

Dorothy put a hand to her chest and gave him a smile that showed both relief and embarrassment. "Oh, yes. Of course. Mr. Summers. I'm sorry. I didn't recognize you."

"That's all right. Can I talk to you for a moment?" He gestured toward a coffee shop up ahead.

Dorothy turned and glanced at it before looking back at him, "I'm sorry. I really don't have the time. I have to pick up some items at the theatrical store just up the street and come back for the rehearsal. Perhaps another time?"

"Just a minute of your time is all I need." Merlin looked around, not wanting to say too much with people around them.

Raising an eyebrow, Dorothy said in a low voice, "I'm sorry, Mr. Summers... but I'm a married woman. And I would prefer if you left me alone. I won't sell Sonya anything about this."

Despite the danger of the circumstances, Merlin saw the irony in the situation. He had a hard time with social situations—with women especially—and here was one who was thinking he was hitting on her. Go figure. Merlin felt he had no choice and he pulled his own passport out, opening it and holding it out to her.

Dorothy glanced at the passport and then looked back at him—then she suddenly looked back at the passport, leaning her head in closer. "I don't understand...." She put a hand to her chin, thinking. "Your name isn't Rhett Summers?" She shook her head, "I don't get it. Why would you lie?"

"Do you see *who* I work for?"

She looked back, eyes narrowing. "Interpol?" There was a shake of her head again, "I still don't understand–"

"Your life is in danger. That's why I'm here."

She crossed her arms tightly, one hand still holding the cell phone. "What do you mean I'm in danger?"

Merlin glanced around, still unsure of who might perform the hit on her. "Can we go somewhere else and talk about this–?"

"Tell me what this is all about."

"Not in the open."

Dorothy was adamant, "I'm not going anywhere with you until you explain what you're talking about."

"It's complicated–"

"Try me. I'm not stupid, you know?"

"I didn't say you were." Merlin still wasn't sure about her involvement either. He watched closely for a reaction. "I've been looking into a Russian oligarch—Dimitri Starkov."

"Dimitri? I've met him. Several times. He's been working to help my husband. Why would you be looking into him?"

Merlin didn't detect any deception in her voice, facial expressions, or body language—although she could be an accomplished lier. He pushed a little further. "Like I said, it's complicated. Starkov has been working to turn some people into assets he can use–"

Dorothy's voice sounded incredulous, "You're accusing Dimitri of infiltrating our government?"

It looked more and more like she wasn't involved in the network. But why was she being targeted–?

Dorothy scoffed. "The next thing you'll tell me is my husband is involved."

That shook Merlin. He now feared he was going to lose her if he didn't give her a reason to trust him. To believe what he was saying. He eyed the crowd again, thinking. "You might not have heard about it because you were occupied with your theater rehearsals...but...Senator Dan Herszman was killed at Dulles International airport. You can check the news on your phone."

That startled Dorothy. She took a moment and then worked away at her phone, nervous and glancing at him as she tapped and swiped away at the screen. A moment later, her blue eyes took on that startled look again. "What happened?"

"A big chunk of concrete fell on him. I saw it happen. I was up there trying to warn him but I didn't get there in time. Starkov and his contacts are using a foldering system to pass messages–"

"I know what that is."

"There was a coded message to someone to eliminate Senator Herszman...through an accident. We just saw one that we believe referred to you...Dot. You're next to be eliminated."

The use of the word Dot caused her to blink several times. Then she glanced around nervously, "You have any idea who is supposed to... to do this...? And why me?"

"Why you is a question I can't answer. I don't know the reason. But the only person we know who could have read the coded message before it was deleted...was your husband."

There was a moment of silence. "Quinn?"

"Right. Like I said...we only know that he saw the message. It could be someone else who will actually come after you. That's why I need to get you to safety until we can figure out who. And why."

Dorothy nodded slowly. "Okay. I understand." She looked down at the sidewalk for a moment, and then said. "Just let me grab my purse. It's inside the theater."

Merlin shook his head, "That's not a good idea. I can send somebody back–"

But she was already around him and headed for the glass doors of the theater.

Moving quickly after her, Merlin kept his eyes on the people around them, conscious that someone could pop out of the crowd at any moment.

The sunlight flashed off the glass doors as they opened and closed. Dorothy disappeared inside.

Merlin couldn't help but mutter under his breath again as he grabbed the door handle and pulled. She was going to get herself killed if she didn't stay close to him—the glass doors wouldn't open for him. He pulled the handle with both hands, trying to shake the door loose. Placing his forehead against the glass, and his hands against the sides of his face, he looking inside.

Dorothy was moving away from the doors, heading deeper into the theater.

It was a full-blown curse that erupted from Merlin's lips. Dorothy Olivaries didn't believe him. She was running from him. Then another thought ripped through his heart. Or Dot *was* part of the whole thing. And he had just told her his assignment. And now the Russian would know.

Chapter 51

STEPPING BACK FROM THE DOORS, Merlin looked up and down the street. He had to assume she was heading out the back way to a parking lot and her car. There had to be a way to get back there. The problem was, there were no gaps between the buildings in either direction. He would have to go to the end of the block and work his way around. And if he chose the wrong end, she could easily get away. He took off to the right, taking a gamble, doing his best to avoid people as he ran. Two buildings down, he came to a sliding stop on the sidewalk. He was staring at the entrance and exit to an underground parking lot. That made more sense. But it was also more of a problem. She would no doubt have a number of exits she could take.

Running down the entrance way to the parking level, Merlin cut back to the left, toward the theater. His footsteps echoed off the concrete walls. The smell of musty concrete and gas fumes was strong and heady.

Within moments, a sign told him he was directly beneath the theater. There was a screech of a tire now and then in the distance but he couldn't see any cars moving for an exit. He glanced at a sign and cursed softly. It told him there were three more levels of parking below this one. She might have continued down to a lower level. Moving to the closest up-ramp, Merlin pulled his Beretta from the conceal holster, held it low in two hands and listened. Everything was quiet. There were no sounds of running footsteps. No sound of a car door opening or closing.

He scanned the underground lot. There were wide structural pillars and sections of walls for stairs here and there that obscured his view. It was possible Dorothy Olivaries had come down another access to the parking areas. He moved slowly, listening carefully, hoping he would see or hear something that told him she was still here. He wondered if he should also wish for unicorns and fairies to brings him a gift.

Chapter 52

DOROTHY OLIVARES TOOK a number of quick steps to slow her momentum. Despite her efforts, those steps echoed off lightly off the concrete walls of the underground parking lot and she grimaced. She had reached the back end of her Jaguar and she dug into her pocket, pulling out her keys. They jangled lightly and she held her breath looking around. Heading for the driver side door and extending her hand, Dorothy nearly pressed the unlock button on the fob. But she caught herself, recognizing the sound of the vehicle unlocking might catch the attention of that Rhett Summers—or whoever the hell he was. Her hands shook as she fumbled with the keys to unlock the door. They jangled again and she mumbled to herself. It was strange how people had become so used to simply pressing a button that unlocking a car was a chore. Especially at a time like this.

The car doors clunked as they unlocked.

Dorothy looked around as she pulled on the handle, opening the door. There weren't any cars on the far side of the Jaguar and she could see all the way back to the far cement wall. The stairs to the theater above her were off to the left and she assumed the man would come from that direction if he could get inside. Everything was quiet.

Slipping inside the Jaguar, Dorothy pulled the door closed slowly. It didn't completely close though. She knew she had to put more force into it. She also knew that would make a sound. But what choice did she have? Pushing the door open a foot, she held her breath and pulled it closed. As expected, there was a bang of sound that echoed off the walls. She continued holding her breath for a moment and then let it out in relief. There were no sounds of running footsteps.

Slipping the keys into the ignition, Dorothy decided to make a call to Quinn. She had to call him, to alert him, to let him know a madman was on the loose. Pulling out her cell phone, she tapped on the number for her home. Putting the phone to her ear, she looked around nervously, chewing on a thumbnail. The phone on the other side rang. No answer. It rang again. And again. She whispered urgently. "C'mon, Quinn. Pick up–"

A thin wire was dropped down over her head and pulled tight.

Dorothy Olivaries felt the shock run through her as the wire bit into the side of her neck. It also cut savagely into her arm just below her left wrist. The phone tumbled from her paralyzed fingers. Her mind screamed. How did Summers find the car so fast?

The garrotte pulled tighter, biting into flesh.

The pain in her neck was immense. Her thin arm felt like it was being cut in two. Her breath was all but cut off. She kicked her legs out, trying to get some kind of relief, some kind of leverage to get away. But it was useless. She pulled at the thin wire with her free hand, trying to breath. She felt a hand gripping the wire and and she slapped and scratched at it, trying to loosen the grip. Her fingernails bit into leather. Spots began to float in her vision. Her chest shuddered, trying to pull in air.

A knee pushed into the back of the seat, trying to gain more power and leverage.

Dorothy got her right leg up, kicking, trying to push against the front console. *Why was this man they had to dinner trying to kill her?* Her shoe fell off. She lifted her leg higher, trying desperately to find something to push against—her toes caught the rearview mirror and it bent downward.

She saw a head in a black balaclava just behind hers.

The lips she could see had a cruel bent to them.

The cruel eyes sparkled in ecstasy–

A gunshot sounded like thunder.

The glass in the right back door exploded inward.

The head behind her jerked—the left side of the black balaclava erupted in a mass of gore that painted the other side window red.

The thin garrotte loosened its deadly grip.

Dorothy clawed at the loosened wire, freed herself from it and jerked her body away. She tried to scream but her throat burned and cut off the sound. Turning on the seat, she pushed with her feet against the driver-side door and propelled herself up and over the console to the passenger side. Her body shook. A hand touched her shoulder and her mouthed opened in a silent, paralyzed scream.

A soothing voice sounded. "It's all right. It's all right. He's dead. He can't hurt you."

Dorothy looked up into the brown eyes. It was the man who had warned her. What was his name? Rhett? No. Why had someone just tried to kill her?

Chapter 53

LEANING IN THROUGH the shattered back window of the Jaguar. Merlin did his best to calm Dorothy Olivares. He noticed a deep red gouge in the flesh of her left arm, just above the wrist. If she hadn't gotten that arm under the garrotte, he was sure she would be dead by now. "I'm going to open the back door, okay?"

Dorothy was having a hard time catching her breath, the fear still palpable in her eyes. But she nodded.

Merlin pulled out from the open window, pulled open the back door and knelt on the back seat. Reaching across, he checked for a pulse first, weapon at the ready. As he suspected, the man was dead. A bullet through the skull would do that. Reaching up, he grabbed a handful of the balaclava and lifted.

There was the gushy sound of bone, brain, and blood.

The face that appeared startled him.

It also startled Dorothy. Her mouth opened and closed. "Quinn?"

Pulling back out of the vehicle, Merlin slipped the Beretta into the conceal holster just over his back right pocket. He looked around, imagining the gunshot had caused someone to call the police. He didn't see anyone coming but he doubted they would have much time. He leaned back into the open doorway. "Dorothy? We have to go. There could be someone else. Do you understand me?"

She nodded. Then her eyes opened wider. "What you mean someone else?"

"It's just a possibility. Can you turn in the seat? I'm going to open the door behind you."

It only took a few seconds but it seemed like a long time before she reacted. She finally nodded, turned, and sat up in the seat.

Closing the back door, Merlin pulled the passenger door open. Reaching a hand in, Merlin helped Dorothy get out. There was no doubt she was shaky on her feet. "Hold onto the door."

Her shaky hands gripped the upper door frame. She closed her eyes in pain, probably from the pressure on the red gouge in her arm. Or maybe the one on the right side of her neck.

Merlin bent down, reached across the console and picked up her cell phone from the driver's seat where she had dropped it. Making sure her call was ended, he slipped it into her pocket. "Can you walk?"

She nodded.

That was good. Merlin would have carried her, if necessary. They had to get away from here as fast as possible. The police would end up asking too many questions. He held onto her elbow, giving her support as they moved away from the Jaguar.

Dorothy's feet were wooden and she mumbled to herself as they walked. She glanced back at the vehicle a couple of times, shaking her head softly.

Their footsteps echoed lightly off the concrete walls as Merlin kept an eye out for another assassin. There was no way of knowing how many people Starkov had under his control.

They were getting close to the exit Merlin had used to come in.

A faint siren sounded in the distance.

Then another one.

Helping her climb the exit ramp to the sidewalk, Merlin slipped his hand around her waist, keeping her moving towards his rental car.

"Put your arm around my waist," he told her, "act like we're just going for a stroll."

She nodded woodenly but obeyed.

It seemed strange that most people were still walking and talking like nothing was going on. A few people they passed were talking about the sirens but it was like an everyday event. Nothing special.

A police car screeched to a half-sliding stop in the street. The wheels were cranked hard, the engine gunned and the police car disappeared down into the underground parking.

Another police car screeched around the far corner and quickly disappeared down through another entrance.

Merlin got Dorothy into the passenger side of the Maserati. He hustled his way around to the driver's side, got in, and within minutes was driving away from the scene of the attempted murder.

Chapter 54

IT WAS DIFFICULT to keep his speed down, but Merlin held firmly to the maximum limit. He couldn't afford to make them look like fleeing felons. It took a good five minutes to reach a major roadway before he could set the cruise control and glance across at Dorothy.

Her arms were tight across her chest. Her hand caressed gently at the deep red depression in her arm. From time to time, she moved the hand to the side of her neck and grimaced.

"Are you okay?"

Dorothy was startled from her thoughts. She glanced across at him, fear still written on her face.

Merlin indicated the red mark on her arm, "Do you need to go to a hospital? How about your neck–?"

Shaking her head, tears formed in her eyes.

"Okay. But if you need to, if things change, just let me know."

Her voice was a tortured whisper, either from the shock of nearly being killed—by her own husband, no less—or from the effect of the garrotte itself. "Who are you? You were investigating my...." She couldn't bring herself to say *husband*. "You were investigating Quinn?"

Merlin looked ahead as they drove, silent for a moment. "My name is Merlin Dragon. As you saw on my passport, I'm with Interpol. Beyond that, I can't say much. And no, I wasn't really investigating your husband per se. Like I said, I've been looking into Dimitri Starkov–"

"My husband was working with him?"

"I'm really not sure what he was doing," Merlin admitted. "It looked to me like Starkov was working with Blackstone Strategies to back your husband politically, eventually compromising him in some way so they could turn him. "But this...this is confusing, even to me at this point."

Dorothy let out a long breath like she was finally coming to grips with something. "I would bet my parents would say they're not confused."

"What you mean by that?"

Rubbing her arm and looking out the window for a moment, Dorothy worked her jaw back and forth. When she spoke, her voice was filled with pain and guilt. "My parents...my father especially...warned me against marrying him. They said he was too...ambitious...too willing to do anything to get ahead." She shook her head, "I was the naïve young woman who pushed back. Not in a rebellious way but... hell... I even thought my mother was jealous of me. How stupid is that?"

Merlin didn't say anything. He just let her talk. He needed information.

She was silent as he went around a slow-moving bus. "I thought he was exciting. He was everything I wasn't. And I thought...by being with him... I would become that same dynamic personality." She cursed under her breath, "How stupid was I?"

Staying quiet, Merlin considered some questions to ask her. He needed to dig deeper into who Quinn was. Maybe finding someone he was working with. A thought—no, the *visualization* of something—struck him hard. "Is...was your husband left-handed or right-handed?"

"Why?"

"Left-handed...or right-handed?"

"He was left-handed. Why does that matter?"

Merlin ignored the question. His thoughts were on something else as he drove. He spoke in a low voice, more to himself, "And the way he walked around...fists clenched, like he was marching...."

"He always did that. Said he got that from his military training. He thought it gave him a walk that exuded power. And that he could use it to stand out in political circles." She snorted, "I used to think it was cute when I first met him. After a while, it seemed more like–" She glanced across at Merlin, "Why were you asking if he was left-handed or right-handed? She stared for a moment. "There was a reason you asked. I think I deserve to know. Especially after...."

Merlin stayed quiet for a moment, still thinking it over "The person who was responsible for the death of Senator Dan Herszman at Dulles International airport...he posed as the chauffeur, hat pulled low over his eyes, sunglasses..." He glanced briefly at Dorothy, "He walked in *exactly* the same way your husband did."

Dorothy put a trembling hand to her lips. She stared into the distance. "Quinn was a thrillseeker. He loved living life on the edge." She glanced at Merlin, embarrassment etched on her face, "He was always urging me to have sex with him in a public place. We did it once when I was buying a dress...in the dressing room...with everyone just outside... I could hear the voices as we did it. At the time...I have to admit I thought it was thrilling as well. But he tried to push it farther, suggesting places where it was more likely we would get caught. Like he wanted..."

Merlin shifted in his seat, feeling uncomfortable. "It's okay. I understand without any more...examples."

Dorothy shook her head, her face flush from embarrassment, her voice low, "But he also kept asking me to wear a dress...and to flash men in public. And he wanted to watch."

"I get the picture. And I think I can see how he fits in. I think Quinn figured out who Dimitri Starkov really was. And I think he saw a double opportunity. Getting ahead politically...and maybe helping himself and his father in business...that was one aspect. The other was the opportunity to up the ante as far as his thrills were concerned."

Dorothy shuddered. "By killing people? That's just sick."

"I agree."

Her jaw clenching, Dorothy spit out the words. "But it makes sense. At least...*after* what just happened...it makes sense to me."

"I agree with that as well–"

A cell phone rang.

Merlin looked across at Dorothy.

She looked down and pulled her cell phone. She shook her head, "It's not mine."

Merlin drove with one hand, pulling his cell phone out. Stabbing the answer button, he put the phone to his ear, not sure who it was, "Yeah?"

"It's Sammy. Can you talk?"

Considering it for a moment, Merlin finally said, "Yeah. What have you got?"

"After I talked to you about that coded message disappearing from the foldering system...?"

"Yeah?"

"Another coded message was dropped in about ten minutes later. Two...words. Kind of."

"Kind of? What does it say?"

"That's just it, we don't know," Sammy told him. "It's either another code that we'll have to break or... these are passwords. I'm leaning toward passwords. To what, I don't know."

That was strange. Merlin glanced across at Dorothy. She was holding herself and staring ahead as they drove. "Send me the message and I'll take a look at it. Maybe it'll mean something. And just to let you know...I have Dot...Dorothy Olivares with me."

Dorothy reacted to the nickname, her eyebrows pushing together as she looked across at Merlin.

"That's good to hear," Sammy said. "Any sign of the husband?"

"Yeah, he's lying in the back seat of her car. He tried to use a garrotte... I had to shoot him."

There was another reaction from Dorothy. She hugged herself tighter and stared ahead.

"That makes another one down," Sammy said.

"Yeah. I'm pretty sure the husband was also the one who killed Senator Herszman at the airport."

Sammy whistled. "That's all F'd up. Why would he do that?"

"I'll explain later. Send me the message and let me know if you break it as a code."

"Will do." Sammy hung up.

Merlin drove on, waiting. The cell phone buzzed in his hand. He tapped at the screen with a thumb bringing up the message. It didn't make any sense. He pulled off the roadway, drove half a block and pulled to a stop next to the curb. He looked at the message again; #gr8m82F4U#. #2moro2nteE123#.

Merlin stared at it. Sammy was right, it looked like passwords. Not necessarily strong passwords because there were a lot of characters missing that someone might normally use. Unless–

"What's wrong?" Dorothy asked.

Looking across at her, Merlin tapped his thumb on the side of his phone, considering whether he should open up or not. "Remember the foldering system I was telling you about?"

"Yes."

"I told you your husband was the one who looked at the message before it was deleted?"

"Yes." She rolled her hand impatiently, "Get to the point."

Merlin turned the phone and held his hand out so she could see the screen. "That message was dropped in ten minutes after the other one disappeared."

Dorothy leaned her head forward, squinting her eyes. "What does it say?" A moment later, her eyes opened in surprise. She snatched the cell phone from Merlin's hand and looked at it closely. "Son of a bitch."

Chapter 55

DOROTHY SAT THERE, staring at the phone. Her jaw was clenched, determination in her eyes to make it all go away. But it was staying right there.

"Do you know what those mean?" Merlin asked her.

Her voice was both angry and filled with self-recriminations at some perceived failure. "I should. I have them burned into my memory."

"What are they? What do they mean?"

Dorothy didn't answer. She glared across at him instead, "*Where* did you get these?"

"I told you. They were dropped in the foldering system–"

Looking out the window and cursing, Dorothy banged a fist against her thigh several times. "I can't believe he did this to me."

"What are they?"

"*These* are my passwords. The first is for my laptop. The second is for my work computer. A *secure* government computer." She shook her head and looked back at the screen, "It's short form for texting but I use them to remember my passwords. I put hashtags on either end. Then it's simple. The gr8 is for the word great. Get it?"

Merlin repeated it and nodded. "Okay...?"

"So it's easy to remember the full password by using the phrase; great mate too fast for you. That's the first one."

Merlin's lips moved as he pronounced it slowly, "Great mate too fast for you. So the word great turns back into the pieces of the password after the first hashtag...gr8."

"Right. The second phrase is; tomorrow tonight easy as 1, 2, 3."

"Tomorrow tonight easy as 1, 2, 3," Merlin repeated. "That's slick." He looked at her, "Where are these computers? I presume the laptop will be at your home?"

Dorothy looked conflicted, "The laptop is in the condominium. The work computer...that I really can't talk about. All I can tell you is that access is limited to people who can get inside the building. Having the work computer password won't help anyone unless they can get inside."

"What about getting access remotely?"

Dorothy opened... and closed her mouth.

"I take it they could use the laptop?"

The conflicted look deepened. "I'm one of the few granted that..." She cursed. Then Dorothy shook her head with some defiance, "No. Quinn wouldn't do that. He wouldn't do that to me."

"Are we talking about the same guy who just tried to kill you?"

Dorothy grimaced. She looked at the passwords on the screen again while rubbing her forehead. She was running through a roller coaster of emotions.

Merlin needed to move her along. Time was running out. "We have indications that sensitive intelligence data was already passed to the Russians." He didn't bother telling her the leak could've come through another source in Starkov's network. He had to get her motivated, looking past the recent trauma and betrayal somehow and working with him.

Tears now formed in her eyes. A moment later, she passed the cell phone back to Merlin. "I'm going to have to turn myself in to the authorities. Let them know that I'm responsible for a security breach."

That was a direction Merlin hadn't considered. The problem was it didn't help him with his assignment, with dismantling Starkov's network. And he was here because 'the authorities' were already having trouble dealing effectively with the Russian.

"Could you please take me to the nearest police station? On second thought, maybe it should be an FBI field office. I can report the matter to them and–"

"No. You're being too hard on yourself."

Dorothy was adamant, "No, I'm not. I'm not even being hard enough on myself. I'm responsible for a security breach. One that could harm American interests."

"You're also someone who was betrayed by the person closest to you—your husband. And he just tried to kill you. I think you deserve some compassion. Don't you?"

She stared ahead, the skin around her eyes bunching up, holding back the tears and pain.

"I need your help. I'm looking to take down the people behind this. And if you work with me, if you do what I ask you to do, you can get out of this and go back to your life. Actually, you can begin a new life, free of all this crap."

There was a long silence. A hot teardrop rolled down Dorothy's cheek. She took in a breath and there was a slight shudder in her throat as she released it. "What do you want me to do?"

"First thing we do is drop you at a hospital–"

"I told you, I don't want to do that."

"Just listen to me. You need to go to the closest emergency room to the theater. Your husband is lying in the back seat of your car in that underground parking lot. The police are already all over it."

Dorothy seemed to shrink in her seat at the mention of the attempted murder.

"You've got the wounds on your arm and your neck to prove your innocence. He tried to kill you. All you have to do is tell them that a good Samaritan shot your husband."

Dorothy looked at him. "Really? A good Samaritan? That's what I say?"

"Everything happened so fast, that's all you know. Someone was trying to kill you. You were fighting for your life. There was a gunshot. You were in a panic. Someone talked to you, but you don't know who it was, you didn't really see them. The doctors and the police will understand your traumatic shock at what happened. Especially when the good Samaritan reached across and pulled off the balaclava...and you saw the man who had just tried to kill you was your own husband."

A gentle sob sounded in Dorothy's throat.

"That's when you fled the scene. You had to get away. You didn't know who the shooter was. All you knew was you had to get away. Understand?"

Dorothy nodded woodenly.

"They'll have a policeman talk to you when you're in the emergency room getting treated for your injuries. You tell him the whole thing, tell him where the car is. They'll put two and two together pretty quickly. And that's when they'll probably ask you some questions, wondering if you killed your own husband."

Her eyebrows pushed together hard. "But I've got the injuries. You said that yourself."

"That's just how it works. They might even think of it as self-defense but they'll want to know for sure. When they do that, they'll eventually ask if you're willing to take a gunshot residue test. Don't suggest that yourself. That could make them suspicious. You can push back a little, do a little acting job, but agree in the end to do it. Understand?"

There was another moment of resignation and she gave him a slight nod. "Okay. I understand. Then what?"

Merlin handed his phone across to her again, "I want you to take my number and call me when you're done. I'll pick you up." When she took the phone in hand, Merlin added, "And I'm going to need some information from you if we're going to get you out of this."

Chapter 56

HOURS LATER, as they rode the luxury elevator to the top floor of her condominium building, Dorothy Olivares stood quietly with her eyes closed. A white bandage encircled her throat, covering the deep wound from the garrotte. Another wide bandage encircled her wrist and lower arm, hiding those wounds from sight as well. But there was no hiding the pain in her face—both from the internal sense of betrayal, as well as those external wounds inflicted by her husband.

One part of Merlin wanted to let her rest. To recover mentally and physically. But another part told him they didn't have the time. And more than likely, she was still in danger from the Russian. Once he knew Quinn was dead, he may simply turn to another agent to eliminate her. Merlin broke the silence. "We were able to access your work computer."

That added more pain and Dorothy screwed her face up. She worked for the Office of the Director of National Intelligence. The organization had been created by Congress in response to the terrorist attacks of Sept. 11, 2001. It coordinated intelligence collection and sharing among U.S. intelligence agencies. The Director produced the President's Daily Brief (PDB), the top-secret document that included intelligence from all the various agencies, given each morning to the President of the United States. Getting her passwords was a major coup for Starkov—it was the perfect focal point of his network, giving him access to the intelligence the American government thought was most important.

Merlin tried to assuage her pain. "No one knows we accessed your computer."

"But I know."

"Yes. But I can also tell you that there is no record of anyone accessing the computer after the last time frame you gave us as *your* last access."

Dorothy opened her eyes and looked at him, "So...the Russians haven't tried anything yet?" She narrowed her eyes and shook her head softly. "That...that doesn't make sense."

"I agree. But we'll take our victories, large or small, one at a time. I'm also told we were able to establish a redirect. Anyone accessing your work computer will be sent to a fake computer mimicking the intelligence collection and sharing your office does."

Her face brightened with the possibility of hope. "You did? So they won't get any real intelligence?"

The elevator came to rest at the top floor and the doors swished open.

"That's that's what I'm told." Merlin put a hand on her lower back and guided her out of the elevator and down the hall. "We'll take things one step at a time. But I'm pretty sure when someone does try to access it, we'll be able to work back, figuring out who it is and helping to build out the network."

Dorothy pulled out her keys, unlocking the door to her condominium. "I'm starting to feel a little better already." She winced as she pushed the door open with her injured arm. "I'm going to be sore for a month. But it's a lot better than the alternative."

Merlin stayed quiet as he closed the door behind them. He wasn't quite sure what to say following comments like that. He wasn't sure if any humor on his part was appropriate despite her own humor with the situation. Her own husband had tried to eliminate her for a foreign adversary. It didn't get any stranger—or more painful—than that.

Dropping the keys to a small table, Dorothy headed for a hallway. "I'll get the laptop." She gestured towards the kitchen area. "You can make a coffee for yourself if you like."

"All right. Do you want one?"

"Yes." Dorothy called out as she disappeared down the hallway. "And make it *strong*."

Merlin headed for the kitchen, found the cups and the K-cup coffee pods...and wondered how he made the coffee stronger with a Keurig coffee maker–

Footsteps came running. "It's gone."

Hearing the panic in her voice, Merlin turned around, K-cups still in hand. "What's gone?" He saw her hands were empty except for a folded piece of paper, "The laptop? Somebody took it?"

Dorothy nodded, "Yeah. And this was propped on the desk like a tepee in its place." She held the paper out to Merlin.

Setting the coffee pods down, Merlin took the paper in hand, unfolded it and looked at. "It's a phone number. Any idea who it is?"

She shook her head. "No idea. What do I do?"

Looking at it for a moment, Merlin chewed on his lip. He had a suspicion on who had left it. "This was in the exact spot where you keep your laptop?"

Dorothy wrung her hands. "Yes. What do we do?"

Merlin didn't answer. He considered the number, nodding to himself.

"Do you know who it is? You look like you do...."

"I have an idea but I don't want to say anything right now. I want you to phone this number. Put it on speaker so I can hear. But I don't want you to say anything about me listening. If you're asked, you're alone. Got it?"

"Yes. I'm not sure why you won't say anything but...' Dorothy took her phone out, looked at the paper and entered the number. Setting the cell phone to speaker, she held it in her hand, palm up.

The phone rang on the other end.

It rang again.

Someone picked up on the other end but was silent.

Dorothy glanced at Merlin, swallowed and then said, "Hello? This is Dorothy Olivares. This number was left–"

The voice was filled with delight and a Russian accent. "Dotty. So nice of you to call. This is Dimitri."

Her face filled with surprise and Dorothy looked immediately to Merlin.

He put his fingers to his lips and softly shook his head.

"Are you alone?" Starkov asked.

"Uh...yes. I... I don't understand, Dimitri–"

"I have your laptop."

Dorothy was startled. "You do?" She glanced around the apartment. At the door. At the windows. "How...how did you get it?"

"Quinn had it with him when he came to see me earlier. At least, he said it was yours. I haven't looked at it, so I'm only going on what he said."

"Why...why would he do that?"

"I have no idea, Dotty," Starkov said. "I was surprised to see it was still sitting there after he left. Would you like to come and get it?"

Merlin shook his head vigorously.

Dorothy was silent.

"Dorothy? Did you hear me? I will be here for an hour, then I'm heading for the airport. If you would like to come and get it...."

Merlin shook his head no again.

But Dorothy made a decision, looked at the cell phone in her hand and said firmly, "I will be there shortly, Dimitri."

Now waving his hands emphatically no, Merlin bent over trying to get directly into her line of vision.

"Very good, Dotty. Perhaps we can have a glass of wine before you go as well." The call ended.

Merlin shook his head again, "No. You can't go–"

Dorothy shut off the phone on her end, her face emphatic, "I *am* going. You heard him, I'm going to get my laptop back."

"It's a trap."

"How do you know that? He didn't even say anything about... about Quinn being–"

"Maybe he hasn't listened to the news yet. Maybe Quinn acted before he was supposed to."

"But–"

Merlin's voice was hard, "Or Quinn gave him a key and he came here after he heard it on the news. It doesn't matter. Starkov is *not* going to let you simply walk away with that laptop. He's a smart cookie. He doesn't get his hands dirty by getting involved in the nitty-gritty of espionage. He's going to find a way to make *you* do it. To blackmail you."

"How would he do that?"

"Because he has your passwords and he can say you gave them to him."

That shook Dorothy. But it was just for a moment and she tried to reason it all away, "But...but we don't know for sure that he has the passwords. We can't just assume that. Right?"

Merlin was emphatic, "They were in the foldering system used in his network. He was communicating with your husband, working with him. You're in the intelligence field. Think about it."

Dorothy licked her lips, conflicted, her voice tortured. "But I have to take the chance in order to get the laptop back. There are things on there that I can't just ignore. I need to get it back, right?"

"Wrong. He's already compromised you with the passwords. And he has your laptop. He probably already has whatever intelligence information you're worried about. And he's going to find some way of compromising you further."

"How much worse can it get?"

"Think about how the Russians collect kompromat—compromising material—on people to bend them to their will. To blackmail them. I've seen Starkov and his friends around women. You're a beautiful woman and he will take full advantage of the situation—both personally and professionally. He'll tell you he will only keep quiet if you have sex with him. And I would imagine he'll have a hidden camera to record every single minute of it."

A shudder ran through Dorothy's body. "Then you're going to have to find a way to keep that from happening. Because I'm going to get the laptop. It may sound funny coming from a woman...especially me...but it's my patriotic duty. I'll do mine...you figure out how to do yours."

Chapter 57

DOROTHY OLIVARES' BODY WAS SHAKING as she walked through the doorway—he had left it wide open for her—into Starkov's sandalwood-scented world of ten-foot ceilings, wide-plank teak flooring, fancy furniture, and triple pane windows overlooking the street below. The strain of soothing, light chamber music carried across the air. But she didn't feel *soothed*. She felt more like the fly being lured by a musical spider. Dorothy wore designer blue-jeans, and a light, black, shell-jacket over a red, high-neck blouse she wore to cover her injuries—she self-consciously tugged the collar higher.

At the sounds of her footsteps, Starkov appeared from somewhere, an oily grin on his lips as he approached. "I am so glad you could come, Dotty. I was hoping to see you again." His gaze caressed her bottom and long legs in the jeans as he passed her.

Dorothy held a cell phone in her hand down near her waist. Her eyes scanned everything she could see without turning, her breath catching when she realized she didn't see a cell phone anywhere. She went ahead anyway, pressing the red icon on the left—she fought back a grimace from the shooting pain in her wrist—then pressed the black icon on the right. "Why are you calling me that? I was always Dorothy whenever–"

Closing the door behind her, Starkov said, "I am sorry if I offended you. It was the name Quinn used whenever he talked about you. I just assumed...."

Dorothy wrapped her arms around herself, hiding the phone against the jacket as she turned to face him. He was right there and she stepped several paces away from the Russian, "You're not family. I'm Dorothy to you. Now, where's my laptop?" She had her thumb hovering over the green icon in the center... she pressed her thumb against the screen, completing the sequence.

Striding across the floor, Starkov gestured to the coffee table in front of a sofa to the left. "You will find it right over there." He headed for the kitchen area. "I will get us a glass of wine–"

"No. I'm not staying." Pocketing the cell phone, Dorothy hustled across to the coffee table. The laptop was sitting there, the lid open. Stepping between the coffee table and the sofa, she saw the screen saver was running. She stood still, looking down at it. "I thought you said you didn't look at it?"

Starkov was in the kitchen area and said loudly, "I lied."

"Pardon?"

There was a moment of silence before Starkov came walking back with two glasses of wine in his hands. "I said I lied to you."

"Why would you do that?" Dorothy's tongue flicked over her dry lips. "What...what do you want?"

Starkov offered her a glass of wine.

Dorothy shook her head. "No. I'm here for the laptop. This isn't a social visit."

"We will see." Setting the glass of wine on the table, Starkov wandered away toward the windows.

"What do you mean...we will see?"

Starkov turned slightly as he walked, gesturing at the laptop with the glass of wine, "Tap on the space bar to wake it up... Dorothy."

She bent slightly, running her hands down her thighs as she looked at the screen saver running. Her hand trembled as she reached forward and tapped the space bar.

The screen saver disappeared and the regular screen lit up—actually, what she saw was a video that had been frozen—and now began playing again. The sounds of raspy breathing rose from the onboard speakers.

Dorothy's butt dropped to the sofa. She looked on horrified. It was her and Quinn, making love. The view was from the ceiling in their bedroom.

Starkov took a sip of wine as he looked out the window. The sun was setting behind the buildings, casting long shadows of fingers toward him. "I take it you were not aware your husband loved to take videos of you together?"

Dorothy's voice was distant, her eyes misting as she watched the movements on the screen. "Why... would he do this?"

Silent for a moment, Starkov turned his head and looked at her. "You are in the intelligence field. Of all people *you* fully understand the Russian term Kompromat."

"But...why would he do it to *me*—"

"Your husband was a very ambitious man. Much more ambitious than you ever gave him credit for." Starkov took a sip again. "He used you in every sense of the term."

Dorothy squeezed her eyes shut. A hot tear rolled through her lower lashes.

Turning, Starkov walked across the floor to stand on the other side of the coffee table, looking down at her. "I also have your passwords."

Dorothy's nod was barely perceptible.

"I will give you your laptop back. And the videos. I don't need them at this point, do I?"

Opening her eyes, Dorothy reached out and closed the lid on the laptop. "Kompromat." She wiped the tear away. "I suppose that means I work for you now. Is that it?"

"Yes. But I want much, much, more from you."

Dorothy looked up at him, "I don't understand–?"

"I want to experience everything your husband experienced." Starkov's eyes roamed her body. "Including filming you while we make love."

Choking back a slight laugh, a cruel smile lingered on Dorothy's lips. "I don't think you could call it making love."

Starkov shrugged. His words were crude. "Fine. Then I will simply spread those nice legs of yours and enjoy your charms. It doesn't matter. Because you will be filmed naked, with me on top of you." He gave her his own cruel smile. "Or maybe you on top of me. I would like that. Either way, a woman like you—in the intelligence community—will be in a compromising position with a Russian like me."

"And I would be destroyed."

"And enjoy the rest of your life in prison."

"Do you really think you can get away with this?"

The Russian shrugged again. "If I get caught, there will be an exchange of spies at some point and I will go home to Russia, to enjoy the rest of my life as a hero of the motherland. And you...you will still be rotting in an American prison."

Dorothy knew she had been warned. But she had pushed ahead anyway. And now the situation was here. Standing up, Dorothy brought her hands prayer-like to her lips, eyes closed.

Setting his wine glass down on the coffee table, Starkov's eye greedily took in her body. "Why don't you take your jacket off...and we can get comfortable?"

Slowly blowing a breath out through thin lips, Dorothy gave him a painful nod of acquiescence. "I...I just need to get some air...first."

Chapter 58

THE SUN HAD SET and the darkness hid everything. Merlin leaned against the five-foot privacy wall that separated Starkov's roof area from this one, trying to discern if there were any figures on the Russian's opulent terraced rooftop on the other side. The wonderful smell of someone's dinner—a succulent pot roast—lingered on the air. Merlin ignored his growling stomach as he looked at the cell phone in his hand. The first part of the plan had been to record Starkov's conversation on the cell phone he had given to Dorothy. The second part was to capture the Russian's cell phone signal so the intelligence people working with them could finally piece together all of the man's network. Once they had confirmed the capture, they were going to alert Merlin and he would go in and get Dorothy. They still hadn't confirmed it. And that worried him. The longer it took–

Strings of soft lights hanging over top of the Russian's terrace lit up.

Merlin's body stiffened when he saw Dorothy emerge from the area around the rooftop door. She walked with her arms wrapped around her, her head down.

Dimitri Starkov appeared next, walking behind her. He wore an expensive, blue-pinstripe suit with a dark blue tie. Even from this distance, it was apparent his eyes were appraising her body. His entire demeanor was that of a predator moving in on his prey.

After ten feet, Dorothy turned her head to Starkov without looking at him. There was a slight nod of her head at something he said, and she walked to her left, toward an area where there was a large, white, U-shaped sofa.

Merlin glanced down at his cell phone. There was still no confirmation. Why not?

Reaching the area of the sofa, Dorothy turned on her heels to face the Russian, her arms still wrapped tightly around her body.

Starkov gestured toward her.

It took a moment before Dorothy unfolded her arms and took off the thin shell jacket. She simply dropped it.

The Russian's head cocked to the side as he looked at the jacket on the terrace floor.

Merlin knew why. The jacket no doubt had the cell phone in a pocket—it was the only place she could hide it as it recorded him—and the garment had dropped too quickly and forcefully for such light material. He was going to have to intervene without–

Dorothy must've realized what had happened as well. She saw the Russian looking at the jacket and she said something to him.

Starkov turned his attention to her. And then at what she was doing. His head uncocked slowly, a lecherous grin crossing his lips.

Reaching up to her neck, Dorothy began by undoing the top button of her red blouse.

Merlin stirred against the wall. *No, no, no.* He glanced at the cell phone in his hand. Still no confirmation.

Taking a step forward, Starkov's movement suggested a definite interest as the second and third buttons were undone.

Dorothy's shaking fingers continued down the blouse, freeing each button, one by one. Undoing the last button, her blouse draped open.

In an instant, Starkov's face took on a serious look. His hard gaze bore into the woman's face in front of him.

Dorothy froze in position like a deer in the headlights. It suddenly dawned on her—she had revealed the bandage around her neck.

And then it all happened so fast.

Starkov moved in on Dorothy, grabbing one elbow.

Merlin's heart jumped into his throat—not because Starkov was going to rape her—but because the Russian turned her roughly, his arm snaking up around her neck in a fierce hold.

Starkov had pulled a handgun from under his suit coat, and he now held it over her shoulder as he used her as a shield. He turned with her this way and that, using her as a shield and looking for someone hidden in the shadows at the edge of the rooftop terrace.

Dorothy's blouse was wide open, revealing her pink skin, a red bra...and the stark white bandage around her throat. Redness and darkening bruises from the use of the garrotte were very evident above and below the bandage.

When the Russian spun around with her and was facing the other way. Merlin jumped the wall. Landing on the other side with a soft thud, he darted into the shadows on the right.

Spinning around at the sound, Starkov pointed his weapon in the direction of the privacy wall, looking for a target. He tightened the grip on his human shield.

Dorothy cried out in pain and she clutched at his arm around her throat. It was followed by raspy, "Please."

"Shut up."

Putting the phone in a pocket, Merlin pulled the Beretta from his conceal holster as he continued moving to his right, using large planters to cover his path as he tried to get closer to the Russian.

Starkov swept the weapon back and forth, calling out. "Whoever you are, I suggest you come out now. Show yourself."

Moving near the rooftop door, Merlin knelt in the shadows, lifted the Beretta, and aimed at the Russian. The problem was he had no shot. Actually, he did, but he would have to be perfect to hit the tiny piece of the Russian's head he could see behind Dorothy–

Putting the gun against her temple, Starkov pulled her back a couple of steps, his eyes trying to penetrate the shadows. "Come out now. Or I shoot her."

Merlin weighed all his options. He couldn't sneak closer without being spotted. And he couldn't shoot without taking the risk she would be hit. But as soon as he did as the Russian asked and stepped forward, he would be in the lights and an easy target. But he couldn't see any other choice. Her life hung in the balance. He took a deep breath. All he could do was play for time and hope another option opened up.

Dorothy cried in pain again as he pressed the gun harder into her temple.

Slowly taking a step into the light, Merlin kept the gun trained on what he could see of the Russian. He spoke firmly, "You kill her and I kill you."

A fierce grin crossed Starkov's lips. "True. But I doubt you will let her die just to get at me."

"I wouldn't be so sure."

"Oh, I am sure. I was trained to read people. To know people. You will not let her die. Put the gun down now. Or we can test my theory."

Dorothy shook her head. And then she cried in pain as the Russian tightened his arm against her neck. She tried without success to pull it away.

There wasn't any choice. Merlin lifted the gun away from the direction of the Russian and raised his other hand. "All right. Just don't hurt her."

"I will unless you comply." Starkov gave him a maniacal grin as he tightened his arm around her neck.

Dorothy's face screwed up and she whimpered from the pain.

"I said all right, you win." Merlin lowered the weapon toward the floor. He looked into Dorothy's eyes, trying to send a message...trying to get her to drop straight down so he could get a shot.

Dorothy shook her head.

Sensing her fear, Merlin had no choice. He placed the gun down, raising both hands. He would have to find another way.

"Kick the gun away."

Merlin hesitated...then complied. The gun whispered across the rooftop, disappearing into the shadows–

Starkov dropped the weapon from her shoulder to a trajectory that would send a bullet center mass at Merlin. He began squeezing the trigger.

Sensing what was happening, Dorothy yelled, "No!" She dropped a sharp elbow into the Russian's lower belly.

His breath shot from between Starkov's lips and he grimaced in pain.

The gun fired.

Merlin heard the shattering of a pot behind him.

Dorothy spun, slapping an arm at the Russian. She struck his gun hand and the weapon dropped to the floor, bounced and clattered off under a section of the sofa.

Starkov reached out with his right hand and grabbed a handful of her blonde hair. His face took on a look of ferocity as he yanked her head down, then buried the fingers of his left hand in her hair as well.

Merlin took off at a run for them.

Dragging her by the hair, Starkov moved Dorothy away from the sofa. She fought feebly against his arms as the Russian manhandled her, Several feet away from the edge of the building, Starkov grunted as he swung Dorothy around hard and tossed her across the rooftop.

Merlin yelled, "Noooo."

Dorothy's side smashed against the railing. She emitted a pained squeak and then there was a brief scream from her as she went over, disappearing to the street below. A faint, dull thud sounded a moment later.

Starkov turned back. He didn't hesitate. Lowering his head, he charged the onrushing Merlin with a yell.

Hitting the Russian with the full force of his shoulder, Merlin carryied him backward until they fell head over heels in a heap of fists and kicks. Elbow blows were added to the melee...and then Starkov rolled away and came up on his feet, turning and getting into a crouch to face his opponent.

Merlin scrambled around to his feet, pulling the carbon fiber ventilator from his shirt pocket, flipped the cap off with his thumb and got into a knife fighting stance, ready to attack. He decided against it.

Because Starkov held a folding karambit in his hand—a deadly weapon with a nasty looking three-inch curved blade that resembled a claw.

To Merlin, this was like bringing a straw to a knife fight.

Chapter 59

AN AMUSED, CRUEL LOOK settled on the Russian's face as he eyed Merlin's weapon. He shifted back and forth in his feet, looking for an opening. "Is your government so poverty-stricken that they give you a child's weapon?"

"Apparently, they are." Merlin shifted back half a step to give himself some additional room to avoid the deadly blade when the Russian began his attack. And sooner or later, Merlin knew he would attack, taking advantage of the odds that were now on his side.

Starkov shifted slowly to his right, "There is a way out of this."

"And what would that be?"

"You could come to work for me."

Merlin's mind whirled through his options. "Do you have a retirement plan?"

Starkov grinned, enjoying the back and forth as they faced each other in a deadly dance, "No. But there will be one if you don't put down your weapon. Do it now." He shifted back to his left.

"I don't think so." Shifting to his left as well to keep distance Merlin's eyes darted to the shadows around them, looking for one of the weapons he knew was hidden somewhere.

Faint voices—faint shouts, actually—could be heard off to their left.

Another cruel grin passed over the Russian's lips, "It sounds like they have found your woman."

Merlin pictured Dorothy Olivares lying eight stories below on the sidewalk, broken. He tried to tamp down the anger. But it was impossible.

The cruel grin was replaced by a look of contempt. Starkov's legs readied to spring forward, "I will tell them you attacked her. And then you tried to kill me—"

"You talk too much." Merlin tossed the carbon fibers ventilator underhanded.

Startled from his preparation to attack, Starkov batted the fake pen away just before it struck his face.

Merlin was already on the move. He took two steps, dove and grabbed Dorothy's jacket before he rolled and came up on his feet. He felt for the weight of the cell phone and then firmly gripped the other end of the light material.

Starkov turned, enraged, and sprang forward, attacking with the deadly curved knife.

Whipping the jacket with a backhanded motion, Merlin struck the Russian in the face.

The cell phone inside the pocket crashed into Starkov's nose, bringing him up short, tears of pain in his eyes.

Merlin grabbed the jacket with his other hand, wrapped the material around the still-extended knife hand of the Russian and trapped the wrist. Leaning back, Merlin put tension on the wrapped material and pulled hard.

Starkov was caught off guard and he stumbled forward.

Pulling harder, Merlin used the Russian's weight to gain momentum as he took several steps back. Shifting his own weight to the left, Merlin continued pulling the Russian around.

The Russian grimaced, fighting to maintain his grip on the karambit as they began to turn like a merry-go-round. He opened his mouth to say something—

Merlin grunted as he pulled the Russian around with all his strength. And let go.

Startled, Starkov's eyes grew large as he was tossed across the rooftop. He knew exactly what was going to happen—he hit the edge of the railing and went over without a sound.

Stumbling back a couple of steps from his own effort, Merlin caught his balance and stood still. He was alone on the rooftop terrace. Moving forward cautiously, he saw one hand hanging onto the railing.

And there he was. Starkov was desperately holding on with his left, his right still holding the karambit. He looked up, his voice strained, "Help me up."

"Yeah, right."

"You...you can't just let me fall."

Merlin's attention was caught by something else eight stories below and to the left.

Dorothy Olivares' body was lying on the top of the heavy canvas canopy that ran from the entranceway and across the sidewalk to the edge of the street. The dull thud he had heard was her hitting the canvas. No doubt the thud had been much louder to anyone below. It looked like the building security were milling around the canopy along with other onlookers. Someone was trying to climb one of the posts. A faint siren sounded in the distance. Then another one.

"Help me up." Starkov's voice was strained.

Merlin turned and looked around for the carbon fiber ventilator. "Why don't you let go of the knife and hold on with two hands?" He spotted the pen-like object, picked it up, spotted the cap and picked it up as well, capping off the slanted, pointed end of the ventilator. He slipped it into his pocket as he went looking for his gun.

The sirens were much louder now, there were at least three or four quickly converging on the scene below. Moments later, tires screeched to a stop. There were faint shouts of instructions.

Starkov's voice sounded weaker. "Help me."

"Have you let go of the knife yet?"

There was silence.

"Didn't think so." Squatting, Merlin spotted his Beretta under a table. Kneeling down, he pulled it out and stood up. Walking back across to where the Russian was hanging, Merlin looked down at him.

The Russian gave him a strained but angry look. "You can't just let me fall. You have to take me into your American government. It's your duty."

"You haven't done your homework, Dimitri...or is that dim-wit? It doesn't matter. First off...I'm not American. And if I *did* take you in, you'll find some way to wiggle out of everything."

"I have information to trade. Important information."

The phone in Merlin's pocket buzzed. Ignoring the Russian, Merlin pulled out the phone and checked the message: finally able to crack password on the russians phone. we have the entire network.

"I have let go of the knife. Help me up."

Merlin looked down at Starkov. He was now holding onto the railing with both hands. He looked into the man's face. It showed the strain of holding on was wearing on him. Holding with one hand for so long had weakened his stamina considerably.

There was also a sudden fear in the Russian's eyes as he looked at the weapon in Merlin's hand.

Looking at the Beretta, Merlin said, "Don't worry, I'm not going to shoot you."

There was now a look of relief. But Starkov's voice was definitely strained, "Help...help me...up."

Turning on his heels, Merlin headed for the rooftop door.

"Wait. No—"

There was silence. Then there was a thud. Only this one didn't sound hollow.

Merlin descended into the Russian's condominium, searching the place until he found a piece of paper with Dorothy's codes written on it. He slipped it into his pocket, grabbed her laptop, and headed out to the elevator. A few minutes later he was walking out the front entrance. Lights from police cars, paramedics, and a large fire engine strobed constantly and lit up the street out front. The fire engine had been parked in such a way as to use their ladder to gain access to Dorothy lying on the canvas canopy over top of him. He was relieved to hear the comments of 'still alive' and 'still breathing'. As he headed for his vehicle, Merlin saw another group of onlookers hovering around a body lying on the sidewalk thirty feet away. The arms, legs, and head were twisted violently. A paramedic was draping a blanket over the body.

Chapter 60

GETTING MORE STRINGS PULLED, Merlin visited Dorothy Olivares in the Center for Trauma and Critical Care at The George Washington University Hospital. He could smell and taste the antiseptic in the air as he sat by her bedside and waited for her to wake up. She looked so frail and her skin so pale he was sure she was going to disappear before his eyes into the whiteness of the sheets and blankets. The critical care team of specialists told him she was in and out of consciousness, that she had suffered a lot of internal injuries and a number of broken bones. A breathing ventilator was working away rhythmically, helping her bruised lungs to do their job. She would be in the hospital for months but the odds were good that she would recover completely. It was six hours and his own eyes were closed, resting when he heard a cough between the beeps of the heart monitor.

Dorothy was looking at him and trying to talk around the breathing tube.

Merlin got up and leaned in closer. The words were garbled and difficult to understand. The slurring from the drugs didn't help either. He put a finger to his lips, "Shhh. There's no need to talk. I just wanted you to know that Dimitri Starkov wasn't as fortunate as you. You landed on the canvas canopy in front of the building. Starkov missed by thirty feet and hit the sidewalk."

Dorothy's lips formed a warped smile around the breathing tube and gave him a two thumbs up.

"And you did your job perfectly, even if the end result put you in here. You were successful in helping us intercept the Russian's cell phone signal. He had some software on the phone that they weren't expecting and it took some time to break through. But they did it. And they backtracked through his calls and messages, unraveling his network."

Her eyes had a look of relief in them and she nodded faintly.

"Everything has been turned over to your office and they're looking to see if they can actually use the network to feed false information back to the Russians."

The mention of her office brought a look of concern to her eyes.

Merlin touched her shoulder, "It's okay, it's okay." He lowered his voice, "I searched Starkov's place and found the paper with your passwords that your husband gave him. I burned it. And then I used your keys. Your laptop is back sitting in its usual spot in your condo. I had someone access it remotely to make sure the Russian hadn't planted anything on it. You can tell your colleagues to go get it, to secure it, so you don't have to worry about it until you get back to work." He moved slightly closer and whispered, "And all the videos have been wiped off."

Relief ran through her and Dorothy gave another two thumbs up.

"And you don't have to worry about anything else. We passed on a cover story. Your husband was working with Starkov. You became suspicious. But before you could do anything, Quinn tried to kill you."

Dorothy's eyes blinked several times.

"Starkov invited you to his place, trying to find out what you knew, and maybe turn you like Quinn. There was a struggle and he threw you off the roof. There were enough witnesses trying to help you when Starkov fell, that it was obvious someone else had thrown the Russian off the roof not long after." Merlin shrugged, "That person is still not identified. Neither was the good Samaritan that shot Quinn. There's enough truth in the story that no one is disputing any of the facts. And I don't think anybody is worried about it."

Wincing at some pain, Dorothy nodded faintly and tried to smile around the breathing tube.

"One last thing. I met your mother and father in the waiting room. Your father and I went for a walk—he's also in the intelligence field you know?"

Dorothy raised a hand and did her best to mimic pulling a zipper across her lips.

"Yeah, well, I explained a few of the extra details to him. And I gave him a duffel bag. He put it in a large safety deposit box for you. He has the key and you can go get the bag when you're released from the hospital."

Her eyebrows knit together.

"It's filled with two million dollars...cash...and I can guarantee it's untraceable. Your father agrees you deserve it for what Quinn put you through. And for nearly giving your life for your country. No matter what happens, you can decide on your own future."

Dorothy's eyes filled with tears.

Merlin leaned over and kissed her gently on the forehead. "Now you get better. And forget you ever saw me."

Two thumbs up.

Chapter 61

REHOBOTH BEACH, DELAWARE

THE SUN WAS HOT on the side of his face, the iced-tea cold on his lips, as Merlin held the phone to his ear and looked out over the blue water of the Atlantic. The cry of seagulls mixed with the laughter of children down on the beach, the sounds of the waves crashing and the smell of the salt water coming off the ocean. There was no doubt about it, Rehoboth Beach was a picturesque vacation town. It was a two hour and fifteen minute drive from Washington. At least, that's how long it had taken him. The lady who had sold him his iced-tea said the town fathers had estimated there were nearly thirty thousand people here this year. The permanent residents were a little over 1,500. The mile-long boardwalk, the eclectic community of shops and restaurants, and the long stretch of beach were coaxing him to stay and relax.

But that wasn't why he was here. He had more thing he had to do. Oksana Pavlovich—Nikki the Cat had called her Miss Boobsalichious—had disappeared. Merlin wondered if she had read the writing on the wall once the spy ship had sunk. Or maybe it was after finding out Dimitri Starkov had fallen to his death. Or maybe the Russians had decided she was a liability and made her disappear. It didn't matter. She was gone. Maybe she would surface again in the future, but for now, she was beyond his reach one way or the other. That was not true about one more individual.

Roland Henderson's voice came through Merlin's cell phone, "Yes, I'm aware Dimitri Starkov was suspected of some nasty business. I had the pleasure of the FBI visiting me–"

"It was more than just being *suspected*, "Merlin said. "The authorities said he was involved in turning some of the people he—and Blackstone Strategies—had been working with politically."

"Well, that's what they *say*, Rhett. You have to realize that these people will say just about anything out of an abundance of caution. They don't have the in-depth understanding of just how you build and maintain America."

"Right. But there is also the factor of all that money that came with the Russian, right? Some people would call it 'dark money'. And it comes with a price."

The greasy smile came across the phone, "Money is money is money. It greases the world of commerce and politics. It makes the world go round. And *sometimes*, to make the world go round, you just have to deal with people who have their own agenda. As long as they can help *us* to advance our policies, it all works out in the end."

Merlin heard the emphasis on the word *us*. He was still trying to pull 'Rhett' into his world of political influence. Merlin spoke his next words slowly, "And just how far are you willing to go for your policies, Roland?"

There was a slight chuckle. "I guess as far as we need to go. Isn't that true, Rhett? We do whatever we need to do?"

"I guess you're right...Henderson." Merlin ended the call.

The seagulls, and the laughter, the crashing of waves, the scent of the salt water and the taste of the iced-tea on his tongue—it all faded into the background. Looking across the outdoor terrace, between the tables, Merlin watched Roland Henderson put his cell phone in a pocket. Merlin wore a ball cap and large sunglasses, so there was no possibility of him being detected, even thought they were only four tables apart.

Henderson pulled some cash from his pocket, setting it on the table to pay for his lunch bill. A moment later, the CEO of Blackstone Strategies smiled, leaned to his right and planted a long kiss on the mouth of the woman sitting with him.

When the lip-lock ended, the woman gathered her purse and slung the strap over her shoulder as she stood up with Roland Henderson.

Merlin had been surprised and not surprised to see Roland Henderson's roommate in the seaside town was Olivia Van Buren. Not his wife. He was here with the beautiful and youthful Chief Financial Officer of Blackstone Strategies. Merlin had assumed she was a whiz with numbers and had risen quickly in the organization. It appeared she was a better whiz at getting Henderson's pants down. And no doubt dropping her own.

Henderson and Van Buren stepped out into the crowd, holding hands as they strolled past quaint shops, cute boutique stores, a dainty teashop, art galleries and more.

Rising from his seat, Merlin picked up the square LunchMe lunch bag he had bought before leaving Washington. It was made of highly durable 600D Polyester. The interior lining was food grade PEVA material, leak-proof, and insulated to keep an office worker's lunch cold or warm for hours. Draping the strap over his shoulder, he followed Henderson and his 'girl friend'. His mind went back to his conversation with the father of Dorothy Olivares at the hospital. Lorne Hightower had been with the CIA for many years. He was one of the few people who was read into the entire situation with Dimitri Starkov. As an American, he'd been happy the treacherous network had been revealed. As a father, he had been livid at what

Quinn had done to his daughter. But he was also quite aware of Roland Henderson's role in helping the ambitious man get into his position of authority. A position that fed his greedy appetite for more and more power. An appetite for more that he felt led to his daughter nearly being killed. The problem was, Henderson wasn't directly linked to Starkov's network. And little could be done to bring Henderson to some kind of justice.

Dorothy's father was going to be that instrument of justice.

Until Merlin talked him out of it.

Hightower had given Merlin a history lesson. There was a thing called the Church Committee hearings back in 1975. Testimony at the hearing revealed a lot of things, including the existence of a secret assassination weapon. The CIA had developed a poison that caused the victim to have an immediate heart attack. This poison could be frozen into the shape of a dart that was fired at high speed from a tiny pistol. The pistol was capable of shooting the icy projectile with enough speed that the dart would go right through the clothes of the target and leave just a tiny red mark. Once in the body, the ice dart would begin to melt and the poison would be absorbed into the blood, causing the heart attack. The poison was still undetectable by modern autopsy procedures.

Merlin found it fitting—or maybe coming full circle—whatever you wanted to call it. From ice bullets to an ice dart. The small pistol was sitting in the bag between a number of cold packs to keep the dart frozen. Merlin had created a slit in the end of the lunch bag, covering it on the inside with duct tape to keep the bag insulated. Casually slipping his hand into the LunchMe bag as he walked with the crowd, Merlin peeled back the duck tape. He gripped the small pistol, feeling the coldness bite into his hand, and pushed an inch of the barrel through the slit.

Henderson was now just a couple of feet ahead.

The CEO leaned his head to Van Buren, "How about if we get you into your bikini and head to the beach?"

Van Buren playfully bumped against him, "I thought you were always more interested in getting me out of that bikini?"

"That works—"

Pulling the trigger, Merlin felt the impulse from the gun. The slight puff of air was hidden under the voices around him.

Henderson's hand shot to his right butt cheek, "Ow." He half-turned as he slowed his walk, letting go of Van Buren's hand, wondering.

The heat and body temperature went to work.

Van Buren's eyes looked startled, "What happened?"

Rubbing his butt cheek, Henderson turned back to her and shook his head, "I'm not sure. It's like a bug bit me. Or a bee stung me." They started walking again. And Henderson turned this way and looking for a flying insect.

Laughing and putting a hand over her mouth, Van Buren said, "Well, stop rubbing your ass. You look like an idiot."

Merlin fell back in the crowd of people, moving to the inside of the sidewalk, next to the wide window of a real estate office. He pretended to look at the beach-side properties for sale, while actually watching at an angle at the reflection of Henderson and Van Buren.

It took ten more seconds in the heat before Henderson's hand shot to his chest. He staggered a step, bending forward.

Van Buren took a quick step to his side, placing a hand on his back as she bent over. "Roland? What's wrong?" She gestured to a wooden bench to their right. "Why don't you sit down for a minute—"

Pitching forward, Henderson landed face down on the sidewalk. His body bounced a half-inch, raising a small puff of dust. Then he lay there, unmoving.

Dropping to her knees, Van Buren shook him. She shook him again, calling his name. Then she called out to the curious crowd around her, "Someone call 9-1-1."

Turning on his heels, Merlin left the commotion that was developing behind. There were more calls from a variety of voices for paramedics or an ambulance or a doctor.

Merlin knew it wouldn't matter. Henderson would be dead before any one of those arrived. As for the politics, there was no doubt someone would come along to replace him in the scheme of things. Right now, it didn't matter.

As he headed for the mile-long boardwalk that would take him back to his car, Merlin repeated Henderson's own words, "Like you said. We do whatever we need to do."

Chapter 62

OTTAWA, CANADA

MERLIN HAD CALLED from the armored limousine on the way home and Sammy was standing in the doorway of his apartment, holding Jigs in her arms. The blue, wooly Chartreux cat was staring back into the apartment. Merlin knew that his pal was probably watching across the room to the birds sitting on the other side of the window.

Sammy scratched Jigs on the head, "Guess who's home?"

The cat's head whipped around in an instant, his orange eyes fixing on Merlin as he approached. A moment later, the cat gave a big yawn.

Merlin frowned as he set his go-bag down and scratched the cat's head, "Thanks a lot, pal. Someone feeds you chicken and you change loyalties overnight." He was actually more than delighted to finally feel the nappy texture of his pal's coat under his fingers.

His ears perking up at the word chicken, Jigs then flashed one of his brilliant Chartreux smiles. Uncurling from Sammy's arms, his front paws reached across to Merlin.

Taking the cat in his arms, Merlin nuzzled the muscular frame with the side of his face as he looked at Sammy, "Thank you for taking care of him. I really appreciate it."

"No problem. I enjoyed it." Sammy reached inside the apartment doorway, picked up a tote bag and slung it over her shoulder. "I have to get going. Duty calls." She gave Merlin a squeeze on the shoulder and then gave Jigs a kiss on the head, "Bye-bye, big guy."

Merlin and Jigs watched her walk away, the cat perking up. "Don't worry, she'll be back," Merlin told Jigs. He then looked in the other direction down the hallway, "But right now I have something else to do." The walk to Jaimie Hartman's apartment felt like a walk to the executioner's chair. Pausing in front of her door, Merlin turned slightly as he held Jigs so he could rap on it. The wood felt cold and unforgiving against his knuckles.

It took a second knock before the door swung wide open.

The smell of some spicy hot sauce from the apartment washed over Merlin and drifted into the hallway. That was both strange and unusual. It was usually the scent of peppermint tea and woody potpourri that gently enveloped him when she answered.

Jigs jumped down from Merlin's arms and disappeared inside Jamie Hartman's apartment.

"Hey, where's that cat going?"

Merlin stood still, knowing full well he had a stunned look on his face. And he was stunned. Because that wasn't Jamie Hartman in the doorway. It was some man. Some man with long curly brown hair, a ruddy complexion, and a slightly overweight body. He had a reddish tinge on the left side of his lip that Merlin assumed was a dab of this hot sauce he could smell.

The man pointed an angry finger at Jigs. "Hey, pal? Did you hear me? What's your cat doing in my apartment? If he does anything nasty in there, I'll wring his neck—"

Merlin moved in close, nose to nose with whoever this man was—friend or relative of Jamie be damned, "If anything *ever* happens to that cat, I come looking for you. Understand me?"

Fear flooded across the man's face. He took a half step back, holding his hands up, "Okay, okay. I get it. No need to be touchy."

"Actually, there is a need to be touchy when you threaten my pal there. Now, where is Jamie? I'd like to talk with her."

"Jamie? Oh, right. She's not here–"

"When will she be back?" Merlin leaned in slightly, looking into the apartment and calling out, "Jigs? Come on, buddy. We're going home."

The man turned his head and looked into the apartment as they heard the padding of the cat coming back across the floor. He stepped to the side to avoid the slightest contact with Jigs.

Jigs trotted through the doorway, turned left and headed back to the open door of his own apartment.

Merlin watched the cat padding down the hallway, making sure he went inside their own place.

"You...you live in the building?" the man asked.

"Yeah. Down the hall." Merlin looked the man in the eyes, "I asked when was Jamie coming back–?"

"She's not. I'm subleasing the place." The man held his hand out, "I'm Leo Boutette. I guess we're neighbors–"

"What do you mean you're subleasing the place?"

His brow wrinkling, Boutette said, "That means I agreed to make all the payments on her original lease–"

"That's not what I meant. When you said she's gone, where did she go?"

Boutette shrugged, I have no idea. All I know is she called me a couple of days ago. I'm a graphics designer and I worked with her on a few projects. I've been looking for an apartment for a while now because they're tearing down my old building for some commercial development. She said I could have her place." He gave Merlin a relieved smile. "I have to tell you, I was sure I was going to be out on the streets when she called."

"And you have no idea where she moved to?"

"No. Sorry, I have no idea. I had the impression she was leaving Ottawa, but I have no idea where–"

Merlin turned on his heels and walked away. His legs felt wooden underneath him.

Boutette leaned out, "And nice to meet you too." He muttered something under his breath and then slammed the door shut.

The world seemed tipsy. Merlin found it difficult to believe that Jamie had simply left without any word. He was sure Sammy would've said something if Jaime had left a note with her. Merlin shook his head. Jaimie *had* left a note of sorts: it was the Can-Can outfit from Paris, left in the bag at his door. She had misread Sammy being there to take care of Jigs. But it wasn't her fault. It was his. She had done everything to move the relationship ahead. Him...not so much. Not because he didn't want to. But because he was that square peg trying to fit into the round hole. Here he was, the man who was given assignments that would save the world—the man who would do whatever was necessary—and he couldn't carve off enough corners to make her stay.

Don't miss out!

Visit the website below and you can sign up to receive emails whenever Eugene Lloyd MacRae publishes a new book. There's no charge and no obligation.

https://books2read.com/r/B-A-AC-OJRZ

BOOKS 2 READ

Connecting independent readers to independent writers.

Did you love *Dark Money*? Then you should read *Box Set: Rory Mack Steele Thrillers Books 1-12* by Eugene Lloyd MacRae!

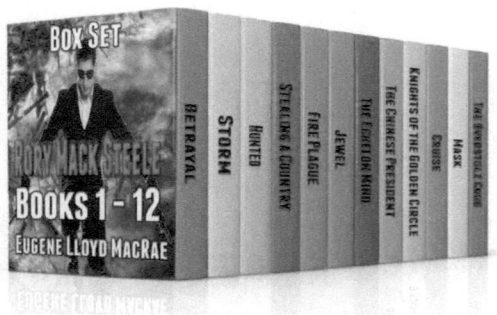

Now in a single box set - 855,000 words - the first twelve action-packed thrillers in the Rory Mack Steele series. Like fast-paced thrillers? Then you'll love to go along with Private Detective Rory Mack Steele and his sister Skye Steele in a set of adventures that will keep you turning the pages.

Read more at eugenelloydmacrae.com.

Also by Eugene Lloyd MacRae

A Rory Mack Steele Novel
Betrayal
Storm
Hunted
Fire Plague
The Echelon Mind
The Chinese President
Knights of The Golden Circle
Cruise
Mask
The Overstolz Code
City
Stealing a Country
Jewel
Box Set: Rory Mack Steele Thrillers Books 1-12

Bulldog Malone
The Diamond Heist
The Banker Case
The Missing Case

The Stopper Files
Iron Pipeline
Economic Hitman
The Gunrunner
Assassin
Dark Money

Whiskey Empire
King of the Bootleggers
Gangsters
'Ndrangheta
Vendetta
Burn Powder
King of the Bootleggers Box Set

Watch for more at eugenelloydmacrae.com.